RIVER OF CHANGE

RIVER'S END SERIES, BOOK SEVEN

LEANNE DAVIS

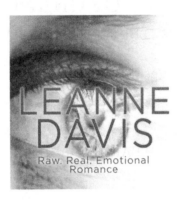

LEANNE
DAVIS
Raw. Real. Emotional
Romance

This is a work of fiction. Names, characters, places, and incidents are either the product of the author's imagination or are used fictitiously, and any resemblance to actual events, locales, or persons, living or dead, is entirely coincidental.

River of Change

Contact Information: dvsleanne@aol.com

Publishing History First Edition, 2018

ISBN: 978-1-941522-57-8

River's End Series, Book Seven

Edited by Teri at The Editing Fairy (editingfairy@yahoo.com)

Copy Editing: Jeannie Brooker

To Sue Krause

For all our years of summer camping trips and the FUN we manage to have together. From Washington Park and our very own "enchanted forest," to Fort Casey, and of course, the endless trips to the property.

Love you always, my dear friend!

CHAPTER 1

~YEAR 8 FROM START OF SERIES~

*C*ALEB HAYES STOOD AT the side of his little brother, watching his brother's *groom* walk towards him. Caleb swatted his neck, tugging on the damn, constricting collar. *My brother's groom*, he kept repeating. Even now, a year later since he learned his brother's shocking secret of marrying a groom instead of a bride, he was still astonished.

Caleb was nowhere he ever dreamed he'd be standing in his lifetime.

Change. For Caleb it was a dirty word. He hated change more than he hated working, which rated a close second. But change was never, ever a positive thing in his experience. The first great change he remembered was when his mom left them. He was only a young teen when she decided their life didn't appeal to her and she moved far away to live with her new boyfriend. He, his brother Jordan, and his little sister, Lynnie, lived with their dad, Chuck. But Mom was out of the picture. No more family. No more motherly love.

Change meant his mom left. That caused pain. Pain, he figured out pretty quickly, must be avoided at all costs. Ergo, pain, both physical and emotional, was the direct result of *change*.

For over thirty years, Caleb tried to live without changing anything. He resisted it until there was no other option. He lived at home without a job until his father threatened to kick him out; and he had no choice but to change and get a job. Change also came when a fire ripped through River's End last summer, exploding the old mobile home they owned. Change meant he was basically homeless now, along with his father.

Last summer, however, was the mother of all change. It started with Jordan coming out, admitting he was gay before proposing to his... *intended* out of nowhere. It happened while they were celebrating their sister's marriage to her longtime boyfriend, Ian Rydell. Now, Ian was Jordan's best man. Not Caleb. Okay, maybe that was because Ian was easy-going and didn't care a shit about the gay factor. Perhaps that affected Jordan's decision. But still. Caleb was his brother's right hand for all their lives and vice versa. Now he chooses Ian Rydell to be the best man?

Caleb wasn't exactly thrilled to attend his sister's wedding to Ian to begin with. Ian was so smart and industrious, while Caleb did all the grunt work for Ian's family. He did anything and everything on their ranch that he was ordered to do. They were real task drivers too. No doubt about that. Naturally, he was ambivalent already about the marriage between Ian and Kailynn. Then his little brother, unexpectedly, and from out of nowhere, got up and made a big speech before he proposed... to another man.

He and his father were sitting together and were both shocked and appalled. No way could Jordan be *gay*. No! Caleb saw Jordan having sex with women before and more than once. He knew he wasn't mistaken on that. But no.

Jordan was announcing his long-enduring love and proposing to... Pedro!

Pedro was younger than both of them by several years, and started working at the Rydells years ago. He was quiet, and spoke only broken English. After several years of working beside him, that was all Caleb knew about him. He might have gone on and completely ignored Pedro. Sure. The guy didn't speak English. What could they possibly commiserate over? Now, however, the quiet, solitary, non-English-speaking man was about to be his brother-in-law?

He shuddered.

See?

Change. Never, ever a good thing.

So, there he stood, not even the best man at a gay wedding.

A *legal* gay wedding.

He wasn't sure about that change. First, the change in federal law shocked him. He hadn't liked hearing about it, of course, 'cause it was *change*. Man and *woman*, not man and man. He was pretty clear on that, although he hadn't been to church in... well, hell, maybe fifteen years. But still, he clearly remembered that caveat.

So now it was legal. He scoffed. Whatever. Had so little to do with him. Until his sister's wedding and the grandiose announcement in front of most of the town of River's End. It completely humiliated him and his dad. Jordan tried to talk to him. Full of apologies, he tried to explain why he didn't tell them first, saying he didn't know how to tell Caleb. He was afraid to lose Caleb. All the usual excuses. *Change*. That day, Jordan completely and irrevocably changed in Caleb's eyes.

Still, Caleb was standing there, wasn't he? A witness.

And he hated seeing how happy his brother appeared. That left a bad taste lingering in Caleb's mouth. He really hated the whole thing. He glanced across at the couple now standing before an arbor overlooking the river on a specially selected area of the Rydell River Ranch.

His brother and Pedro rented a small, one-bedroom house across the river in town. *Together.* They would now live together. That chafed at Caleb's craw. He and Jordan were living with their dad until the fire burnt them out. Now, Dad lived with Ian and Kailynn in their big ass house near the river. He and Jordan lived there too, sharing a room, but Jordan was moving out. He was about to be without him. Sure, he figured one of them might someday marry a broad and raise a mittful of kids in River's End. Maybe they'd share beers at neighborhood barbecues and watch their rugrats playing together. Sure, he understood they'd eventually have to change. But to change like that?

No. Never.

He glanced over at the attendants he saw on Pedro's side. He ignored them, of course. Not like your typical, normal bridesmaids. No. They were Pedro's... what? Best men too? Two other men Caleb didn't recognize were there. And... what was that? On the very end, he spotted a woman.

Who knew? His blood zinged. He drank several nips off his flask to muster the courage to go through with it. His fingers twitched, aching to draw it out of his inner pocket and take another nip.

A woman was part of the wedding party. He tipped forward just a few inches so he could see her over the bodies of his brother, Pedro, and the other men. His brother and Pedro were holding hands as they exchanged their rings and vows. He flipped his gaze up to the woman. He needed a distraction to get past the odd and, to Caleb, *so wrong* sight of his brother holding hands in a most loving and tender way with another man.

The woman might have been around his age. Yes, she

didn't seem as young and coltish as a twenty-year-old. But heck, no wrinkles, and he could live with that. She had dark, glossy, black hair that cascaded over her shoulders and down to her waist. She also had the gold-tinged brown skin of her Latino heritage. Her face was pleasant; heavy eyebrows over thoughtful, black eyes.

His gaze scanned downwards towards the more inter-esting goods. *Nice...* he thought and almost said out loud as his gaze gobbled her up. She had a nice rack too, set off in the ruffled, scoop-necked blouse she wore. It was tucked into a skirt that skimmed her knees and swooshed around. She wore wedge-type sandals that added several needed inches. She wasn't tall. He almost rubbed his hands together in a salacious manner. He liked 'em small. He was tall, and it made him feel so much bigger and manlier when they were petite like her. And she was enticing. Her waistline was narrow, and her hips were voluptuous. She had womanly curves and he really appreciated those.

He blinked when she suddenly started clapping before the few in attendance joined her. His gaze reluctantly left the señorita and returned to his brother before he jerked his head away. No. He should have been blinded. They were *kissing*. Each. Other. Two men. Right there in public. Well, maybe not in public, as it was on private land and a private wedding, but still, they were not in a bedroom.

Change really, really sucked.

Finally, it all ended. They were smiling and holding hands as they walked. Jordan was visibly thrilled, and Caleb could not figure out what to do about his brother being so elated in this way.

He followed behind, loath to appear too joyful a partici-pant as if that would make him seem gay too.

He straightened up suddenly when he realized he was right next to the busty little señorita. Taking out his flask and tipping a generous portion into his mouth, he assumed she wasn't Pedro's one lesbian friend, and hoped he'd maybe find a way to make this evening turn around into something less… odd. And so full of change. Right down to his brother, whom he thought he knew better than anyone else in the world. If that weren't change, then what should he have called it?

JOSEFINA RUIZ CLAPPED her hands together, blinking rapidly as hot tears threatened to fall from her eyes. He did it. Pedro finally came out. And in a fully surprising fashion. She worried constantly about her little brother. He was so quiet and incredibly sensitive. Most people didn't know he was in a room even if they were standing behind him. His English was much better than he pretended. But using broken English made most white people assume he couldn't speak well so they generally avoided him. The trouble they had understanding his thick accent outweighed any urge to communicate with him more often than not. She frequently admonished him for doing that. He always responded with a small, heart-melting grin and ducked his head without ever changing. He barely even spoke to her in their native language and she could speak as fast and fluidly in Spanish as he could. But he rarely gave her the opportunity.

She found it hard not to worry about Pedro. It made her worry constantly about him until Jordan Hayes came into the picture.

She had to admit being shocked when she learned about the relationship. But that was years ago. Four, or maybe five? She couldn't remember exactly, but her then twenty-year-old brother was acting very strange. Back when Jordan and Pedro first got together, he was secretive and often gone for unexplained periods of time. It was hard for her to miss. At the time, all six of them lived together in a single-wide trailer in Brewster, Washington, about twenty minutes from River's End.

When Pedro was eighteen, he was hired on as seasonal help for the Rydell River Ranch. It was the biggest private operation in the area. After that, they kept him on pretty much all year round, except perhaps in the dead of winter.

He flourished there, and he met another worker who was on a par with him: Jordan Hayes.

They started working together and eventually became friends. Most astonishing to Josefina was that Pedro was speaking in English to Jordan. Jordan was the best listener. Most people talked *at* Pedro, but rarely *to* him. For some reason, Jordan managed to get through to him and drew him out of his aloofness.

Josefina was extraordinarily protective of her little brother. He'd always been freakishly small for his age, and never, ever talked. When he reached his teens, she started to suspect he was gay. She believed he'd always known that. But quiet Pedro never felt the need to state it.

Until Jordan Hayes came along. Jordan started hanging around a lot. Like crazy amounts of time and one day, Josefina had asked him, "Are you sleeping with my brother?"

Jordan was absolutely appalled at her question and stormed out of their small trailer, only to return a week later.

"How did you know? Did he tell you?" Jordan asked Josefina.

"He never tells me. You know how Pedro is."

He nodded, his eyes flashing at her words. "Yes," he said softly. "I do know him. No one else does."

"No. They don't. So, you must understand how unique you are."

Jordan's back went rigid and he stared at her open-mouthed. "No. Never. I've never been unique a day in my life."

"I don't mean because you're gay. I mean because of the connection between you. Your relationship."

"No. I'm not gay." Jordan's head shook vigorously, and he was adamant. She scratched her head. Did he not realize having sex with her brother was gay sex? Not that she cared.

"Um. Okay. But I meant, he doesn't really let anyone inside his inner world or thoughts. So, you're unique."

Jordan was a white, slim guy whose hair was a little too long and he usually wore nothing fancier than a stained t-shirt and a pair of jeans and boots. Josefina was a little shocked to realize that he was Pedro's taste in men. A quintessential, red-necked cowhand, to be honest. And he appeared heterosexual in a strong, beer-drinking, light-your-fart-on-fire way. Which she saw as a man that could protect Pedro.

But with Jordan? No one would suspect. Jordan swore all the time and his English was grammatically off.

Eventually, Pedro grew tired of hiding it and having Jordan act like he wasn't gay. She wasn't sure what Jordan thought. That he was bisexual? It was just because of Pedro? For a while, he seemed angry at Pedro, as if it were Pedro's fault that Jordan wanted him. But that slowly changed into a fierce protection of Pedro. Then Pedro dumped Jordan and told him it was over. Six months later, Jordan surprised everyone when he unexpectedly proposed to her brother during his sister's wedding. Josefina desperately wished she'd been there to witness it.

But even better, now she was witnessing this.

As a brand new married couple, they chose to hyphenate their names together as Hayes-Ruiz. Josefina was surprised when Jordan took their name. He looked at her strangely.

Jordan Hayes was surprisingly accepting of all. She loved that about him.

Her brother finally had someone who could protect and love him. Someone he could trust and be open to, which wasn't an easy endeavor for her brother to achieve.

The wedding parties were split right down the middle. Jordan's side was white. Josefina didn't know any of them personally but had heard mostly good things about them.

On Pedro's side, the number of attendees was huge. Starting with her dad, siblings, and two sets of grandparents, aunts and uncles and cousins. His family numbered in the dozens perhaps. Friends and family all interacted without prejudice or intolerance and all lines crossed.

Her heart warmed and swelled with rejuvenated hope for all of humanity. Pedro's family and friends were a boisterous, warm group. They catered the affair while the Rydells provided the setting and wedding decorations.

"Good evening, my little señorita. May I interest you in a drink?" The voice rolled the word "señorita" in an exaggerated Mexican accent. Offended by the lout, Josefina's mouth dropped open. Who the hell thought that was an acceptable way to come on to anyone? Josefina glanced to her left and found the man who so rudely insulted her culture and dared to treat her like an object.

Caleb Hayes. She wanted to stomp on his foot. He was a tall man and swarthy in complexion. Even today, he hadn't bothered to shave, and his face was buried under too much stubble that suggested a few days of not shaving. He had dark whiskers, black hair, and blue eyes. Dulled now, no doubt, because he was half drunk. She recognized him from his brother and seeing him around town. He worked with Pedro and Jordan.

Over the years, she and Jordan had grown closer and had many conversations, something she never had with Pedro because he didn't do that. But Jordan was a talker. And she knew how badly he feared his brother finding out.

For many years, Jordan avoided saying he was "with" Pedro. She restrained her eye rolling. Still. She knew Caleb was intolerant and a terrible womanizer. He was often drunk in town or being hauled home in the back of a police car. He was the complete redneck that Jordan turned out not to be. Jordan held off his claim on Pedro for years, primarily because of his fear and insecurity, and that was owing to Caleb. Jordan most feared losing his brother. He feared being disowned and even despised by him. She was repulsed and disgusted by such an individual as Jordan's brother. She seethed at his unwelcome presence.

Of course, he had no freaking clue who she was. She realized that when his eyes dropped down to her breasts. Nothing was visible. No cleavage, not even for his viewing pleasure. But he was explicitly determined to find some.

"Oh. Sorry, but my girlfriend wouldn't like that." She smiled sweetly as she spun on her heel and escaped. She was surprised he even attempted to make a pass at her. She bit her lip. No. She didn't need that kind of ass in her life.

She wondered, however, if Señor Dickhead Caleb Hayes would soon realize they were, in the loosest of terms, *family* now. She shuddered at the thought. He'd, no doubt, believe every stereotype about anyone and everyone he'd ever heard. Sighing, she made her way towards her brother and her new brother-in-law. She was excited to congratulate them and welcome Jordan into their family. She just wished his horndog brother wasn't so freaking gross.

CHAPTER 2

*C*ALEB WATCHED THE TWITCHING legs of the pretty bridesmaid scurry away in what could almost be called a run. He squinted his eyes. Was he really so bad? What caused all the panic that she felt she needed to get away from him? So, what if she swung to the opposite side, why the brush-off? Why did she hurry off so fast? He tipped the flask to his lips. Maybe she was intimidated by his looks. Because she was tempted. He shuddered as too much liquor dribbled down his throat. He licked his lips and wiped his mouth with the back of his hand. His gaze wandered around. *Damn.* He felt awkward. He wasn't sure what to do with himself and that was never the case. Not in River's End. He'd lived, worked, and recreated here his entire life, although there were rare moments he didn't feel exactly right being here. This was still his place. His people. His family. His philosophy and politics.

Except now? Not at all. Nothing felt normal or regular. It felt… changed. One hundred percent turned on its head, changed. His brother now was placing his hand on his… *groom's* shoulder as he leaned closer to say something to

Pedro. Something very intimate was exchanged between them obviously. Jordan leaned close, and they spoke before they—Caleb shuddered—they shared a *look*. An eerie, loving, caring, connected look. Pedro smiled at something amusing and funny between them. It was not a friendly look. Nor a look between co-workers. No. It was a lover's look.

Caleb sucked in a breath that hurt his chest. It was so odd. And hard. Now that he knew and really understood their relationship, all he could do was watch his brother and his brother's former-boyfriend-now-groom with a near obsession in his level of interest. Every interaction from now on would be different.

Caleb saw it all. Until last summer he had not seen it. Oh, but now he did. He saw it so clearly. He'd worked with them both closely for a full seven years. He'd always known they were close friends. Bros. He never considered anything like... this. That he'd be standing in attendance at a celebration of their union.

He drank more, scowling after them. Something sharp kept stabbing his gut. Jealousy? Anger? Disgust? All of the above. He erroneously believed he and his brother shared the closeness he now realized that Jordan really shared with Pedro. In fact, their relationship was much more intimate than he and Jordan ever had. Not to mention his realization that for years, Jordan lied to him. Bald-faced lies.

Sensing that *he* was the outsider startled and shocked him. It was a bitter, jagged pill for him to swallow. He hated it. Which led to frustration and anger. For being lied to. For having his entire view of his brother irrevocably altered. It tainted their relationship and how he viewed Jordan. That extended to how he saw the entire world and people in his community whom he'd never doubted before.

If his own brother could so successfully lie to him for so long, how the hell could he trust another person? Or a relationship? Damn. There was no way to truly know anyone. If he were that wrong about his own brother, a brother he worked with daily, and lived with, hung out with, and interacted with on an hourly basis, what could he be right about?

Chuck Hayes, his dad, was talking to Jack Rydell, whose ranch they were currently using as a backdrop for his brother's nuptials. His dad looked as uncomfortable as Caleb felt. He rarely spoke to Jordan anymore and only attended the ceremony today because he lived with Ian and Kailynn Rydell.

Ever since last summer when their family's trailer burned up in the fire that took out the entire valley and then some, he'd been living at their house. Ian threatened both of them and said that Chuck and Caleb either had to go to Jordan's wedding and show their respect for both grooms, who worked on the ranch, as well as their gratitude to the Rydells for hosting the wedding there, or both of them had to get out of his house.

That was that. No negotiations.

Caleb drank more as his thoughts reviewed that critical moment and Ian's ultimatum. Stupid prick. Ordering them here. Threatening their place of residence. Blackmailing them. How dare he? Only because he was rich and had a family who never failed to support him. That was the only reason why he could do so. It made Caleb bitter. He might not have been standing there today were it not for Ian and Kailynn.

His dad remained near the back of the crowd. Caleb hadn't witnessed him interacting with anyone else and if he had, Caleb knew he would have said nothing to Jordan. Chuck finished speaking and Jack walked away and then, so did Chuck. Limping on his bad leg, he started down the road towards Kailynn's home. Not a word did he speak to Jordan.

Caleb's gaze, growing fuzzier by the gulp, focused on his

brother. He lifted his head from where he and Pedro were chatting together to stare after their dad. Jordan stilled. He stared longer. Pedro grazed his hand with a brush of his fingertips. Jordan didn't move. He kept staring. He flinched, and his gaze fell back on Pedro. He stared at their clasped hands before Pedro pressed his lips together and lifted their linked hands to his mouth and... and kissed them.

What? Was he just saying, *Screw the old man?* If he couldn't accept them as they were, then so what? That distinctly seemed to be the message Pedro conveyed to his new groom. But Caleb saw Jordan glancing down the road once more and the hurt he felt visibly flashed across his face, although quickly. It was there and then it was gone, but Caleb saw it.

He winced and hurt for a brief second for his brother. The rejection was so clearly directed at him through Chuck's snubbing him and his unwillingness to even address Jordan by himself, let alone, Jordan and Pedro.

But Caleb tried to rationalize the situation. Jordan shouldn't have hidden this for so long and lied to them all. Maybe he could have prepared them better. Maybe if he just stopped being gay, they could all go back to being *themselves.* The real them. The *them* they were for years and years and years. The same. Guys. Men. What were they supposed to be now?

And there went the flash of anger. Damn Jordan. He ruined everything. Every memory. Every ounce of comradery. The future. The plans to raise families together, and grow old with their families intertwined.

He'd known it as soon as Kailynn hooked up with the likes of Ian. There couldn't be that relationship with her and her future family because Ian was the employer and not the employee. Not one of *them.* Which was fine, for Lynnie. But for Jordan and him? They were going to be together, always. The same. Then... this?

"Does it make you feel better?"

He turned and glanced back to find Lynnie stomping up to him. Anger emanated off her too. What for? What had he done?

"What?" Maybe she was frowning about the concealed flask.

"You and Dad making Jordan feel like shit. Like he was less than a man. Like he failed you. Like he lost all of his manhood? What the hell do you want him to do?"

He winced. "I didn't do anything, Lynnie. I'm right here. Dressed up and joining the party." He spread his arms to show off his dark suit and loosened shirt, but it was a button-down and clean.

"What Dad just did, walking away? Snubbing him. Not a word? That's as cutting and hurtful as if he were yelling at him. And believe me, I clearly understand the only reason Dad doesn't say much is because he knows Ian and I will kick him out. It's unacceptable to us. So, he retaliates like this instead."

"Well, it's against his deepest beliefs. His son living like that."

"Well, it's not for him to say, is it? Nor can Jordan help it. If hiding it for a decade doesn't convince you, I don't know what will. He was the most important part of your life until that singular moment at my wedding when you learned about this. Are you really willing to lose him and us over this?"

"I'm here, ain't I?" he grumbled at her.

"You can be here under protest, or as a part of your brother's life."

"That's Dad, not me. I haven't left."

"You haven't said anything to him either."

"What do you want from me?"

"Support him. Care about him. Be his brother again. You

15

should know what to do, you spent over twenty years doing it before you knew anything about this. Now you won't speak to him."

"It just changes everything."

"Things change. People change. People grow up. People get spouses. Things were going to change despite our sexuality because we all have to grow up and enter the world as adults. Nothing ever stays static. I know how you struggle with this, but you've got to learn to embrace change or you're going to be the real loser. You'll end up losing the people you love and never meeting new ones."

"I don't see any struggle with it," he tossed out, knowing it was all untrue.

"You want the three of us to continue living with Dad in the trailer. You'd have stayed in place for the next three decades. Never moving on, or moving out, or growing up. Drinking your fill and carousing on the weekends. You can't handle change, but I'm telling you, change will happen no matter what you think or do. Do you get it? Do you see what I'm saying? You. You, Caleb, were and are the greatest influence on Jordan's life. And what do you stand here doing? Drinking. Glaring. Grumbling. Wallowing in your pity party. A childish view you can't overcome. All I'm asking you to do is love your brother."

"Why are you coming after me like this, Lynnie?" Confusion, anger, hurt, and fear swirled around his brain and churned his gut at hearing her scornful words. He didn't know what to make of it.

Self-reflection wasn't something he ever spent any time doing. He just knew he loved his brother and they had a blast hanging together, carousing together, as well as working together. Now? To be summarily replaced, and not by some chick, as the natural law and order of the universe dictated, but by another dude, a man, whom he also worked with was a hard row to hoe. He didn't know how to begin to accept this break from tradition. Worst of all, he didn't like the changes from his usual expectations. What he expected usually gave him a sense of security.

Her expression softened. "You really don't get it. For years, I was miserable after I graduated high school. But in contrast, the best years of your life were living in that trailer with me and Jordan and Dad, the four of us. They were the worst years of mine. I felt so trapped. Limited. Like I'd never see my dreams come true. And yet, you never noticed I was so unhappy and unfulfilled. You obviously thought it was enough for me. You never noticed Jordan was always struggling with something deep and shameful to him. You didn't even notice that Dad was going to rot away and die if he didn't start taking better care of his health. We weren't okay. We weren't ever happy or healthy. Yet… you were. You were happy. You loved it. You wanted us all to continue living together. You valued the sameness so much, you didn't even realize how miserable and unhappy everyone else was. We were right there, living right beside you and you had no clue, Caleb. Do you realize that?"

He stiffened. That wasn't true. They… were a family. A tight unit. They had bonfires and potlucks. They drank together and went to church together. They were happy. There were long nights of talking and laughing. They had plenty of friends who liked to come over.

What? What was she talking about?

"Caleb? *We* weren't happy. *You* were. You never even realized it. Maybe… maybe you need to consider that. You're clueless to other people's needs, especially once yours are met. Life isn't a snapshot in time. It's a living, breathing, vital, changing organism. Embrace your brother, who is right there. He wants your love and approval and yet you are clue-

17

less, as always. So focused on things not changing, what if you miss the very changes that could improve your life?"

He stared at his sister, his mouth hanging open and his head spun in near dizziness as she rewrote their childhood and upbringing. According to how she made it sound, it was unhappy. A bad thing. His scowl deepened and he passed her and stomped away. His brain was hurting, his stomach kept tightening and his heart was racing. No. No! That wasn't reality.

Too much alcohol. He was buzzing. No driving tonight. He glanced up, looking towards the ledge of land that his family still owned, where their mobile home once stood. He stared out over the vast expanse of Rydell land. Looking higher up, he began climbing the now faded trail that used to connect their land when he considered the Rydells his friends. Shane and Ian. Jordan, Shane and he spent years, decades even, running back and forth to each other's house. Walking, running, riding ATVs and horses; they used different modes of transportation but always followed the same path back and forth. They hung out drinking, talking and BSing with each other. It was a golden era. Wonderful. Fun. Now? He suddenly learns that his brother was tortured without him ever knowing anything about it?

Darkness was slowly descending over the land. He could hear the buzz of the partygoers below. Lights that were strung all about illuminated the party and the farmyard lights only added more atmosphere. In his sloppy walk up the hill, Caleb reached the top and found himself on the land where his home once stood so proudly. He stared around.

It was gone now. All of it. The fire gobbled it up as fast as a hungry, greedy demon with an insatiable appetite. Only a few pieces of twisted metal from the trailer's frame were left, now bent and blackened. Empty propane tanks were off to the side, but otherwise, it was barren. The trees that outlined the perimeter of the property were singed into skeletons but still had not fallen. The sagebrush was starting to reappear slowly again.

He kicked the dirt. His dirt. Their dirt. All the Hayes owned in this world was this barren plot of land. All the outbuildings and various tools and items that filled them were destroyed in the fire. Everything was gone.

Caleb was already a little disgruntled when he learned that Lynnie was getting married to Ian. To Caleb, she still seemed too young, his little, baby sister. How could she become a wife? Then, his brother announced he was in love with Pedro Ruiz and barely a week later, their family home exploded. It freaking exploded. Pop. When does that happen? How often does a home actually explode? Theirs did however.

The strong force of firefighters managed to save a lot of the residences, mostly in the lower valley neighborhoods and many of the pricier homes. An old, dilapidated trailer rusting out in the dust bowl of Gunderson Hills? Not exactly anybody's priority. Even if it represented all that Caleb loved and cared about in the world.

Sure, it was lucky no one died or got hurt. But they lost everything. Sure, it might not have been no freakin' thousand-acre ranch filled with material riches like the Rydells, but what they had was all theirs. Their home and their way of life.

Now it was gone. Poof! In no more than a week, all that Caleb knew and accepted as his life had either morphed, changed, or vanished.

He found the old fire pit. God, how many bonfires did they burn here? The rocks around it still remained, along with the hole they dug. The debris was all gone of course. How many days, no, years, did he and his family and friends, mostly Jordan, sit around the fire pit, ruminating over the woes of the world, or the valley, or the latest goings-on? How often did they sit there drinking beer and having fun? So what if they weren't deep or philosophical discussions? They were *their discussions, about their times, and their lives.* He used the tip of his shoe to stir the ashes. Those days weren't all bad. Not like his sister insinuated.

Finding some broken, snapped, charred logs and branches, he pulled his lighter out and started the dry pine needles underneath it until the wood caught, and flames sprung up. He stared at it against the darkening sky.

The only real wealth the Hayes owned lay in the view their land offered. It looked out for miles toward the horizon. The river wove a bright blue strand of color through the green fields and golden, dry spots of unirrigated land. Horses roamed the rolling acreage, cows grazed, and only a few houses were interspersed, surrounded by the mountains that seemed to rim the entire world. Vast and deep, jagged and rounded, the diverse landscapes provided a three-hundred-and-sixty-degree view, all featuring beautiful pine trees. Caleb loved pine trees. Their fresh scent and the way the needles sparkled under the hot, dry summer sun—that was his wealth.

No, it wasn't all bad.

He swallowed and flopped down on the ground. Flames flickered in the breeze. Screw the burn ban. What could possibly happen? The land would burn? Again? Destroying everything, from his brother and their relationship to his sister and how he felt about his dad?

Lately, Chuck confined his rants about Jordan strictly to Caleb's ears. A sickening knot formed in Caleb's stomach whenever he thought about the things his dad told him over the last year about his brother. Chuck wouldn't dare to speak that way to Jack or Ian, especially not Kailynn. His dad knew that much.

But this was about Jordan. *His brother.* It was so much harder to talk that way about his brother, his flesh and blood, not to mention, his best friend in the entire world. He didn't know how to accept the truth about Jordan. But that didn't stop his dad. The nasty names he called Jordan made Caleb want to speak up.

In his heart, he longed to tell his father to shut up. But of course, he never did. He just stayed quiet while his dad vented and ranted. Caleb just sipped his beer or other alcoholic beverage a little faster and he made the drinks a little stronger. He was usually trying to get drunk to ease the moment and his guilt. The sickening knot that was lodged inside him yearned to protest and exclaim, "That's my brother. And your son. How dare you speak about him like that?"

It wasn't about being politically correct anymore either; it was strictly about decency. And loyalty. It was about his friggin' brother this time.

And since that day last summer, when this all came out, Caleb found himself in a quandary. It was so personal now, learning a secret about his brother, his best friend. He didn't know how to handle it.

He liked Jordan more than anyone else on the planet, much more than his dad. And now? How could he suddenly hate him? According to Chuck, he should have. But he didn't feel like that, so he couldn't voice it and he stayed quiet.

All the while, his guts were being gnawed away because he did not speak up. He failed to protect his brother by not telling his dad to shut up. So he was disloyal to both of them. Up until last summer, Caleb was nothing if not loyal to his family. Not only to Chuck, but to Jordan most especially. He felt loyal to Kailynn too. He readily admitted his many faults and was well aware of them.

He wasn't exactly a thinker, or particularly intelligent. He barely earned a high school diploma. Work was always hit-or-miss for him. He drank too much and partied way too often. He slept around too and with lots of *women*.

His dad often questioned him about that. That only resulted in him becoming more promiscuous and less discriminating with his sexual partners. Staring at the dancing flames with some chagrin, he had some regret with how he'd spent the last year.

He knew he wasn't worldly, but he also had no interest in being so. He rarely read the newspaper and barely could remember who the president currently was. Never mind the town's local goings-on. He didn't know and didn't care.

He liked to listen to country music, strictly country, and drinking at the River's End tavern. He also enjoyed a good fire with friends and beers and BBQs. He adjusted to working full days and full weeks even, only because he liked the comradery at the Rydell River Ranch with his brother, AJ (the foreman), and even Pedro.

They were synchronized like a team. Now two of them had become lovers and Caleb felt like the odd man out, literally. He had no idea how to handle it.

Caleb wasn't great at anything. He was impulsive and did things just because they crossed his mind. He always was like that. In school, he spent more time being in trouble than being in class. Doing anything from vandalizing school property with spray paint or carving swear words into a door, to letting off fireworks inside the city pool, he was incorrigible. That last stunt was pretty epic.

The point was he did lots of things mostly because they seemed funny at the time. In school, Shane hung out with him. They caused a lot of the trouble often together. They both enjoyed women, drinking and having fun.

But hell. Shane suddenly fell head over heels with a new, redheaded school teacher. He just about underwent a total reformation he changed so much. Going from biker to husband and father. He ran the Rydell Rides and worked all the time. Suddenly, it mattered that Shane was Shane Rydell, and Caleb was no more than one of their lowly workers on the ranch.

It never mattered before, of course. He and Shane approached life the same, and it was never an issue. Shane never snubbed him or acted like he was any better than Caleb and his family. Until all at once, he did. He embraced his identity as a Rydell and the family ranch that defined their unlimited success.

Suddenly, Shane became one of his bosses and Caleb was relegated to being the hired hand. All at once, he lost his compadre in crimes and misdemeanors.

Now there was no more Shane, and no more Jordan.

There was only Caleb.

He sighed and threw a few pebbles at the fire. Goddamned fucking change. What good did it ever bring? At one time, his life was awesome. Full, fun, and hilarious. The stories created by Shane, Jordan, and him as well as all their friends from the valley were nostalgically being relived in his mind. The laughs they had. The fun they shared. Now what did they have left? They all fucking worked or were involved with their families. Big, freakin' whoop.

"You know there's a burn ban on. And your smoke is visible for a five-mile radius."

Caleb sighed, drinking a big gulp from his second flask. He didn't turn towards his brother's voice but stared harder at the flames. "Yeah? Well, I was never too good at following the rules. Why start now?"

Jordan stood off to his left. Caleb still didn't turn his head. He noticed his black dress shoes, which seemed so odd and wrong for standing in the ash-covered dirt that Caleb was sitting in. "What the fuck you doing up here, Jordan? Don't you got a groom somewhere you should be fucking?"

Caleb instantly regretted the cruel words. He bit his tongue and shook his head before pouring more alcohol into his filthy mouth. Damn. Why did he say things like that? Mean, crude words he didn't really mean. His heart sank with the disappointment he had for himself, yet he still said them. "Once you say something," Chuck always taught him, "if you were a real man, you didn't apologize for it." He tilted the flask back and let the alcohol burn his throat.

"You'd say the same thing to me if I had a bride in place of a groom except there would be nothing but cheers and sincere wishes of congratulations," Jordan answered after a long, silent pause. Caleb was sure he was staring hard at him.

"But I can't say that, now can I?"

"No. You can't." Jordan kicked the ashes near his feet.

Caleb winced at Jordan's uncharacteristic display of emotions. And anger. "What are you doing up here?"

Jordan sighed loudly as he kneeled down near Caleb. "I saw the smoke up here and knew it was you. I know you only came to my wedding today because Kailynn pretty much threatened you and dad. Either go to the wedding or get out."

"So?"

"Yeah, so?" Jordan's tone was hollow. "One last time, Caleb. This is the last time you can give me shit about being gay. Don't you think I know how you feel? How Dad feels? I was there too, listening to it all through my childhood and adolescence. It just... was always the truth. I never knew what to do with it. But you know what? I've accepted that this is it. I'm gay. I love Pedro and we've just vowed to spend the rest of our lives together. He's now the most important person to me. My spouse. So if you can't respect and accept that, then fine. I've given you almost a year to adjust. But you

24

know what? I gave you and Dad more than a decade before that. But no more."

Caleb swallowed the odd lump that lodged in his throat at hearing his brother's words. "Kailynn cornered me down there and told me the same thing."

"I've spent too many years regretting and trying to punish myself simply for being who I am."

Caleb sucked down more off his flask and handed it to Jordan without a word. Jordan took it and did the same. "I didn't know."

"That I was gay? I know. I made it my life's mission that you, especially, would never know."

"Well, that, too. But no, I mean, I didn't know that it was so hard for you."

"Yeah. It was."

Caleb blinked his eyes against the sudden pressure. Shit. He drew in a breath. He quietly asked, "Is it still bad?"

"No. Not since I just decided I had to be truthful. I have Pedro and his family for support. They've helped me a lot. Josie probably most of all."

"Josie?"

"Yeah, Josefina, Pedro's older sister. You were talking to her tonight."

He cringed. "The Mexican chick with the big titties?"

Jordan rolled his eyes and his eyebrows rose up as he snorted in disgust. "You didn't say that to her, did you?"

"No. Nah. I just didn't know she was his sister."

Jordan flicked the dirt at him. "You hit on her though." Statement, not a question.

"I might have given her a warm and friendly greeting."

"Yeah, I'm sure I can predict what one of your warm and friendly greetings is like."

"They accept you? Pedro's family?"

"Yeah. They do. I let Pedro go, thinking I could get over

25

him. I thought I could be with someone else in secret. But I couldn't. I couldn't think of living without him anymore. The thing is, Caleb, you have to accept me and him together, as one, and treat both of us with the same respect and tolerance or… or this is it. It'll be goodbye for us. We're done. Accept me or don't. I've finally realized that's on you. I can't make you think or do anything. Because I don't need you anymore, I finally have plenty of other people that accept me."

"By people, do you mean this Josefina and Ian Rydell? Does he accept you? That why you picked him to be your best man?"

"I didn't think you'd even come today," Jordan said softly and so sincerely that Caleb winced. "But the stupid part is? All I ever wanted was to tell you and have you accept me. So many times when we sat before a fire at this very spot, in the middle of the night, all alone, talking and drinking and bonding, so many times I wanted to tell you. I needed to tell you, actually. But then I knew you'd just call me names, or worse, like Dad always warned he'd do if he had a gay son. So, in my need to survive, I kept silent. Ian knew long before anyone else. He told Kailynn who made it comfortable for me to admit it to her. They supported me wholeheartedly and helped me like I always dreamed you would, if you knew."

"But you knew that would not be so."

"Well, you haven't been so far, and you've had a year to get used to it." Jordan shook his head and shrugged. "Dad always knew, Caleb. That's why he kept saying all that shit. He wanted to shame it out of me. Pretty powerful stuff coming from your old man. In the end, I had to recognize the situation: my family would never accept me. I chose to accept myself. Now, I'm asking you to."

"Sounds more like an ultimatum to me."

"Sure. It is. But I think I have every right. Nothing else has changed about me. I'm the same guy, Caleb."

"But I saw you. I saw you having sex with women."

"I hated every second of it. I only did it to prove to you and Dad... as well as trying to change my preference."

"You couldn't change it though?"

"Nah. Never. It just is. No substitute. No choice. It was always this way for me. And what I finally accepted is that I don't even want to change it. I'm done regretting it for you and Dad or trying to change my true feelings."

Jordan slowly rose to his feet. He stared at Caleb and threw down a handful of dust. "This place was a hard place to grow up in. If you didn't fit the mold, no allowances were made. Kailynn didn't fit for her own reasons and neither did I. You were lucky because you always did. But you never seemed to catch on that we didn't fit. Or how miserable we were here. I'm glad in many ways that it burned down. It held a lot of negative memories for me. And I think in order to move forward I've had to let that go."

"And me? Did you let me go too?"

"That's where it's at, which means, now it's on you. Tonight. We can be done or we can be brothers. No more apologizing for things we cannot change. Decide."

"I don't know what you want me to do with all this," Caleb answered, hedging. He didn't like the ultimatum.

"I guess nothing. And in doing nothing, I guess you do something." Jordan waited a beat before he took a step back, then another. Turning around, he started back down the trail he'd come up on. Wearing his fancy-assed suit and shoes, he had actually climbed up the dusty, dirty, black ash-strewn path to ruin his shoes and cuffs. Just to see Caleb. Jordan's words struck a chord in Caleb.

The pain his brother and sister lived in wasn't something he managed to realize. It shamed him now and hurt him.

Suddenly, it was like having a bucket of ice-cold water being poured on what he recalled as a lukewarm but pleasant childhood.

Sure, there was sadness all around when Mom left. Their family split up. Anger and resentment naturally surrounded her abandonment. But they all had each other. They all lived here together.

And the experience was not the same for any of them.

But Caleb never knew. Not any of this. The changes that were whirling in his brain made him feel incapacitated. He could not believe this was what they'd become. He didn't, however, get up. Or move. Or yell after his brother. Instead, he finished the flask he'd been nursing and opened another one. Toasting the fire and the empty, torched land that was once his home and the empty spot beside him where Jordan used to sit.

CHAPTER 3

A STEADY THUMP KNOCKING against his bedframe awoke him. Startled and disoriented, Caleb blinked his eyes open. Instantly, the sensation of his head splitting overcame him. Oh, lord. His head was pounding harder than the steel-toed boot he saw on his bed. What the hell? He lifted his aching head upwards. Fuck. Ian Rydell was standing there dressed to go outside and shoving Caleb's bed to awaken him.

"Wake up, Caleb."

He rolled the other way, his stomach heaving. Sitting all alone beside the fire last night, he stayed there for a long while. Passing out eventually, he woke up and stumbled home. He came in and fell on his bed in his sister's house when the sun was just beginning to rise. That was mere hours ago. Like two. He groaned. "Go away. It's Sunday, and I don't work for you today. So fuck off."

Mondays belonged to Ian and he had the right to tell Caleb what to do; and Caleb eagerly had to jump up and respond. Not on Sundays. Sundays, Ian wasn't his boss any longer, but his brother-in-law and Caleb didn't have to get along with or be nice to his damn brother-in-law.

"Then get out of my damn house. Believe me, I won't miss you."

Caleb groaned as he flipped upright. "What do you want? You on some kinda power trip?"

Caleb blinked against the bright daylight, noticing Ian was still standing there and dressed to go outside.

"Get up. We're dealing with some stuff right now or you're getting outta here."

"Why?" he grumbled. "Where's the fire?"

"You made your sister cry, and therefore, you pissed me off. Get up."

Caleb glared at Ian. They engaged in a long death stare before he got onto his feet and his stomach instantly rebelled, shoving the harsh acid upwards. Damn. His eyes bulging, he breathed in some deep breaths if only to keep from hurling. "What did I do to Lynnie?" His head was all fuzzed up and aching so bad. Leaning forward, he pressed his hands into his temples.

Ian brusquely shoved Caleb's shoulder. "Get up. Your room stinks and I can't even breathe in here."

Caleb scowled at the retreating figure of his sister's husband. Stupid prick. He sniffed. It didn't smell... well, not all that bad. He glanced around. Maybe it was time to wash some clothes. He stood up and the room began spinning, making him sway on his feet. Damn. He needed to sleep off the hangover.

But Ian... oh, the bastard. He constantly used Caleb's occupation and residence there as a bargaining chip in his bribery. Was it his fault he had to live there? No. His fucking house blew up. What else was he supposed to do? Live on top of all the ash and rubble from his exploded home? No. Some damn family he had, and he regretted ever helping Ian out before.

Caleb steadied himself and pulled on a pair of jeans and a t-shirt. He sniffed the shirt. Okay, he worked in it on Friday but it was all he had to put on right now. Stomping in his bare feet towards the front door, he saw his boots off to the side.

Kailynn was very fussy about having any dirty boots in the house and he always made sure to leave them outside the door. Yes. Of course he did. But nothing he did was ever noticed or appreciated around here. They only noticed the things they didn't like.

He groaned and squished his large feet into the cold boots. Before him stood the horse trailer, fully loaded with Ian's truck idling in front of it. The only good thing about that was Caleb didn't have to hook it up. When he trudged over to the cab, he got in and sat down with a huff. "Why?" he asked after a few moments.

"Because I feel like riding. And it smells better than your stinky room, which is located, last time I looked, in my house."

"My sister's house too, you sexist prick."

Ian flipped the truck into gear. "Yes, it is." Ian grumbled before adding, "but somehow, I take ownership of you."

Caleb flipped Ian off and they rode in complete silence up towards a trailhead. Caleb recognized it as one that ended in Sunset Lake. Great. He got out of the truck, glad to escape the cab and its driver before he waited. Ian was busy bringing out the two horses and opening the trailer's door to grab the tack.

Let Ian work for him for a change, Caleb sneered as Ian began grooming the horses before bringing out the bridles and other gear. In no time, Caleb got bored, rolling his eyes as he stepped forward to grab a saddle and heft it on the steed's back. Pulling on the cinch strap, he tightened the girth of the saddle. Ian nodded and tossed him some water bottles. "Drink up. Might help you with the spins."

He glared back, hating how easily Ian predicted what was wrong with him. Hauling himself onto the back of the white and black paint, he started down the trail without waiting for Ian. Not too much later, Ian caught up with him. Caleb grimaced and faced forward as they rode for three hours without a single word to each other.

In the third hour, Caleb's stubborn hangover started to release its vise-like grip on his temples and his bouts with nausea began to fade. The warm morning air started to clear out his thoughts and the clip-clop of the horses' hooves was hypnotic, soothing, and helping substantially to ease the effects of the alcohol.

The lake came into view. They dismounted and hobbled the horses before tossing their saddles aside, without a word still. Usually, Ian's work commands were all he had to say and Caleb knew how rare it was for Ian to speak without any provocation, especially without his sister's presence. She was the only one Ian liked to talk to.

He swallowed some water to soothe his dry throat and rinse out his foul-tasting mouth.

The lake was spring-fed and one end was covered in rocks that extended to the top of the peak as it was below. Trees whispered in a creaky breeze and only the horses neighing intermittently disturbed the perfect peace. The best thing, however, was how much it helped his hangover.

Another half hour. They sat near each other, but still didn't speak. Caleb threw a rock in the calm water. He had to break the tension. Gritting his teeth, he felt slightly annoyed that it was he and not Ian who had to shatter the long silence. The man was a freaking robot.

"What's this about? Why am I up here with you this morning?"

Ian skipped a pebble across the water without glancing at Caleb. "You don't remember?"

"Remember what?"

"I figured as much. You have no concept of what you've done. Your brother gave you an ultimatum last night. He told you to accept him or he'd be done with you forever. You chose the second option."

Caleb froze. Fragments of the previous night's conversation flashed in his mind. Maybe... yeah, maybe he and Jordan argued while they were by the fire. He'd been drinking pretty heavily by then. Sure. Whatever. So? It was only one of dozens of fights they'd had throughout their lives together. They'd come to blows plenty of times before. One little fight wasn't anything to get so dramatic over.

"I didn't *choose* anything. It was a stupid argument."

Another pebble across the water. Ian's gaze stayed forward, but his face was blank. Something about the serious demeanor he saw in Ian sent a ripple of raw nerves down Caleb's spine. "I suspected you were too drunk to realize what you did. You ended the relationship with your brother. Your sister knows it, Jordan knows it, I know it and yet, you still don't know it. Do you, Caleb?"

He rolled his eyes and shifted forward, grabbing a handful of pebbles and throwing them in a shower above the placid lake. "Hell, it was just a fight. I'll apologize, don't worry."

"No. It was an ultimatum last night. He gave you a choice. You made the wrong one."

"What do you know about my brother and me?"

"I know because when he came down from meeting with you, he told me he was quitting the ranch. He no longer had a brother and there was nothing more to discuss."

Caleb's eyebrows shot up. "So you're saying he just quit like that?" He shook his head and denied it. "Nah. Just ignore it, Ian. He didn't mean it. Just blowing off some steam. Like I said before, I'll apologize today."

"What don't you get? Caleb. Listen to me. Your brother quit his job. All because of you."

"He was overreacting in that case. It wasn't a big fight."

"Apparently, it was to him. I think it meant everything. It was your last chance and yet you still don't realize it." Ian's placid demeanor irritated Caleb and he threw another rock. Then in an even, placid tone, he asked softly, "Drunk again, Caleb?"

Caleb bristled at the accusation. "It was a wedding. Not uncommon for partygoers to drink."

"A wedding in which I was best man. Not you."

"Whatever. So you got the honor to be best man, so what?" Caleb hunched forward with a huff. Stupid Ian, ever the know-it-all and full of shit. What did he understand about Jordan and their shared brotherhood? Yeah, there was plenty of fighting and ribbing each other. Ian just didn't understand their closeness meant that they could be honest with each other and sometimes that honesty caused shit to occur, like harmless fighting. It meant nothing.

Ian stopped talking. Caleb stuck his middle finger up behind Ian's back. Ian said, "I never liked you. I got stuck with you. First, because of Shane's friendship with you and then because of Kailynn. You came with her like a package. I accepted that. I accepted you even though I had to tolerate you. But I always liked Jordan. The thing is, I started to respect you, and would have before you found out about Jordan and Pedro. You were hard-working, holding your own, showing some incentive, and determined not to mooch off your sister for the rest of your life. But when the fire happened, and your brother came out and admitted he was gay, you didn't respond with the least bit of tact or hell, much less, decency."

"Who are you to judge me? My family's home burns up and my old man and I are rendered instantly helpless and homeless. You're damn right I wasn't happy about it. What do you know about what it's like to be me? What have you ever lost, Ian?" Caleb fisted his hands. "And even if you did happen to lose anything, you'd buy a new replacement, right? You don't have a damn inkling of what it's like to be me, to have so little to begin with and then have nothing."

Ian didn't rise to the bait, but nodded, and remained calm. "And here you are living with me."

"So was Jordan." Caleb was quick to point out. What was this about anyway? Piss all over Caleb weekend?

"Jordan came to us a year ago with a goal and a plan. He asked me and Kailynn if he could stay at our house for nine months, after which time he planned to marry Pedro. They wanted to save money for a nice rental and that's just what he and Pedro did. He apologized for needing our assistance, but he also scheduled a date when it would end. We had no problem accepting that, you see, and we were glad to help them. But you? Not a goal or a date of termination from you. An assumption instead, that at thirty-fucking-one years old, you could just live on and on with us indefinitely. You're a young, able-bodied, healthy man who should have more self-respect than to mooch off everyone you know. I don't get it. And then, if you add all this shit with Jordan…"

"What are you saying?"

"Kailynn can't even look at you today."

"So she sent you?"

"No. She doesn't know I brought you with me today. I told her I was going out for a ride."

"What do you want, Ian?" he grumbled.

"This is your last chance. I figured last night, you were

too drunk to know any better, but today, you won't be. Jordan is giving you an ultimatum. Accept him now as he and Pedro are, or never see him again. And in order for that to happen, you both can't work for the ranch. He was right about that. However, I didn't accept his resignation. I told him I'd be requesting yours."

Caleb stiffened as he shot onto his feet. He kicked the rocks and replied, "How dare you? Drag me all the way up here and then threaten—"

"I'm not threatening you with anything," Ian stated. Softly. Ian-like. Final.

Shock and something akin to fear rippled through Caleb. No. He glanced at Ian. No. Ian, married-to-his-sister Ian. He could not be terminating his job now, or could he? His only livelihood. His only means for making money. And for what? A lame fight with his brother?

"And realize this, Caleb, Kailynn and I are the acting managers of the ranch right now, so there's no debating any decisions with us. We will be sympathetic to Jordan's side. So…"

"Wow, it's my job, my livelihood, and my place to live. Talk about strong-arming me."

"Do you really see yourself as the victim here?"

"Well, you sure as shit ain't being extra nice, Ian. What would you call it except blackmail?"

Ian's jaw tightened, and he suddenly stepped forward. Swift and sure, he grabbed Caleb's shirt and shoved him backwards until Caleb's body bumped hard into a tree. Ian stayed calm but said in a tight-lipped voice as he pressed on Caleb, "I am offering you the favor of your life, you stupid idiot, but you're too damn selfish and ignorant to see that. I'm trying to make it so you won't lose your family. The family I think you truly love. But you're just too damn pigheaded and blind to see it." He shoved Caleb's torso.

Caleb's mouth dropped open, his brain too stunned to process Ian's words. He felt the jabs from the tree trunk and the pressure on his chest, but his brain failed to register what was happening. Was Ian really threatening him? How could this calm, placid, quiet Ian who so rarely talked, suddenly attack him like that when he never commented on anything before? He was manhandling Caleb and threatening his job as well as his place of residence.

An epiphany waffled through Caleb's addled mind.

Had Jordan maybe, actually, been serious?

Caleb glared at Ian, but his mind raced at Ian's last words, shocking him back to reality. They both stared, taking ragged breaths and glaring hard at each other. "You're for real?"

"I'm for real."

Caleb pushed on Ian to get his hands off him and walked away to stand at the edge of the clear mountain lake. He was staring out over all the wildflowers and pristine waters beneath the craggy mountain cliffs.

His brother hated him. His sister wanted to kick him out. His brother-in-law was prepared to fire him.

He couldn't even remember what he said. Snippets, but not everything. It didn't seem at all profoundly different from anything he'd ever said before. So what was this? All this hostility toward him that seemed to spawn from one horrible night? One thoughtless conversation? One apparently substantial fight? He shook his head and kneeled down to cup the cold water and splash it over his face. The shock of the water temperature woke him up and cleared most of the hangover.

Just as he supposed Ian was trying to do right here and now.

Ian's boots came to a stop beside him with a crunch of the

37

pebbles beneath them. "You ever consider how goddamned mean you get when you drink?"

"No more than anyone else."

"Yeah, much more than most. Just saying maybe you should consider this a wake-up call."

"Wake-up call to what?" He rose and stood up but his tone was calmer now.

"Maybe sober up, listen to what Jordan said, and what I am promising if you don't straighten up and fly right."

"Accept him as he is? I already do. He's my brother."

"He meant *accept,* not tolerate. Or ridicule. Not another slight or negative word or glance or sexist joke about him and Pedro. That's a whole different thing than merely tolerating him."

"I don't have a drinking problem," Caleb replied.

Ian put his hands up. "Okay, if you say so. Just pointing out that it seems to cause you most of your problems. And as for the rest of it? I thought maybe you were hearing me, but I still don't know. So that's the end of it. All the pleading you get from me, Caleb. You have to decide. You have until the end of the day to get back to me."

"Ultimatum one and two?"

"Yup." Ian turned and walked away. Caleb stared after him.

That was it? Ian goes that far and body-slams him, then insults and threatens him before he just walks away? As if he didn't care what option Caleb chose? He shook his head and slowly clambered to his feet. He was feeling less pissed off and self-righteous than he was twenty minutes ago. Maybe *some* of what Ian said rang true. Alarmingly so. Was he… did he… could he possibly act a little differently when he drank too much? It happened on a nightly basis. What was Ian saying?

No, damn it. He wasn't a drunk. So what if he *got drunk*? Big difference.

Ian called out to him. "Looks to me like a storm could be moving in. Better head back."

Caleb, moving by rote, re-saddled his horse and followed Ian out. Sure enough, a rare rain shower came down just before they got back to the truck. Caleb made quick work of unsaddling and loading his horse in the trailer—doing his half of the work this time—before he got inside the truck.

When they were halfway back to the ranch, keeping his face averted, Caleb asked Ian, "Do you... do *you* think I have a drinking problem?"

Ian didn't answer for a long time, enough for Caleb to chance a glance and see if the man even heard him. But Ian leaned forward to turn the air conditioner down. "I don't think it does you any favors. What positives are there when you drink?"

"Fun." He scoffed.

"Fun? You're entering your thirties and you still live with your married sister. You have nothing to show for your life until now, except *fun*."

"Like you'd even know what that's like."

Ian glanced his way before he looked back at the road. "Are you somehow trying to insult me?"

Caleb twisted around. Okay, it was a lame insult. "Just saying you don't enjoy much in life. Not like I do."

"I also still talk to all the members of my family and they live with me. I do not live with them. See the difference? You can't possibly compare your fun to what I have earned and which constitutes an actual life." Ian sighed. "Then again, maybe you can and that's what you choose. I'll guess we'll know today, Caleb, won't we?"

"So you think you can strong-arm me into what? Being

all hearts and roses about my brother and another man? Is that what he wants?"

"No. I don't. But I'm willing to let you stay if you can manage to try."

"Where do you think I'll go? I have nowhere else to live but here."

"That's the thing, guilt-free, it would no longer be my problem. You would no longer be my problem and with your sister's blessing, it's almost a win for me. And who is left to party with? Shane doesn't hang with you any longer. Neither do Jordan and most of your old group, because two are in jail and one got married. There's no one left, Caleb, just you."

Just you. The words echoed eerily and pathetically in Caleb's brain because they were true. Alarmingly true. Okay, maybe there wasn't a whole lotta fun left. But... shit. He was the pitiful loser, still drinking himself to oblivion and partying, even when there was no one left. Not even his little brother. His sidekick, the one person he thought he'd always have.

"I'm not a drunk," he muttered, arms crossing over his chest as he sunk down lower.

"If you say so."

"I'm not," he insisted, too sharply. Too grumpily. Maybe a little too defensively.

"You're a pretty heavy drinker then."

He didn't argue that and stared out the window silently.

"Do you remember what you said last night? To Jordan?"

Caleb waited a long beat and then conceded. "No. Apparently, not fully."

"You might consider slowing down. You should try to find Jordan today, they're leaving tonight, and going to be gone camping most of the week. So if I were you, I'd choose my answer before he goes. I think he truly meant his ultimatum and maybe if you go after him today, he'll reconsider, but if you wait..."

Caleb didn't reply but continued glaring out the window. He stomped away from the truck when they stopped and didn't turn back once to help Ian with the damn horses. Not his. Nothing belonged to him. Beyond the boots on his feet and a few changes of clothes and his old truck, Caleb owned nothing. Even the old truck belonged to his dad. Been around for twenty years. He, Jordan, and Kailynn all shared it equally.

He didn't remember what he said to Jordan last night. Just some grumbling and complaints. An argument? Maybe. It wasn't... shit. It wasn't important enough to alter their relationship. They were brothers. Flesh and blood. They could argue all day and night. Or fight. Or hate each other even, but they'd always be family. He remembered vague images from the day before. Being at the wedding. The pretty girl, named Josefina, wasn't it? He remembered the fire. Being alone. Jordan and he talked briefly. He rubbed his eyes but couldn't remember what they said.

Caleb was stomping away from Ian when he heard Ian say, "This isn't like the other times. This is for real. You don't shape the fuck up, then you lose Jordan. As I said before, we'll take his side and that means no job and no home for you. You better decide."

All this because of a little intoxication? A trace of an attitude?

Whatever he'd said and done must have compelled Ian Rydell to talk to him. Nothing before this ever made Ian talk to him before.

Shit.

Maybe... maybe this was really the last line he dared to cross. But hell if he would go quietly.

He turned around and stomped into the house. "Did you sic your husband on me, or did he do this all on his own?"

Kailynn glanced up, startled from her work balancing the ranch books on the computer. "What?"

"I just lost a day of my life listening to how Jordan will hate me forever, and I'm a worthless mooch who puts you and him out, and oh, yeah, I'm also a mean drunk. You put him up to this? Or was this all Ian in his shining glory?"

"Ian? You? No, I didn't put him up to anything. But... yeah, I know what happened with Jordan and the rest..."

"Well... Do you think I'm a piece of shit who drinks too much like Ian does?"

She slowly set her pen down and rose up from the desk chair. "Where is this coming from?"

"Your husband," Caleb snapped grumpily. "Now, do you?"

"Yeah, I think alcohol doesn't do any good for you. Makes you... mean. Lazy. Shiftless."

"Ain't I just all those things?" He hurled out the accusation as he paced. Though his heart was thumping hard, his head starting banging with it. Kailynn agreed. They thought he was a mean drunk... a shiftless loser... and Jordan? Shit. He'd somehow lost his brother without even realizing it.

"Caleb?"

He paced, ignoring her, and pacing some more.

"Caleb, please."

He stopped and stared at her. Her face softened. His heart thumped at the realization that he was all those horrible things. Maybe, just maybe, he didn't really want to be. But what the hell was he supposed to do about it? Was it just him?

"No. Not when you're sober, you're not any of those things. You wouldn't have lasted with Ian so long if you weren't a good worker. He wouldn't tolerate BS in the fields, not even for me."

She got up and walked towards him. Caleb flopped down on the couch and stared at his fingers. "Wh—what did I say to Jordan?"

She flopped down beside him. Blowing out a breath, her hair ruffled as she replied in a stern tone, "Jordan gave you a last chance to be his brother or be done with him forever. Accept him and the man he loves or never speak to him again. He chose Pedro. Not you. You could have accepted him and his lifestyle right then, which would have been good. But you... you opted not to."

"Not to what?"

Kailynn's face contorted. "To be his brother anymore. You didn't get how serious this was? How real?"

Caleb's heart skipped a beat and he didn't move for a moment. "Jordan's ultimatum was I either accept his marriage or we're done as brothers?"

"Yes." Kailynn's eyes filled with tears. "You really didn't get that?"

"And I refused to accept him?"

"You did. Quite clearly." Her voice cracked. "It's why I cried most of the day. I love you both... but I can't side with you..."

He stayed stoic. "No. Of course not." He shot onto his feet, spinning on his boot heel before he walked out.

Furious now, he stormed past Jack Rydell who was casually strolling on the same path. Jack had been acting weird since the fire last summer. His son coincidentally disappeared, and no one had heard from him since. Jack's odd behavior was the primary reason Ian and Kailynn decided to stay at the ranch. They left Seattle and moved back to the ranch permanently. That was the only reason Caleb had a place to live.

Ignoring everything, he got into his truck and barreled down the road, heading towards Brewster... to go where?

See his brother? What would he say? That he was sorry? He could handle all the changes? Could he say that to Jordan? And more, could he handle it?

Or should he merely let the ultimatum stand? Was this better? It was certainly easier if he just let Jordan go and went on about his life. No more disappointing everyone.

Besides why should he have to change to support Jordan's way of life? Why didn't Jordan just change? So, he might as well have kept on driving because he'd soon have no home anyway. No job. No sister. No brother. No father either, only because his dad would side with his sister in order to keep living there. That left Caleb completely alone. Aimless. With no one to talk to and nothing to do.

He rubbed his hand through his hair. Was he really that mean when he got drunk? Maybe he drank a little too much. Got a little surly sometimes, but Jordan never took it personally or thought he was serious before. But that was before Jordan came out. Now Jordan was a completely different person all around. How could Caleb learn to accept that?

He knew where Pedro lived with his father so he parked and stared at the single-wide, old trailer with the sagging porch and weed-peppered lawn. What was he doing here? Intending to go off on Jordan for ruining his life? Or to ask him if they could still be brothers? He didn't yet know.

He shoved the truck door open and it protested with a loud squeak. After crossing the short, gravel walkway to the rickety front porch steps, he banged hard on the door and waited, but got no answer. He banged again. Turning, he jumped off the porch and went around the corner of the trailer to the small back deck before he stopped dead.

Josefina. She rose from the chair. "You're not just going to go away quietly, are you?"

"Were you purposely ignoring my knocks?"

"Hoping to." She got up and strolled past him. Dressed in

a pair of jean shorts and a t-shirt with low-riding cowboy boots, her long, waist-length, jet-black hair swung free. Her breasts were as big and full as Caleb remembered from the wedding.

He didn't let his gaze linger there too long, however. Straightening up, he asked, "Is Jordan here?"

"Jordan doesn't want to see you… pretty much ever again."

"So you know. What did they do? Hold a press conference to broadcast what an asshole I was last night? Look, just tell me where my brother is."

Her eyebrows lifted. "Wow, you are an even bigger asshole than Jordan described. No. They stopped by this morning to grab Pedro's stuff. But I'll be damned if I'm siccing the likes of you on them."

Caleb shut his eyes to regain his patience and repress the nasty things that nearly slipped off his tongue. Heartless things. Flippant things. Things that would annoy this woman to the point that she would not do what he wanted. "Look, Josefina, right?"

"You remembered my name?"

"I remember bits and pieces of the day." He swept the hat off his head and held it in his hands, spinning it while stepping closer to her. She glowered at him all the more. "I gather I was offensive, to you, and Pedro, and Jordan. I don't remember. Not clearly enough."

Her head tilted. "What? Are you saying you were drunk?"

"Yeah. That's probably an understatement though."

"You didn't seem that drunk to me."

"No? I can put away quite a lot of liquor before it catches up to me."

Her gaze lowered, sweeping over him and back up. "Something you must be proud of."

"No." He sighed. "Not at all. I'm sorry for whatever rude

45

remark I said to you." He cleared his throat. She had a way of staring right through the heart and soul of him.

"What exactly are you doing here? Haven't you done enough damage already?"

"It sounds like it; yes, I have. That's why I'd like to talk to my brother and apologize." He resented having to explain himself to this stranger, a girl who had nothing to do with his relationship with his brother.

"They're already gone."

Caleb's shoulders fell. He'd waited too damn long. He dropped his head in defeat. "Do you know where they were going to stay tonight? They couldn't have driven all the way there already."

"Yes. I know where they plan to stay."

He all but groaned at her sharp retort. "Could you possibly tell me?"

"Why would I do that?"

"Because I intend to go there and speak to them."

"They're on their honeymoon. I know you don't believe in their relationship, and the vows they exchanged don't mean much to you, despite what everyone else thinks, but I'll be damned if I'm going to let you ruin the first night of their honeymoon. This is the official start of their lives together. For once, they can be truly free and clear of shit like you."

His temple throbbed as he clenched his teeth, finding it harder and harder to keep listening to her. "You don't even know me."

"Oh, yes, I do. I know you, Caleb Hayes. I've known your type all my life. I also know how mean you are to my brother, and have been for years."

He started to speak but shut his mouth. Mean to her brother? What was she talking about? Maybe just last year, considering all the changes that occurred between them, but was he ever mean in general to Pedro? No. Nah. He never was during the whole time he worked with Pedro. He hadn't been mean to him ever before. He just worked with him. Man to man. Why would Pedro consider that mean?

"I have not been mean to him. Okay, maybe just recently. I had a hard time accepting their... you know, but..."

"Their love? Commitment? Relationship? Believe me, I know you still are having a hard time. What I can't figure out is why. If you were around them more maybe you could learn to be a nicer person."

"Yeah, I know all that."

She tilted her head. Her eyes were huge with heavily accented, black eyebrows that captivated him. He could not shift his gaze from her perfect face. Her gorgeous looks socked him in the gut. How could he begin to approach her now? First of all, she was way, way out of his league. Only a sufficient amount of alcohol could make him believe otherwise.

Her mouth tightened. "You need to leave now."

"I came off pretty bad at the wedding. I see that now. But I'm not always that bad. Please. If I can make up with Jordan, won't it make everything better for both of our brothers? Consider the favor you'd be doing."

She tapped her foot, crossing her arms over her chest. "That charm of yours usually works most of the time, huh?"

He threw his hands up. "I'm not trying to *charm* anyone. I mean it. What does it take to convince you?"

"You can't convince me because I know your reputation." Her mouth temporarily tightened and then relaxed. "But I saw how upset Jordan was. Unfortunately, he cares very deeply about what you think. You should be ashamed of yourself. Not only for hurting him so much by your rejection, but bringing that hideous attitude to his own wedding."

She passed by him, surprising him when she went inside. He was unsure of what to do with himself. The growing

47

disdain of his siblings and Ian now included Josefina. It must have been a pretty epic bender for him. She came back out and handed him a piece of paper. "They're staying here."

He took the address, setting his hat back on his head before doffing it towards her in a mock salute. "Thank you, Josefina. I promise to make good on this."

She scoffed at his comment. "I'm just hoping you won't make it any worse." Turning on her heel, she walked away, disappearing around the back of the trailer again. He sighed, realizing she detested him. He probably deserved it but that did not make it any less disheartening.

Sitting in his truck, he stared at the address. A three-hour drive lay ahead of him. He glanced at the clock, guessing it would be dark long before he got there. And if he did manage to get there, what would he do? He was homeless. Jobless. Friendless. Familyless. He didn't have many options to choose from, did he? He knew he had to do this though. Despite being boxed into a corner.

He took the address of the motel and looked it up on his phone to let the navigation guide him there. It was dinner time before he got to the destination. He stared at the generic roadside motel and his stomach twisted and churned. What should he do? Just knock? Crap! They were on their honeymoon.

He hated feeling homeless, jobless, and without the comfort of his siblings. He was on the brink of losing everything, which wasn't very much, in his life. He didn't have a goal or purpose to occupy his thoughts. No kidding. That void seemed startlingly more obvious now, more than he could ever remember before.

One conversation could not destroy it all. His job, home, and family. He had no control over any of those things. Perhaps Ian had a valid point... fun didn't compensate for all those other things.

What he could have lost might not have meant too much to anyone else, but it was the entire world to Caleb. His family. His job. What the hell else could he do but continue working for the Rydells? He'd never lasted more than a week or two when he worked for the other ranchers and orchard owners in the valley. The Rydells offered him work whenever he asked. It was work he could do and it was always more or less the same. He couldn't change it.

Most of all, he didn't want to lose his siblings. They were his friends as well as his family and his only social connection. They were all he valued in his otherwise pointless, shallow life.

After mustering up his nerve, he walked down the outdoor corridor, heading towards the room number that was his final destination. He stared at it, standing a few feet away. When he lifted his hand after a moment or two, he stepped forward and knocked very hard three times before stepping back and waiting.

Minutes passed before he heard his brother opening the door. Caleb cleared his throat. Jordan's gaze narrowed, and he squinted at him.

"What the fuck do you want, Caleb?"

"I got the motel address from Pedro's sister."

"I know. Duh. She already texted Pedro and told him the whole story. You're so sorry. Why? Did Ian threaten to kick you out?"

Stunned, Caleb pressed his lips together. "He might have spoken a few words with me."

Jordan crossed his arms over his chest. He was so cold and harsh towards Caleb. His shoulders sank, and Jordan sighed. "Go home. I don't want to see you. In case you missed the fucking memo, I'm on my honeymoon. I want to stay here and be happy, not miserable and drifting and shiftless like you are. I might be gay, Caleb, but at least I'm not an asshole. I found someone to love and who loves me back. What the fuck do you have? Nothing. Whatever you're looking for, go home and find it. There is nothing here for you."

Pedro stood behind Jordan and set a hand on Jordan's shoulders for moral support. Caleb glanced at him and then at his brother. His heart hammered hard in his chest. Shit. Ian wasn't understating this at all. Caleb wasn't wanted here anymore. No, he was hated here. He must have really fucked up. He'd never seen Jordan so cold, final and hell, so real. His brother truly meant it.

Caleb's head was pounding harder than the morning's hangover. He grabbed his neck and pressed into the stiff muscles as he started shaking his head. "Jordan... I'm so sorry. I didn't comprehend what happened last night. I was drinking, and I didn't realize..."

"What? That I'm a person? Of course, you were drunk again—"

"I'm going to stop drinking," Caleb interrupted quickly. Desperate for his brother to forgive him, he wanted to quit tapping into the events of last night. He would have done anything. He would have said anything to make that true and real and permanent.

"You're going to stop drinking? Good luck with that." Jordan started to shut the door.

Caleb shoved his arm through the door in near panic. "Wait! Please! I mean it."

Jordan was shaking his head. "You always mean it. Until the next time... and the next drink. I don't plan to be around for your next binge."

"You think I do all of that because I drink too much?"

Jordan's eyebrows rose. "I hope that's the reason. Other-wise, I'd have to give your personality all the credit for the cruel, prejudiced shit you like to spew. Whatever. None of that concerns me anymore." Again, Jordan tried to get him to move his arm so he could slam the door shut.

"Wait. Wait! I'm not homophobic. I'm... just a little unsettled by it."

"Unsettled? Is that what you call it?" Jordan's face dropped, and the anger faded from his expression. "Please just go. Leave us alone. We'd like to enjoy our chance to be happy without having you around. For six long years, I let you and those who were like you, come between us. For six years. I can't... I can't do it anymore. I have no more patience or forgiveness left inside me for that. This is me, get it? I'm gay. I love Pedro. And if that means goodbye and good luck, Caleb, then GOODBYE AND GOOD LUCK!"

Goodbye and good luck? He couldn't be serious. This couldn't be the end of their brotherhood. Caleb could not and would not accept that. They had a fight. A mild disagreement, not the end of the world. No. Never. He said, "You've never said anything to me about it before. Nothing like this."

Jordan shook his head. "I was always playing along, Caleb, and hoping if I did it long enough you'd... I don't know, you'd suddenly change and be nice to me. Crazy, I know, on my part. But you're just a mean son of a bitch inside and outside. Having a contrite moment now? My guess it that's only because you finally got cornered. Never been called on it before. Who knew wimpy-assed me would be the one to end it for you? But I already knew how Kailynn and Ian reacted, so, yeah. I'll bet this is all a big role for you to play, isn't it? A way for you to hopefully keep your job and home. When have you done anything for me?"

Jordan started to shut the door again, but Caleb pushed inside forcibly. Jordan scowled at him harder. The only thing he had on Jordan was his brute strength, which he used now to gain entry. Caleb was hoping to salvage whatever was about to end for them. "Wait! Just please wait a minute. I'm sorry I hurt you. I'm sorry for all the mean things I said to you and Pedro. I promise you..." he glanced up and saw Pedro staring at him.

Although a small guy, Pedro worked with the endurance and strength that outdid Caleb. He could work all day in triple digit temperatures without a drop of sweat. Caleb knew that. He never once acknowledged it to Pedro however. Or complimented his stamina. But Pedro's cold face reflected Jordan's expression. These two had obviously talked long and hard about this and were now joined in a completely united front against him. Caleb never considered that they could freeze him out or go against him. Especially Jordan.

Caleb's heart started to pound and speed up. No. NO! Family relationships didn't just end like that. Not because of a few off-color remarks. He never thought his brother could be so unwaveringly serious. Heart attack serious. Death serious. Vowing not to speak to him again serious. His breathing started to increase. His heart rate skyrocketed with panic and it felt like something suddenly zinged through his entire body.

He was about to lose his brother.

Jordan turned his back on Caleb.

How could it not be hard for Jordan to end their brotherhood? Their friendship. Their everyday part of each other's lives. Could Jordan mean that? Holding his back tall and straight and his head high, Pedro watched Caleb with a cold, stony look in his eyes. They both meant it.

Panic overcame him. Babbling, he started pleading. "I promise both of you, I'll shut up from now on. I'll change. I'll be better. I'll find a way. I'll quit drinking. I'll be... I'll be how I should have been from the start. Jordan... Please. I can't lose you. You're my brother, man. I should have come after you last night and told you that you'll always be my brother.

You're my fucking brother. That's all that matters. I don't have shit to show for my life but you and Lynnie. And... mostly, just you. Please don't cut me off... please let me at least try and change. You don't have to forgive me or anything, but at least, just let me try..."

Jordan turned towards him and his head tilted. "I've never heard you beg for anything before."

"I'm begging you for your forgiveness."

Silence met his reply. Dead, long silence. Then Jordan said, "I'm sorry but one conversation doesn't fix decades of shit."

"No, of course not. But I could start there. I'll try... I just didn't know how you felt. Not this bad. Please. I'll do anything." He'd never begged anyone for a single thing before. His entire body went taut with nerves.

Jordan said with a stony, cold facial expression and tone of voice, "We plan to get back from our honeymoon next Friday and we're moving into our new place on Saturday. We could use that giant, strong back of yours when that happens. Perhaps, we could start there."

Moving furniture? It sounded so normal and easy. Something a lot of people did. Caleb's heart jumped with glee. Yeah. Of course, he could do that. "Do you... mean it?"

"Yeah. My sincerity never has been in doubt. Only yours. So that's it. Pedro and I will give you a chance to redeem yourself, but nothing can be assumed. You'd better start changing, Caleb, and real fast."

Caleb nodded over and over while smiling. He put his hand out. "I can do that! I can help you move. I know how to do that."

"Unfortunately, not much else. You'd better figure it out."

"I will. I swear. Thank you. Have..." he glanced at Pedro and then stared into his brother's eyes, saying, "have a great honeymoon. I'll go now."

"Yeah, that would be greatly appreciated."

"But I'll see you on Saturday?"

Jordan grunted. "Saturday." Then he slammed the door on Caleb. Caleb wilted. It was enough though. It was a chance. A chance for him to change. Probably his last chance to change, and Caleb clearly understood that now. Even though it cost his former life, and home, and way of living, as well as being isolated from his brother, sister, and father before he realized it, he definitely knew now that he had to change.

He just had to figure out how the hell to do that without messing everything up. To date, all he'd done is screw things up. Now, he had to alter his lifelong behavior patterns and attitude. He had no choice anymore, and had to learn how to do just that.

But where did he start?

CHAPTER 4

"CALEB'S COMING TODAY," HER brother announced with a grimace.

Josefina dropped the vase she was wrapping in paper and set it into a box. "What? That asshole? That Caleb?"

"Uh-huh. That was my first reaction too. But Jordan and he had a conversation, and Jordan set the bar and the ultimatum pretty high, and shockingly, Caleb complied with the terms. It astonished me too, but it made Jordan so happy. If you could have seen him that night in the motel room after Caleb had gone to so much effort to talk to him. Caleb's never bothered doing anything like that before."

"So, does that mean he's back in the family?"

"Yup. Vows say *for better or worse*."

Josefina turned her head away, muttering, "You can definitely count that as the very worst of it. Damn."

"No, not damn. Good. This is good. Jordan has spent all our time together, working toward this moment, when he finally laid down the law with Caleb. His heart has ached with grief over Caleb and what his brother's influence and approval mean to him. He even failed to put me and our relationship over Caleb's opinions and sneers, which is why we initially broke up. It's huge to know he's done this, and yes, even bigger still that Caleb actually came through for Jordan. I believed to my core that only Ian and Kailynn were Jordan's real family, the ones that would always stand by him."

Josefina stared open-mouthed at her brother. He was busily packing more dishes into a box and didn't notice her shocked gaze. He lifted his face up. "What? Why are you staring at me like that?"

"I'm sure I've never heard you string that many words together in one sentence."

Pedro grinned, slightly lifting his lips into a boyish, small smile. "I'm just happy. For once, I feel like talking."

Her heart swelled, and she reached over and touched his hand. "I love to know that you're so happy. Of course, I'll be nice to Caleb. For you, and not only because you asked me, but also because you're doing it for Jordan after a huge, emotional breakthrough."

"And maybe Caleb did come through. When a push came to shove, the shit was real, and final, Caleb had to see Jordan. For that, I'm grateful. If not, it would have devastated Jordan. I'm tired of watching him get hurt and having to sacrifice his own thoughts and feelings because of his family's careless attitude about him. I woke up every day during the last year and especially since the wedding, wanting to keep my eyes shut. Why? Because I'm so afraid it's still a dream and not my true life. I fear that I'll open my eyes and Jordan will not be there. Especially now that I can be with Jordan out in public as my husband. That's all I ever wanted. We're poor as church mice and probably always will be, but we love each other genuinely and that makes me feel like the richest man in the world."

"I hope someday to be blessed with the same kind of relationship you two have." She hugged her brother and he squeezed her back, grinning.

"You need a good man too, huh?"

She laughed. Rarely was Pedro so easy going or gregarious. He shamelessly revealed the jubilance he so obviously felt inside, something uncharacteristic of him. Jordan was at his sister's house collecting his things, and she and Pedro were collecting Pedro's. They had minimal furniture to load, and some hand-me-downs they scrounged together, but their excitement over moving to their new place made it seem as if they were relocating to a castle.

A loud truck roared into the driveway of the trailer her father had raised all five of his kids in, including Josefina. She eagerly moved out to a small apartment when she was twenty-four and made enough money to do so. The oldest of five, and half white from her mother's side. Her mother died of complications from diabetes and her dad remarried a lady named Izzy with whom he had two more kids. Izzy also had two kids from her former relationship, which her dad raised as his own. Pedro was the only boy. Her dad struggled at first when he learned his only son was gay, but Josefina was Pedro's champion from the start and her dad came around.

She glanced out the window and spotted the beast: a bright red truck, two-toned in color with a large bed and a rack that featured oversized lights on it. Oversized tires and a loud diesel engine are what made it the *beast*. She sighed as she recognized the driver, none other than Caleb Hayes.

But it was heartwarming to see Jordan sitting on the front passenger seat. When he got out, she did not fail to see the giant grin on his face and the bounce in his step as he ran up to the front door and burst in without knocking. Caleb had purposely driven Jordan there, and that, in itself, was huge.

She hung back, and Caleb lumbered in behind Jordan. He was a big guy, with wide shoulders and a strong, barrel chest and arms. He had a swarthy complexion with dark black hair and he often sported a sparse beard, that looked scratchy on his chin and neck. He stood back, glancing around, shifting his feet, clearly uncomfortable. But Jordan reached forward and hugged Pedro. Right then and there. As if it had been a matter of days and not merely two hours since they separated. She grinned at their affectionate display while Caleb stayed back, half scowling. She sighed. That man had a long way to go before he could prove he actually "changed."

Caleb noticed her and straightened his back. His eyebrows rose with obvious interest and he distinctly perked up. She gritted her teeth, reminding herself to be nice. *Ignore the asshole.*

They separated and turned towards their joint siblings. "So let's throw this stuff in."

Everyone grabbed boxes and walked them out to the back of the pick-up truck, shuffling past each other with different loads in their arms. They left them beside the truck until after the furniture was loaded up.

Taking the end of the bed frame, mattress, sofa and dining room table, Caleb bore the brunt of the weight quite effortlessly with each item. She stood back and let him nearly singlehandedly carry the sofa into the back of the long bed truck. He secured it all down neatly before jumping off the load. Begrudgingly, she'd have to give kudos to his horse-like back when it came to hauling crap.

He stared at her a few more times and she felt his gaze on her, which was so intense at times, it seemed to be stripping her naked. She managed to keep her eyes off him and consciously aimed them anywhere but toward him. Consequently, they still hadn't exchanged any pleasantries.

"Well, let's get this shit delivered," Caleb said, rubbing his hands together. Her brother jumped into the back seat of the crew cab. Reluctantly, so did Josefina. She guessed Caleb spoke crude and rude all the time and wasn't trying to be offensive. That was just him.

She kept quiet on the ride from Brewster, where they lived, to downtown River's End. Caleb followed instructions and drove down the side street where Jordan and Pedro rented a single bedroom, small house. It had a miniscule yard but what it lacked in acreage it made up for with the view.

The drive was uncomfortable for Josefina. She kept seeing Caleb's eyes leaving the road to glance in the rearview mirror *at her*. She was sure of it. She kept her gaze confined to outside of her window, but she was sure he never stopped checking her out. Why? Was he trying to guess her bra size?

They discussed rental prices and Caleb obviously knew nothing about it or his brother. It was all news to him. Josefina could have patted herself on the shoulder, since she not only knew all about it, but she'd also been privy to the decision-making.

They pulled into the driveway of the small, old, quaint house. It needed some work, some paint and had a few gaps where the siding needed replacing. But Jordan convinced Pedro he could do the repairs and they managed to negotiate a lower rent with the owner in exchange for any improvements.

The lawn needed mowing and tending, naturally, but Josefina expected they'd take care of that. After piling out of the cab, they walked towards the house. Jordan withdrew a set of keys and opened up the place. They entered the musty, dimly lit foyer. Caleb walked over and opened the shades. Instantly, the sunlight made it better. "What do you think? A little airing out, some coats of paint and it should be pretty damn nice."

It wasn't, not at all, but Josefina remembered where

Jordan had grown up. Yes, all of them grew up in crowded, old trailers. At least hers was clean and fresh as a daisy. Her father had an obsessive need for constant cleanliness in the home. But Jordan? Not so much.

"What do you think? Josefina has gifted us going half on the price on interior and exterior paints." Jordan asked. Caleb just stood there, a big, hulking, menacing presence in the tiny space. She moved back, giving herself more space from his bulk. She was glaring laser bullets at Caleb. His brother so eagerly longed for his approval. He'd better freaking give it to him.

To her shock and surprise, however, he did. "It's kinda nice. Yeah, some paint would make it a lot nicer though. I could help you paint it. Whip it all out in a weekend."

Jordan stilled. His unmasked hope for Caleb's acceptance just about broke her heart. Jordan wanted that more than anything. She mentally commanded Caleb not to revert to his former history, being an asshole all the time and hurting his brother thoughtlessly. Jordan nodded, and his tone became offhand and cool, so opposite of the little boy he was just a moment ago with so much eagerness in his eyes. "Yeah, sure, that could happen. We'll have to see what else we can work on."

Caleb rubbed his hands together. "Well, let's get all this inside before the heat hits."

They worked as a team and Caleb ran the show. The natural leadership he demonstrated surprised her. He easily took control without even trying. Was it because of his bulk and strength or his deep, often too loud voice? Probably all of it. The old alpha male dominance. She hated reducing it to that, but also knew how attractive it was to both men and women alike.

Caleb methodically worked through the web of knots he

tied to hold the load down. She shifted uneasily as soon as she realized her brother and Jordan were inside.

They were discussing the placement of the furniture and she was all alone, standing below Caleb who continued to work through the layers of knotted twine and rope. He got it all untied and he stood on the open tailgate, wrapping it into a loop around his bent arm. He finished and jumped down, coming closer to her when he set the rope off to the side in the back of his truck.

"So... you're Pedro's sister?"

"That obvious, huh? You're a quick study," she snapped sarcastically.

He turned and jumped up until he sat on the tailgate. "I deserve that. I must have offended you at the wedding. I'm sorry about that."

"Only because you realized whose sister I was? That's not much of an apology."

"I didn't know. Again, I'm sorry."

She tapped her foot, visibly annoyed. "You know, it speaks pretty poorly about your relationship with Jordan considering you didn't know who I was. They," she waved her hand towards the house where her brother and groom stood, "have been together for close to six years now and yet, you had no idea who I could be? Sounds like a pretty shitty relationship you've had with your own brother, huh?"

Swinging his legs, he stopped at hearing her sharp retort. "No. I didn't know... Anything. Let alone, who you were."

Silence descended between them. It was already a quiet street. An empty lot occupied one side of the rental and the chirps of crickets and frogs were all that filled the air as well as the occasional whooshing of the river in the distance. She should have let it go, but it festered inside her. "Did you learn anything from that? Your own brother's entire life had to be kept a secret. Was it worth it?"

He shifted around, growing rather uncomfortable with her questions. Granted, they were intrusive, but it was her brother. Someone he deeply hurt with his cruel behavior and prejudice. And Jordan's feelings were valid too since he was someone she had long considered a second brother, not just an in-law.

"I don't know. I'm trying my best now. But…it's hard for me. When I see them embrace or talking like… couples do, hell, I don't know. I worked with 'em both nearly every day and never had the slightest clue. I realized they were close friends, sure, I just never knew about this…"

She restrained the urge to roll her eyes. He was so generic and antiquated, he was unwilling to get out of himself if only to understand someone else who was different.

"Jordan's stipulation was that you accept both of them or not. I never heard the word, *try*. Trying is a pile of shit at this point."

Josefina was deeply entrenched in her brother and Jordan's journey after personally witnessing the pain of unacceptance from other people, including their own families.

"No. I do. I accept them. I'm not just *trying*. It's pretty new for me… and unlike you, my brother *does know* me. He knows how hard a time I have with… with change and variability. Any change. All change. This is a huge change for me."

"So just like that, you excuse it? You tortured him. You do realize that, I hope? I doubt your brother made that explicitly clear. Your constant disapproval and his innate fear of you destroyed him. You owned such a huge presence in his life."

He sucked in some air. "You don't pull any punches, do you?"

"About my brother? No. Hell no. I'd do anything in his defense and support. That's called love. That's what's real.

But you obviously don't even know how to treat your brother with love, do you?"

"No," he agreed quietly. His face was impassive. She had no idea how he'd reply to her ranting anger. And she was angry too. He hurt her brother and he never had the right or the reason to. Pulling a knee up, he hooked his arm around it. "No…Josefina?"

She was startled when he said her name, an husky timbre in his voice. "Yes."

"Well, Josefina, I'm working on it. Maybe you could give me a break."

"It's hard to when your attitude and prejudice nearly ended their relationship. No one should suffer that much over another person's opinion or advice."

He shifted around. "I didn't know he was gay."

"What a shit excuse."

"It's all I got. I know now. I'm working through some stuff that's long overdue. But can I add, in my defense, that I was raised…"

She scoffed. "I know how you were raised. I watched what it did to your brother."

Caleb's face lost its neutral scowl and he winced. "It's not okay, what I did. I know that now, but I didn't know it then. Not even last week. But now it has been clearly drilled home to me. By multiple sources." He flipped his hands up in the air. "What else can I do but start to change what always seemed second nature to me? Why should I bother to even change if no one will stop talking about it or forgive my past? Give me a second chance. That's all I'm asking for. Jordan's agreed to give it to me. Can't you too?"

She tugged on her lower lip with one finger and her thumb. Was he sincere? But maybe he had a point. He wanted to change now, so what more could he do but try?

"Don't hurt them then. Walk away if you can't handle it but don't hurt them again."

"That's all you want from me?"

"Yes. That's all I want."

"I promise to do that. Does that mean you could eventually not detest me? Quit bawling me out every time we meet?"

She stiffened at his words and rolled her eyes as she sighed. "You can't help being so offensive, can you? Are you a product of your unhappy childhood too?"

He grinned this time. "Yeah, actually I am but I didn't consider it all that unhappy."

The front door opened and Pedro and Jordan came up to them. She faked a smile and asked, "So are we ready?"

The guys started lifting the heavy furniture. Josefina followed behind with boxes, which she directed to all the different rooms. She stopped dead in the bedroom when she heard Caleb say, "Pedro, help me?"

She forgot sometimes that they worked together daily at the ranch and had another relationship. In this interaction, Caleb was putting the bedframe together, but the brackets were bent in transit and he couldn't muscle them in. Together, they kept adjusting and refitting them until it worked. She was a little impressed at Caleb's patience in such a tedious process. When the brackets clicked together, Caleb glanced at her brother, grinning. Over his bed. So maybe the damn galoot was trying.

He stayed through the rest of the afternoon and they started the smaller tasks of arranging all the personal items in the drawers and cabinets as well as the odds and ends, which ended up in the garage. There was another trip to Ian and Kailynn's house for some tools and whatnots that Ian offered to them, including a small, push mower.

"I could mow the grass. It's ready for a haying if you all don't get on it soon," Caleb offered.

Jordan's joy over his brother's involvement was obvious and celebratory. And Caleb did mow the lawn and rake the clippings. She was surprised he even noticed the excessive growth. Judging him harshly, she knew that, but she never pictured such a crass man to care about the menial chores. He worked outside while she set up the kitchen, every so often, staring randomly at the big, handsome man in the backyard. Damn, chauvinistic asshole. He had good looks and a devastating smile, which were almost enough to make his macho, alpha male act slightly charming. That is, if you were the kind of stupid woman who would fall for such blatant crap. He was a guy who would cheat as often and as easily as he went to the super market. No thanks. She knew better.

Still, he was kind of handsome.

But even that vanished as soon as he opened his damn mouth.

Munching on chips and salsa for dinner, Jordan and Pedro's new place was now livable at least. Caleb leaned back on the chair of the dining room table and said, "This is good shit. Where'd you get it?"

"Didn't buy it. Josie made it," Pedro answered.

Caleb wagged his eyebrows. "Good cooking like this? Marry me, Josefina," he said, grinning with mock sincerity. She scowled and elbowed her brother. The last thing she needed were his comments to solidify his opinions about her.

Twilight dimmed the sky and Pedro let out a huge yawn. "I'm beat." He stretched his arms and rested one hand behind Jordan on his shoulder, squeezing it. Jordan glanced at him and leaned forward to kiss his hand in a quick smooch. It was so sweet. A loving gesture. Delivered with the ease they deserved, after all these years. They were engaging in normal, affectionate gestures, as any couple who recently got married would do.

Caleb, however, suddenly dropped his chair down from where he had it balanced on the back two legs. He swallowed and rested his gaze on the chips in front of him before stuffing a handful in his mouth.

Trying, her ass. His disapproval was louder than the thunk of the chair when it dropped. "Me too. I think I'll go home."

"We can run you home," Jordan volunteered. But he looked pretty beat too.

Caleb's gaze jerked up. "Yeah. I'll take you, Josefina. It's no biggie."

She cringed, forgetting he was her ride. Jordan's truck was there, which he brought over earlier, and Pedro didn't have his own. She smiled, and her lips went into a tight line. Fine. Otherwise, she might have overreacted to the simple truck ride. It was nice of him. It was definitely out of his way. He lived across the river, about a four-mile drive, so taking her home would have easily added thirty miles roundtrip.

Jordan glanced at his brother, clearly pleased with his offer. "Really? It's out of your way."

He replied, "It's fine."

She let it go only because of the joy she saw on Jordan's face at receiving his brother's help and being here. Caleb's acceptance seemed to include all of this thus far. Crumbs, yes, but Jordan gathered them with delight as if they were specks of gold dust.

She followed Caleb to the door and Pedro gave her a huge hug while he said thanks, as did Jordan. She stared back at them in the doorway of their first home together and something lodged in her throat. It was huge and new and shocking and hard-fought and hard-won for them to be standing there, both tired after a long day of moving and now they could sit down and relax together. *In their own home.*

That left her alone with Caleb Hayes.

~

CALEB GLANCED out of the corners of his eyes towards Josefina as she pulled on the seatbelt and clicked it in. Even the way she did it seemed pronounced and judgmental toward him. Wow, did she have some opinions. Strong, loud, hypercritical opinions. He cleared his throat, his mind helplessly straining for some kind of conversation starter.

Mostly, he was wishing he were smarter, brighter, and better read. She was so quick to answer and articulate her angle on things, obviously far smarter than he. He was no mental giant and barely managed a word snippet here and there, so unlike what she so obviously breezed through. That's why he eventually decided to start mowing the lawn. It was loud, and it kept him quiet. He could not say things to irritate or piss her off, or make her, yet again, gnash her teeth.

Yeah, she really disliked him.

Usually, Caleb didn't give a cow's ass who liked him. Or not. But he, for some reason, wanted her to like him. Of course, he thought she was gorgeous with that killer body and smile. He recalled her delicate face and long, thick, midnight black hair, reminding him of a horse's mane. And in a good way. Naturally, it was not something he'd admit out loud to her.

Still, she hated him.

"So... they seem to really like their new place."

She scoffed. "Yes."

Sighing, he shifted himself around, growing uncomfortable at her tone. "Look, I get that you disapprove of how I handled my brother... well, at least for the last decade and especially, for the last year. But he forgave me, so why can't you?"

"Because he's a much nicer person than me. That's why I like him so much. And furthermore, it's because of how you negatively affected and hurt *my brother*. It's not about you though, as hard as that may be for you to understand."

He gnashed his teeth this time. "I don't think it's *all* about me." Or did he? What she so clearly believed and said instantly made him reconsider his robotic denial. Did he do that? Make everything about him? His sister just finished telling him she'd been equally as miserable and unhappy as his brother, all during their life together that he now missed the most.

"You equate my inability to like you as a direct reflection of your masculinity. It's driving you nuts, isn't it, that I'm not so easily floored by that boyish grin of yours? It's obvious that it usually works for you."

He flashed the famous grin at her and shrugged and even wagged his eyebrows. "Well, I can't help it. Yeah, it has before and still does... but I didn't think you noticed."

"I noticed that you fail to add any substance to all that pretty."

"I'm not pretty," he said automatically, frowning at her.

She smiled sweetly, but it was cloying and fake. "Oh, I'm sorry, was that too scary to hear? Threatens your manhood? Is that why you're protesting now so much? Don't worry. Just because your brother is something, like successful and loved, don't worry. None of us think you are too."

What hurt Caleb most was left unsaid: all of Jordan's good traits, those which she didn't believe Caleb also possessed. And obviously, being attractive wasn't on that list.

"I have substance."

"Really? What would that be, Caleb?" Again with the sugary, sing-song voice.

"You want me to itemize all of my strengths? You already dislike me, so wouldn't that make me sound arrogant?"

"Make you sound arrogant?"

He heard the irony in her voice.

"Fine. I came off as an arrogant prick the night I first met you. I had a tough time with it too. I'm working hard to change it. The threat of losing a brother makes you rethink things. Realizing your sister and brother were miserable in the same life you loved and longed for nostalgically, yeah... I've been doing some thinking."

"You have?" her tone, again, was too amazed to accept the fact.

"Yes, I have. That's why I came here today."

She pursed her lips, crossing her arms under her breasts. They pushed them up an inch or so, he noticed, before chastising himself and staring forward. He was behaving better. He was also growing and changing as a person. Right? It was all he attempted to do.

He just wished he had a damn idea of how to accomplish it. There was no clear-cut path to his goal. There were so many different ways to think and live and view the world, and Caleb was never very good at discerning the best choices. He'd never been a champion at self-reflection and logical conclusions. Especially now, after having the change or action result from all the self-reflection.

He didn't know how to share himself like he was trying to with Josefina. This stranger. But he was trying. 'Cause she was hot? Well, yes. That was merely the initial attraction, however. He couldn't help liking busty, small women. He also liked her looks. Did that mean, in order to be deep and better and not what he'd always been, he should attempt to become her friend?

And not seek more of her company to have sex? And what? Hang out? *Talk?* He shuddered to think about it. Talking. To. Her. But there they were. The drive was only halfway over. She obviously disapproved of his usual approach with women. Sure, he'd run into that plenty of times before. Women rolling their eyes or tightening their mouths in displeasure, clearly conveying their cold rejection to his charm and appeal.

But there was always another woman or girl waiting in the wings for him to try them out on again. There was always someone else, so he merely ignored the uninterested and headed toward the interested. It was successful enough, not to brag, just stating facts, and there were a lot of women who found him hot, handsome, attractive—but not pretty—and hooked up with him because of it. But not this one.

And for some reason, this one's rejection stung him a lot more than usual. Her continued, sharp-tongued retorts only further annoyed him and instead of making him grow used to her, he was irritated by her and wished he simply did not like her.

He was confused as to why she enjoyed hurting his feelings. So, he might not have been her type of guy, he was considered by most to be harmless, funny, and engaging. Even if he wasn't interesting, cultured, smart, articulate, or thought-provoking. He sighed. The list of what he wasn't, however, was growing much longer than he ever dared to admit, even to himself.

Self-reflection sucked, but maybe he should have done that a decade ago. He knew it was already hopeless with this woman. She detested him and everything he stood for. The way he lived and interacted in the world. The way he treated her brother and his own. She had him there. Caleb scooched around on the bench seat again, more uncomfortable after his profound revelation.

His head started to hurt. God, he hated revelations. They always hurt. Regrets pained his heart. Anger toward himself rose from his gut.

And Josefina witnessed all that through the lens of the brother she was caring for and supporting who was now married to Caleb's brother. No wonder she hated Caleb so much. It was justified too. That awkward fact hit him harder than everything else.

"I get it."

She lifted her dark eyes and looked his way. He shook his head, his mouth twisting up in scorn, mostly at himself. "What do you get? That I don't want to jump you?"

He didn't answer her snarky sarcasm but kept driving, gripping the wheel tighter. "That I hurt Jordan."

"That's where you and I differ. Family loyalty. Pedro is my brother. I would never turn my back on him for anything."

"I get it, Josefina. Okay? I finally got what I was and did. But I didn't until my sister and Jordan went off on me the night of his wedding. That was after I hit on you. I didn't know. And before you start railing at me, I know that's the worst part of my meanness. I didn't even know how mean I was. Jordan was always my shadow. For our entire lives. And yet I never really knew him. It's been a bitter pill for me to swallow. But three decades of acting one, narrow way is hard to drop in only a few days time."

Her mouth hung open as she stared at him. "I did not expect you to say all of that."

"Why? Because you don't think I'm capable?"

She bit her lip. "Well…"

"Don't answer that," he grumbled, glaring towards the road before him.

She laughed, and he looked at her in surprise. Her laugh had a husky, sexy tone that evoked all kinds of thoughts she

71

would not have approved of in his mind. Until then, she hadn't laughed, or shared any genuine humor with him.

They entered Brewster, passing huge spreads of orchards that bordered the highway and Columbia River. The bridge spanning the river glistened in the late afternoon sunlight. "Take the next right, and go towards the high school."

He did. "Are you close to the boat ramp?"

"Yes."

"So, you don't live with your family anymore?"

"No. I'm twenty-eight years old."

He flipped her a glance and got her insult, since he was thirty-one and still lived with his.

She kept guiding him on several turns until they stopped in front of a four-unit, single level building.

"Here?"

She nodded. "Here."

He swallowed and put the truck into park. It wasn't much. But far nicer than where he lived. "What do you do?"

"I work as a translator."

"Oh." He didn't guess anything like that. "You mean for Mexicans?"

Eye roll. "For anyone who speaks Spanish, Caleb, and little or no English. Do you want to know something even more shocking and appalling?"

"What?" He heard the rebuke in her tone for not including *all* people who spoke Spanish.

"I also speak several other languages besides Spanish. Awesome, right? I'm also proficient in German and French."

"Wow. You speak multiple languages?" Then the question he had to ask, which seemed so obvious, spilled before he could stop it. "Why? Why learn so many languages?"

She rolled her eyes again. "Because I have an ear for it. It interests me too. However, you were correct in your assumption that I'm only certified to work as a translator in Spanish.

I'm also a certified provider at the Department of Social and Health Services, along with being a CMI."

"What's that?"

"Certified Medical Interpreter. I mostly freelance, however. I do a lot of work on written documents and run a website. All kinds of people, especially those in business and government, hire me for multiple types of projects. I work a lot in the hospitals, schools, and sometimes, I get brought in by DSHS."

"You were certified to do all that?"

She nodded. "All of them. I spent several years slowly building up my reputation. There is a shortage of people with my credentials in this area so I tend to stay pretty busy. Not wealthy yet, nor anytime soon, but yes, I support myself." She waved towards the dumpy building before them. "This is just for a little while. I'm saving to someday buy my own house. Someday, but until then..."

"You help your family too, don't you?"

Her eyebrows jutted upwards. "How did you know that?"

He shrugged. "Your unconditional dedication to Pedro suggested I take a guess."

"Yes, I help them out as often as possible. My dad works as a foreman on the Oslow Orchards and he's often in charge of the loading areas. Pedro? Well, he got in gold with the Rydells and I started translating after I graduated. I have since started my own business."

He stared at her, his eyes flashing with new appreciation. "That's impressive." He had no idea how one went about starting and then sustaining their own business. He wasn't nearly smart enough, let alone, industrious enough for any of that.

"You know, I've always been decent to your brother," Caleb said, almost biting his own tongue. It was a quiet moment and right before she was about to jump out of his truck. But he felt compelled to tell her. Seeing how much she cared about her younger brother.

"You have?" Her eyebrows rose up again, this time slower, methodically and with disdain, as if she were ready to catch him in a lie.

"Yes. I have." He frowned. "Why, did he say I wasn't? That's not true at all. Pedro, me, and Jordan always worked together as an in-sync team for at least half a dozen years. I admit I was flaky the first year… maybe two. But it took me awhile to get the hang of a full-time day job."

She scoffed. "Yes, working a full-time job in your twenties. How awful to expect such an ambitious attempt from you."

He gave her a sour look, but went on, "Anyway, after that, we always worked together daily. I saw him and interacted with him probably twice as often as you did."

"You didn't even talk to him. You didn't know he spoke English," she exclaimed, quick on the attack.

"All right. I thought he spoke limited English, but we did work and interact. I saw you eyeing me while we were putting our brothers' bed together. He and I did it in a snap, like we always do when we work together. Quick. Efficient. Quiet. Okay, I could talk a lot, I guess, without realizing… I'll work on that too."

"What am I to gather from this?"

"Just pointing out that I liked working with Pedro. I always liked him."

Her lips pursed shut. "Oh. You actually like him?"

"I do. He's quick and smart and quiet. Things I appreciate. He always does what he says he will and gives it everything he's got, all of his tenacity."

"Do you work like that too?"

"Not as faithfully. He regularly picked up my slack. I noticed that. I'll—"

"Work on that?" she interrupted. This time, however, her lips were pressed tightly together as she subverted her obvious amusement. He smiled back.

"Yes, I'm going to work on it."

"Why did you want me to know that?"

"I guess..." he frowned and shifted forward, uncomfortable with her close scrutiny. "I guess I didn't want you to think I was as bad as you obviously do."

"What difference does that make? I'm nothing to you, Caleb. The latest girl you like to ogle. Pedro's the one to whom you owe the apology. First, because he's your brother-in-law. Second, because he's your co-worker. Third, because he's the one you wronged. Don't start off with an apology to me. Do you not see now how easily you dismiss Pedro as a person? A person in his own right, a person with standing and dignity. Pedro's the one to whom you owe an apology."

Caleb winced. *Brother-in-law.* His brother-in-law. "Oh." Shit! He missed the rule that he should have started with an apology not just to Jordan, but to Jordan's husband. Caleb's brother-in-law.

"Another damn brother-in-law," he grumbled after a short groan.

She cocked her head. "What?" Her face scrunched up in quick anger.

He held his hands up. "It's just that I have irritating brothers-in-law. First, Ian Rydell, my damn boss. The in-law that I take my orders from. Smart, smug, and all that, to now, Pedro. I didn't even realize what a dick I've been to him even while working too. Just pointing out... damn brothers-in-law."

To his surprise and bewilderment, she started to smile. "It's nice to see you're not making it about his sexuality."

"That's all I need to do to convince you to hate me a little less?"

"It would go a long way, I'll admit…"

"And apologize. I—damn. I didn't think about doing that. I'll do it." He shook his head. "I know I need to change. This has vividly illustrated it to me, maybe like nothing else could. I probably needed to be cracked over the head with it. Thick-skulled, stupid, dense jerk that I am. But I got the point, Josefina. I just don't know how to begin to fix it."

Her head tilted. "Are you being sincere? Or playing me? Or trying to get at me again?"

"Sex? God, I'm not that dumb. I already accept that's a *never* between us. I didn't have a clue how offensive I was to you and now I'm beginning to get an inkling. Believe me, I get it now."

She squinted, and a small smile emerged on her face. "You're not dumb."

He responded with a huge smile. "That's about the nicest thing you've ever said to me."

She grabbed the door handle and the door creaked as she pushed it open. "You're smart. And you have much more decency than your father ever could. So there is potential, Caleb, in you as a person," she added quickly. Perhaps she intended to clarify the potential didn't involve sleeping with her.

He rolled his eyes. "I know what you meant."

"There. Then see? There is potential. Your dad hates your brother and mine. I can see that you're trying, doing the opposite of what you did before, and being the other way."

"I'm trying to."

"Trying," she conceded as she stepped out and he stared after her. His heart blipped in a weird way when she tilted her face downwards, and her long lashes swept against her lower lid. She was breathtaking. She possessed classical beauty. The kind he'd never admired before but was inexplicably drawn towards.

"Josefina?"

She glanced up. "What?"

"Painting." He blurted out the first thing that came to his mind and winced at the bumbling announcement he made for no real reason.

"What?" Her expression scrunched up and she looked puzzled.

"When we start painting their place, do you wanna help?" Paint? He wanted to ask her out so he asked her to help him with home improvements? "I could use your guidance, you know, in acting better around our brothers. I want to be better. I swear, but I'm... I'm still not comfortable. I want to be though. I'm sure I will be, but as of now, I worry I'll keep flubbing it up, you know, sticking my foot in my mouth—"

"You want me to help you be nice to our brothers when you interact with them?"

"Well... shit. Yeah, I guess so. It just sounds so stupid when you word it like that. I don't want to hurt anyone else. Okay? Maybe you could watch how I usually behave around them. Do like you just did then, and give me some pointers. Like apologizing to Pedro and not just assuming Jordan did it for me. See? I wouldn't have ever thought of that. You don't take any shit either and maybe I could use some of that."

She squinted her eyes at him. "You're not trying to seduce me, are you? Because it won't work."

"No." He held his hand up as if he were taking the Boy Scout oath of allegiance. "I swear. I'm not."

"I will withhold judgment, but fine. I'll help you and give you my advice. But remember, you asked me. I won't go easy on you either. He's my brother and you did severe damage. I don't forget or forgive that easily."

"I gathered as much. I get it. If anyone else had done to Jordan what I did, I'd have kicked their asses, but now? What do I do when the perpetrator turns out to be me?"

"First? No more ass kicking. No more fighting. That just shows what a typical ass you are. Be more than that. Be better."

Be more. Be better. Simple. Straightforward. He chanted it a few times. Yeah. Be more. Be better. He could probably do that.

"But... that's all I am. A hick. An ass."

She squinted at him as if he were under heavy scrutiny. Her hand held the door and she leaned into it. "I thought so, Caleb. Until today. Until this drive. I believed that's all there was to you. But you know what? A long time ago, I thought that's all there was to your little brother too. I've learned a lot since then. Maybe, just maybe, I can learn something new about you too, and now, I think I can. Maybe there's a whole hell of a lot more inside there."

If he were a dog, his ears would have pricked up with interest, pleasure, and total adoration at hearing her praise. But instead, he nodded and swallowed. "I hope you're right. It's the first time I've ever wanted to improve."

She tilted her head. "Not what I expected today. Thank you for the ride."

"Next weekend? Should I arrange it for Saturday?"

"Okay. Next Saturday. I'll plan on hearing from you. If I don't? I don't. No sweat off me. But it's your chance."

He sucked in a breath as she slammed the door shut and strolled towards her front door. He stared after her, thinking, his *chance*. She said it herself. She was giving him a chance. Okay, it was the complete opposite of what he expected, but a chance never the less. A chance to prove himself to her. That he was capable of much more than unsubstantiated hate and short-sightedness. He was capable of much more than hurting innocent people and treating women like objects.

He winced as he relived their short time knowing each other. Yet she had a wealth of knowledge about him, gleaned from a distance over the years and what she saw was extremely unattractive. Maybe, just maybe, he could change that. He sighed, shifting the truck into gear to go to his sister's house.

There was that word again.

Change.

Goddamned change everywhere and even he was doing it now.

CHAPTER 5

*C*ALEB HAYES HAD PROVEN her not exactly
wrong, but maybe only partially right about him.
She stared out as his truck pulled away, driving at a slow,
sedate pace until he reached the stop sign. Kids played in
their yards and all around the street. It was nice that he
noticed and didn't go barreling through there as if he didn't
give a damn. But still, Caleb... hell, what was this? He wasn't
exactly a likeable person, but not as detestable as she first
believed.

He must've had a true epiphany about their brothers and
their lifestyle in general. He was very helpful today. She had
to give him that. She, Pedro, and Jordan were slimmer and
weaker than Caleb, so he compensated for his lack of
compassion with sheer brawn. The man was strong and
made light, easy work of what would have surely exhausted
her and Jordan and Pedro.

He was handsome too, when sober and not saying stupid,
crude things. He had thick, dark black hair that flopped
around in an annoying, boyish manner. He was so damn
clueless too, but what touched her and surprised her the

most, was his insecurity. That was a complete shocker. His ego and arrogance were a thin veil designed to cover his little boy eagerness to fit in.

It made it harder not to forgive him when she witnessed his astounding insecurity. He wasn't dumb. She had to give him that much. He was also trying very hard, for some reason, to get along with her, his brother, and her brother.

She wasn't sure how she felt about that, so she decided to let it sit on her brain for a while and seep in. She refused to let his good looks sway her. Pedro's well-being was first and foremost in her heart, so she was willing to help Caleb change if he truly meant what he said, especially about their brothers. Her only stipulation was that he had to be legit in his desire. She intended to withhold her judgment until then, but decided to give him that chance.

Or discover that he was making it all up just to get laid.

She'd soon know the truth, she supposed. Sighing, she turned away to take a shower. She couldn't wait to wash off all the dust and sweat of the move. She emerged fresh and clean and slipped a pair of shorts and a t-shirt on. Then she went into the kitchen to heat up a frozen dinner and make a small, fresh salad.

She wandered out to her front stoop to sit down and eat. She never ceased to enjoy the sounds of kids playing. Otherwise, it was mostly quiet in the neighborhood. Far off, visible from the cracks between the houses, she could make out Brewster Bay, where the Columbia River's broad expanse created shallows, making it resemble, at least for a mile or so, a huge lake. Then it continued flowing to the next dam, a few miles downriver.

Perhaps she overreacted to Caleb's advances. But she was pleased when he stopped immediately after receiving her disapproval. He might not have been as bad as she first pegged him, but she was convinced she wasn't completely wrong about him. Funny thing was, he seemed to realize that about himself too.

~

He and Ian had barely spoken since their day at the lake when Ian had all but dragged him kicking and screaming from his complacency into apparently what he had to become if he intended to stay in his family and keep his job and home.

He reported to Ian that he and Jordan were on the mend, but offered no other details. It wasn't Ian's damn business. But he managed to keep his job and his residence.

However, Ian and he were barely civil to each other. At work, Caleb preferred to deal with AJ most of the time anyway. AJ took orders from Jack and Ian and relayed them to the rest of them, assigning the crews where to work and on what. AJ ran a tight ship and didn't tolerate any dicking around or feeble excuses. He expected everyone to work long, hard work days whether it was rain, shine, or snow; nothing stopped AJ and that work ethic extended to all of them.

First day back to work after their honeymoon, his brother and Pedro drove into the worksite and got out, laughing before they walked up to where the crew was meeting. Everyone was assigned their tasks and break times for the day. There were a few extra hands on staff with the summer harvest coming up. Pedro and Jordan didn't touch each other, but Caleb sensed a distinct, overt and unconcealed warmth he never noticed before.

When Caleb and Pedro were all alone, working on the orchard in the afternoon, Caleb mustered up the guts to face Pedro. "So, Pedro, all these years you understood me?"

"Yeah. *Si, señor,*" Pedro mocked in an exaggerated, fake

accent before he flipped into an American accent, sounding like Caleb. "Sure, I understood you, Caleb." He grinned and lifted his eyebrows comically.

"Why? Why didn't you tell me?"

"You assumed it right off the bat, and since I didn't want to talk to you either, it worked out better for both of us."

"I—I shouldn't have done that shit."

"No. But it doesn't stop you from doing shit like that."

"I'm sorry. For that. And for assuming. And for being a dick, in general." At least a dozen altercations and offenses flashed through his mind and he could have gone back and individually named and itemized them separately to apologize for. Pedro knew it. Caleb knew it. He probably deserved to be called out for it.

Pedro paused and gave him a once-over. "Do you mean what you said before? I'm surprised to hear you apologizing to me, but what about accepting me as your brother-in-law and the spouse of your brother? Or is this all an act so you can stay employed and be generally un-hated by the rest of your family?"

Caleb sighed and stopped moving. Dropping his shoulders, he stared up at the sky and the sun nearly blinded him. "Honestly?"

"Yeah. Please, that's what I prefer."

"I think it's a little of both. It started out, obviously, with me scrambling in panic and trying not to lose my job and home, but later, well, maybe... I mean I think, now I mean it."

"That's far more honest than I've ever known you to be."

"Well, I've never tried to be honest before."

Pedro stared at him. Caleb nodded. "Then I guess only time will tell."

Caleb's bottom lip lifted up on one corner. "Yeah. I guess time will tell. That's fair enough."

Pedro's eyebrows rose. "Yeah, it's fairer than you were to me."

Caleb winced but ignored Pedro's hint of wrath. When Pedro turned to get a tool, Caleb said, "Thank you."

Pedro paused and glanced up. "For?"

"You could have convinced Jordan to hate me and told him not to give me a chance. I know that and from what I've done, I surely would have deserved it too. It was only your support that allowed him to give me the chance and I know I don't deserve it, but I have you to thank for it."

Pedro sighed. "Damn it, Caleb," Pedro replied, "I don't care one way or another about you. Jordan does. You might as well know that I don't trust you either. But Jordan needs you. Don't you dare do this, or pretend like you've changed, not unless you mean it. And you intend to stick with it. You have to understand this can't be a free trial. It has to be *real*. Something you've never been very good at. You're serious one moment and in the next, Jordan could become the butt of your jokes and satire. You've already hurt too many people."

"And now you think I'm just assuming I can get your forgiveness. You're not wrong about me, Pedro. I didn't care before. I care now though and I'm trying my best to prove it now."

"We'll see..." Pedro replied as he turned and sauntered down the ranch road. The sun's rays were hot and bright around them. Horses were grazing in the pastures and they flicked their tails and moved their ears while their mouths chewed away. A few walked up to the fence line as Pedro passed by, curious by nature and always trying to draw his attention to them, no doubt. They reminded him sometimes of little preschoolers, always seeking the attention and approval of the adults.

Caleb nodded. Volumes of things unsaid could have easily

fueled the anger in Pedro towards him and Caleb knew he deserved it. His prior treatment towards Pedro seemed as if the man had no feelings or humanity, not even anything to say. Yeah, he had to admit he treated him badly. He had a lot of work to do.

Caleb pressed his lips together and gave a single nod. Eventually, Pedro would see the changes. Jordan would see them. In the end, everyone would notice because he was determined and motivated now. He refused to think the way he used to any longer.

JOSEFINA HAD A BUSY WEEK, working at least fifty hours although she was pleased with the added padding to her weekly salary. Slowly, but surely, her meager nest egg grew. Four long years she'd been saving it. Her pride soared each time she transferred ten percent of her weekly earnings into it. Soon. Very soon, she'd be a homeowner. Her. Josefina Ruiz. But not today. As she thought of her annoying neighbor, that wonderful day could not come soon enough.

Friday night, she answered her cellphone when it rang with an unfamiliar number. "Hello?"

"Hey. It's Caleb. I got your number from Pedro, *after* I apologized to him." Caleb ran all of the words together in a quick, frantic spiel, as if he feared she would hang up before she knew the purpose of his call.

She smiled. "You apologized to Pedro?"

"And that's not all. I also called to follow up about tomorrow. The painting? Do you still want to come?"

Her laugh surprised her. "I guess so."

"Then I should tell you about my apology…"

She sat down, lulled by his teasing tone. To her surprise, she even stayed on the phone for a good twenty minutes with him. Nothing was really said or discussed. The only thing they managed to decide was that he would pick her up at nine tomorrow and she'd help him select the paint. That was because both of their brothers insisted Josefina would make the better choice. She agreed; they didn't have much taste when it came to interior decorating.

But the conversation delighted her and when she got off the phone, she was smiling. Huh. Not the usual result after an interaction with Caleb.

Maybe she judged him wrong. *Maybe.* But if she had, it was his own fault. Until now, she never observed the smallest act of kindness or decency toward Pedro and Jordan. But strangely, now that he was demonstrating another side, it seemed excessive, although heartfelt. It didn't match her initial opinions about his indifference and willingness to remain ignorant about anything beyond his limited vision of the world. Actually, from what she knew and observed, that was just Caleb Hayes. The risk of losing his brother seemed to captivate his attention like nothing else could. It meant that Caleb loved his brother, which didn't come through until now.

But then again, this all could have been a small blip on the radar and could just as swiftly disappear. She couldn't trust him, not just yet.

He pulled in at the exact time he said he would. His promptness made her raise her eyebrows in an expression of pleasant surprise. They stopped by the hardware store. Despite a modest selection of colors, she managed to find several that complemented the existing décor in the home. Although it wasn't much to work with, anything would have improved and brightened up the dingy, yellowish hue on the walls now.

"What about this for the exterior?"

She turned toward Caleb when he held out a color swatch.

"Or is it too girlie? Oops. I mean, is that… maybe that's what it should be?" He pressed his lips tightly shut and shook his head. "Please don't get mad. That came out wrong as soon as I started to say it. I just meant—"

"Because they're gay the exterior paint should be a pretty color?"

"No. I didn't mean that and I don't think so. No. There's nothing about Jordan that is—"

"Gay?" she supplied, her tone crisp and a little haughty.

"No," he insisted sharply, running his hands nervously through his dark, silky, straight hair. "No. I didn't mean anything insulting. Jordan prefers simplicity is all I'm saying. Black, grays and browns, or shades of those colors. That's all I meant to say."

Josefina let out the laugh and smirk she'd been restraining.

He stared at her, his expression growing more serious before he realized she was deliberately goading him. "You did that on purpose?"

"Maybe. Just a little bit." She giggled to ease the harshness.

"That was kind of mean."

"So mean." She agreed. Then she nodded at his left hand. "But I think we'll go with this white and dark gray trim. That'll look nice, simple, clean and bright."

His shoulders sagged in relief as he nodded. "Glad that you're the final decision maker."

They left their orders for the colors and waited until they were mixed and the interior and exterior five-gallon buckets were given to them. When the time came to pay, Caleb frowned and yanked out his wallet. "Let me pay for half. I only got them a damn coffee maker."

"Something I'm sure they needed too. They owned

nothing but their clothes and beds as far as I was aware. I know your sister and Ian gave them some yard tools and a lawn mower as a present."

"Ian is very generous, I know. But then again, he has plenty of resources so he can be."

"Well, thank you, Caleb. I'll be sure they understand it's a gift from both of us." She tilted her head his way. Did he have the funds to pay for this? She knew how much her brother made for the Rydells. But Caleb's salary wasn't any of her business and he did owe Jordan a decent wedding present.

They loaded the paint into the back of his truck as well as the rollers, brushes and drop cloths. "That is a full day's work, at the least."

"Oh, yeah. To cover both inside and out."

Their conversation back to River's End was half as contentious as the one a few days previous. He asked innocuous questions about her family and job and they discussed some local people they both knew. Not hard, since it was a terribly small area.

She was surprised but pleased at the change and ease she found between them now. After parking, they pulled all their gear out and knocked on the door. Pedro answered. He was wearing sweats and a light t-shirt and standing with bare feet. He smiled, looking so happy and fulfilled, and Josefina's heart lifted. For years, Pedro was burdened by his tumultuous relationship he shared with Jordan Hayes. It absolutely warmed her heart to see them together now and forever, so light and happy and content with each other in their new home. Married life obviously agreed with both of them.

"Come in." He kissed her cheek and took the load from her hands as he glanced over her shoulder at Caleb. "Hey."

"Hi, Pedro. How's it going?" Caleb's tone wasn't as natural with Pedro as it was with her. Dear God! The man just couldn't get over it, could he? She coughed to cover a snort of amusement. He glared at her when his head whipped up and he caught her watching him.

She waited until he passed her and leaned in and said, "Breathe. Stop acting so odd."

"I just feel weird with Pedro after you so epically pointed out how awful I was," he all but hissed it at her.

She pressed her lips to stop a smile and quickly caught up with her brother as Jordan stood up from the kitchen table. "Coffee?"

She smiled. "Sure. I heard you have a nice new maker."

Jordan nodded eagerly. "Yes, Caleb got it for us."

She took the cup he offered her and added, "And the paint. Caleb also bought half of the paint for your new home."

Jordan froze, his gaze falling on his brother who hung back in the living room. Caleb's stance showed how uncomfortable he felt. "Really? You did, Caleb? You bought us some paint?"

"Well, Josefina bought half too."

Jordan's eyes flashed. "Yes, she did. But, thank you, Caleb. That's awesome."

Josefina knew Caleb's gift meant far more than a paltry bucket of paint. When Jordan turned away, she gave Caleb a small wink. Caleb grinned, happily realizing his gesture went a long way towards making the reparations he claimed to want to do.

But even more than the money they spent was the day. Everyone was working together. At times, Josefina worked with each of them, including Caleb. She'd always heard that Caleb was lazy, ineffectual, late, disorganized, didn't finish things right, and took shortcuts. Granted, all of it came from Pedro, especially during the first several years that he worked with Caleb. But despite his previous laziness, Caleb was very detailed, kind, thorough, and hardworking. He significantly helped them move forward on the improvements.

It was close to ten before they finished. Speckled in different colors and splatters of paint, they were all a mess. Josefina's hair was pulled back in a tight braid, but her hands, arms, neck and even her face revealed specks of paint. She accidentally leaned back against a recently painted wall so her entire left behind was a light shade of blue.

"Well, that's it." She put the last stroke on the corner wall of the final room. Caleb and Jordan tackled the exterior, and she and Pedro painted the interior. She told Caleb to touch up the trim while she finished the last room before she stuck her paintbrush in the empty can.

"It looks so much better."

"You made a great choice with those colors."

"I did." She beamed and glanced over at the recent handiwork.

"You guys go now. We'll finish the clean-up. Thank you, again, both of you. This is so above and beyond," Pedro gushed with glee.

Josefina and Caleb wandered out to Caleb's truck after a few more gracious thank yous. They pulled out and Jordan put his arm around Pedro's shoulders as they leaned their hips together and both waved them off.

She watched Caleb's eyeballs straying up to his rearview mirror and they stuck there for a long moment. She waited for a grimace. A sneer. A comment. He stayed neutral. Then he said, "They are pretty happy, aren't they?"

"Yeah, they are."

"They appreciated the paint and all of your help. I think they must have told me a dozen times."

"Yes. Imagine never believing that something, which meant everything to you, could finally be attained."

He shook his head. "I can't imagine."

"What do you mean? I don't mean you have to imagine what it's like being gay, I meant, spending your time, all the hours in your days, with the person you want to spend it with most."

"No. I meant, I can't imagine what that feels like. Wanting someone like that. To see all the things you want in someone else as if they are your everything."

"You've never been in love before?"

"No. Have you?"

She sighed. "No, not really. I sometimes get jealous of their closeness and intimacy. How easily they manage to interact and agree to stay together forever."

"I failed to notice it before. After I knew about it, I purposely tried not to watch or pay attention because I was so against it…"

"Wow, pretty honest."

"I'm trying to be. Anyway, watching it now, it doesn't bother me. I'm getting used to it. The affectionate touches and glances, and little, silent understandings and messages. I can't imagine being that close to anyone."

"It's kind of easy to get jealous."

"Yeah, maybe it's not so much jealous as it is envious."

She smiled at his thoughtful distinction and he blinked once before he jerked forward. "Anyway, the tavern's still open. Want to stop in for a quick drink? We sure deserve it. We worked hard."

She gave him a look and he intercepted it. "Just because we're both exhausted, and I feel too strung out to go straight to bed. Gotta relax. I only invited you out of friendliness and to cap off a job well done."

"A job well done," she mimicked. "If it's strictly for that, then yes, I can."

He pulled into the parking lot and they entered the establishment. Country music played in the background. It was moderately crowded so they found a small table in the middle of the room. She ordered a glass of house wine and Caleb had a beer on draft.

"You only drink beer?" Josefina inquired.

"Yup. Simple guy. Simple taste. You didn't have that part wrong about me."

She tilted her head, sipping hers. "Actually, I'm starting to believe you're not at all simple, and a whole hell of a lot deeper than you pretend. But what I find most startling is what a shock it seems to you, more than anyone else, including Jordan and me."

His expression morphed into confusion and pleasure. For some reason, he liked earning her approval. That surprised her. He seemed to find her particularly smart or something. She considered herself plain and average. Normal. Unextra-ordinary. His expression clouded up again. With a long sigh, he pushed the drink away. "Damn. Why'd you have to go and say that?" he grumbled. Leaning back in his chair, he frowned and crossed his arms over his chest.

Startled, she could only stare at him in wonder, open-mouthed. "What? What did I say?"

"All that crap about being a good guy."

"That's a bad thing?"

"No, but now I have to listen to the nagging voice in my head, when I was planning to ignore it indefinitely. Tonight. Tomorrow. Maybe always. I usually ignore it anyway. I mean, I have the little voice always telling me what I should do, I just prefer to ignore it. I was already intending to back out on my promise and beg for a chance to prove myself. And now, I can't."

"Again, what are you talking about?" she asked, bewildered.

He nodded at the drink before him. "I wanted to spend more time with you," he grumbled before he began fidgeting.

Annoyed. She almost apologized for him wanting to be around her more, and nearly chewed him out for clearly having other intentions. "There is nowhere else open. Except this damn tavern. So I figured, sure, why not? One beer won't hurt anything…"

"Caleb, what are you talking about?"

"I promised I'd quit drinking."

"Whom did you promise?"

"My brother, my sister, my boss… everyone."

She watched him. "You're an alcoholic?"

"I don't think so. I don't know. They all agreed I was mean and lazy whenever I drank. I admit I drink too much and too often. I blamed a lot of the shit I did at the wedding on drinking and I promised Jordan—"

"Not to drink anymore. That's a tall order. I mean, if you have a problem, I think you're undertaking a huge struggle to suddenly, you know, not have a drink."

"Yes. But look at me."

She was torn. Was she angry that he chose a bar and ordered a drink, probably using that to come on to her? She was a little surprised when she found herself saying, "Look at you now, with the beer pushed away and you're not drinking it." Taking the drink, she set it down on the empty table next to them. "Then keep your promise and find out."

He nodded. A smile appeared on his lips as he stared at the beer. "Okay."

She smiled right back. "Okay. And Caleb? You started to change it. Don't sell yourself short."

"You did."

"I did." She admitted it willingly. Eagerly even. "I'll always admit when I'm wrong and I'm glad to do it. I'm glad I was wrong about you. You came through for our brothers and even the way you treat me has seen major improvement."

"I didn't mean to be so awful to you. I just thought you were pretty."

She smiled at his simple words, but saw the hurt in his eyes. She would never have guessed that before she started interacting with him and their brothers. "Thank you. That's a nice way to feel and you didn't have to communicate it to me. Insulting me with lewd looks and advances and calling me 'señorita' were not ever appreciated or good feeling."

"I'm sorry." His hands fidgeted with a napkin. She sensed his distress in all this. His hand drew her attention and she stared at his big knuckles. A brief ripple of sensual awareness overcame her as she viewed his forearms, dusted in black hair, which seemed so strong and powerful even when he rested.

She ignored her odd, unexpected attraction. Perhaps the source of it was his contriteness, or his willingness to listen to her and apologize, or his attempts to be different. No longer the simple light-your-farts-on-fire redneck she originally pegged him as. "Is it something that you could forgive?"

"Yes," she said with a husky timbre to her voice. Regaining her composure, she purposely let go of his hand. "Yes, of course."

He sat back. "My sister is a lot like you. She's real smart. She went to college, you know, and got a degree from the University of Washington. That was her dream. The most important thing to her. I—I never even knew that before. Not until she was about to receive it. I've known her for her entire life and I never knew her one great dream. Same with Jordan." He shook his head. His voice was dripping with pride when he spoke about his sister. He cleared his throat.

"She's back here now and works side-by-side with Ian. He defers to her like she's the leader. He asks her for advice and her opinions and then he follows them. Anyway, my point is: she isn't like me. She's very special. Not meant for this kind of life or the single-wide trailer we were born and raised in. Definitely too good for the likes of me as her brother. But she said a lot to me that night, stuff she said before, but it finally hit home. Maybe I refused to hear what she said before. You remind me a lot of her."

She tilted her head. That was much more of a compliment than knowing he found her pretty. She scrunched up her eyebrows listening to him. The "Aw, shucks" shtick could have been a total act. He was being respectful with the sister comparison. Leery of Caleb's true intentions and what could so easily be a contrived run to get her, she decided to take him in stride. Not fully trusting him yet.

"I always liked her," she settled on saying.

"You just despised me," he stated with a glint in his eye. Was it regret? Hurt? Both, it seemed.

"I did then. But now perhaps that opinion could change."

They shared a surprising smile and she marveled at the sudden stream of understanding that suddenly flowed between them. Glancing down, she said, "Well, this was an enlightening day. But I'm pretty beat."

"It was enlightening and in more ways than one."

Startled at his statement, she looked up to find him watching her. The smile on his face was different and sweet before he glanced away. It wasn't the aggressive grin and cocky smile she remembered. It seemed much more sincere.

The rest of the ride was quiet, but pleasant. Different than before, because they were amiable. She bid him good night, beginning to believe something in Caleb had truly shifted.

CHAPTER 6

*C*ALEB WATCHED JOSEFINA CROSS her yard quickly and step into her building. It was an ugly building. Beige with peeling paint and some old, dented, scuffed, and bruised doors. The building had not one feature to soften the painful exterior of the four doors and dirty windows beside them. The lawn was brown and long dead with dust and a concrete walkway that led to the front. There wasn't even an awning or an overhang to soften the appearance. Rocks scattered the yards and the dumpsters at the end of the parking lot were overfull and bursting with detritus.

He shuddered, not only was it ugly but awkwardly stuffed in between other small buildings and broken-down cars. The sprawl of cookie-cutter housing was far more distasteful to him than the condition of the building where she lived. It would have suffocated him to live there, and made him unable to breathe.

It was almost Main Street Suburbia. Only the mountains made it tolerable. He needed plenty of air. Space. Trees. Mountains. Especially, the mountains. He needed a hefty dose of River's End. Driving back to it, his breathing automatically regulated as he passed through town and into the valley, following the winding Rydell River, and heading to the ranch.

It wasn't his. He lived in his sister's house on her husband's family's huge, thousand-acre swath of impressive land. The only job he managed to hold consistently was there. He couldn't even consider working anywhere else. He knew how the Rydells functioned as a family, and how each brother's personality affected him and them. They were awfully predictable, which he valued. He also valued the placid calm he saw in AJ, their foreman, as well as Jordan and Pedro, his cohorts and fellow farm hands.

He parked his truck. Ian built the house while they were still living in Seattle. Who could afford to do that? The only people he knew that made more than six figures were the Rydells. He just didn't know anyone else with that kind of money.

Certainly not from this area and most especially, not from Gunderson Hills where he and his siblings were born and raised. He went inside the glass-fronted house that he still couldn't believe he was allowed to enter, let alone admit it was owned by his sister.

It was fancy, in a way he'd never known people could live. It wasn't like he ever perused home and garden magazines to get a glimpse of how others outside the area decorated, and he'd never been an avid TV watcher, rarer still, a movie watcher. Home. Here. The people of River's End were his type of people and the only kind he knew. He was far more content in their presence or up in the hills than he was even inside his sister's house.

All the leather furniture and high, vaulted ceilings with fancy wood floors, varnished and finished until they shone, filled him with worry for fear of scratching them. Hell, give him a trailer he could freaking walk in and lounge in and relax in any day over this money pit.

Unfortunately, there was no insurance on the Hayes mobile home. To make matters even worse, when the fire consumed it, they were even broker than they were ordinarily. Caleb never paid rent before. However, he was liberal in the vast amounts he spent on his booze and late nights out. Generous to friends, he truly had no idea where his wages went. Some paid the bills, like the medical insurance, gas, and food, but he lived pretty damn cheap.

So, he should have had something left over. But he didn't. That was why he had to move in with his sister. After he settled in, Dad soon followed so it felt more comfortable and normal. All his siblings and dad were living under the same roof again, even if he had to tolerate Ian's continuous presence.

Ian was quite clear when he told Caleb he had long overstayed his welcome. Well, hell. Yeah, maybe the time was overdue for him to have his own thing going on.

He just didn't know how to make that happen. Sighing, he flopped down on his bed. Jordan's bed was still there.

Caleb stared up at the ceiling. Tonight was fun with Josefina. He liked talking to her. She was so different from anyone else he'd been with. Sharp, sarcastic, and disdainful, traits he usually didn't enjoy, but since he liked her, he found them tolerable. He didn't have a clue why, but he thought she was intriguing, not to mention likeable. Usually with women, Caleb never felt like that. Women never interested him long enough to lie on his bed and think about them before he fell asleep. But here he was now, thinking about Josefina and the idea of them together.

Owing to his attraction toward her, Caleb realized it wasn't enough for him to change just to keep his job and get his brother back. No, he had to mean what he said now and do better.

With that in mind, the next evening, he parked in front of his brother's place, arriving there unannounced. He swung in carrying a bucket of chicken and fries that he picked up on the way. He also brought beer for his brother and iced tea for himself. Jordan stared at him, slack-jawed, when he saw it was Caleb at the door.

"What the hell?"

He lifted the bag up. "Dinner. Wanna let me in?"

Jordan stepped back, making room for him to enter. Caleb set the food down and the beer clicked loudly when it hit the table. He turned towards his brother as Pedro sauntered out from the kitchen. Pedro nodded at Caleb, resting one shoulder against the door jamb.

"Do you guys mind? Thought as long as I was out... and there's a Mariner's game on tonight. Thought we could watch it together. Unless... you know, if you guys have other plans..." Caleb shifted his feet uncomfortably. A sudden realization dawned on him and it hit him much harder than he expected; they weren't just his brother and friend anymore. It was like dropping in on his brother and his brother's new wife. They might cherish their privacy, being newlyweds and all. He winced as he made the connection.

Jordan nodded, and his eyes were both bright and weary. "Yeah... yeah, sure..."

They all sat down and ate, Jordan and Pedro beside each other, and drank a few beers, which Caleb politely skipped. He caught Jordan eyeing him several times over the glass of iced tea he drank. He shrugged and did a mock toast to them. Pedro and Jordan held hands, and Pedro even put his head on Jordan's shoulder at one point.

Theatrics, big ultimatums, and any other antics were not necessary. Sitting beside them as a couple on the couch and watching the game together, Caleb realized this was the real thing.

The "only time will tell" that Pedro mentioned. Anyone in a panic can come up with all kinds of big gestures when their back is up against the wall and they risk losing something they dare not lose. But living what one preaches and promises? That was harder, stricter, and more demanding than any grand gestures. That was where the real test was. Where the real evidence of any changes would be.

First, he was sitting beside two men who were cuddling.

Second, he held a glass of plain iced tea in his hand.

And he had to admit he was very uncomfortable and felt awkward. He made a few comments, but they felt forced and sounded flat.

But. It wasn't the worst evening Caleb ever spent.

So maybe a future potential lay ahead.

It also wasn't so bad to be getting out of Ian's house. Caleb spent way too much time at the ranch. The few friends that were left in the area were scarce and not like in the past. Things changed. Jail. Marriage. Relocation. Careers. There were a number of good reasons, but essentially, there weren't too many people left for Caleb to hang out with.

He came back to Pedro and Jordan's house two or three evenings a week, usually arriving with the evening meal. It was on the third week of one of his visits, when, as he started to leave, Pedro said to him, "We're having some friends over Saturday. You know, a housewarming get-together." Pedro glanced towards Jordan who flushed and Caleb didn't fail to see it. "Jordan wasn't going to invite you because he thought you'd think it was lame…" Pedro had a challenging look. "But if you would like to come and be nice, by all means, do and bring your choice of drinks."

Friends? Caleb thought hard but could not think of what *friends* they could possibly have which he didn't also know.

He scrunched his face up. Puzzled over who they could be hanging with that he didn't know, he nodded, feeling a little curious. And he felt sure he knew most of Jordan's friends… so… he could handle it. A housewarming party. Who knew? He could think of no one else who did such things. Or if they did, they never invited *him*. The reasons were obvious, even to him.

"I will. Yes. I'll see you then."

Saturday, he showed up with a jug of iced tea in one hand. He also brought a large bag of pretzels, his contribution to… whatever this was. A housewarming party.

He was surprised to find Ian and Kailynn already there. He hadn't spoken to his sister or asked her if they were coming. After a round of hellos from them and AJ, who was also there with his wife, Kate, Caleb saw a few others whom he didn't know. There were men and women who worked in the area and some were people he knew well.

His nerves began to relax and he sipped his glass of iced tea and made small talk. He straightened up when Josefina walked in, carrying a bowl and a bag of tortilla chips. Her salsa again? He hoped so.

She wore shorts and her thin, graceful legs were nicely muscled. His eyes lingered on her as he downed half a glass of iced tea. He lost track of the conversations and bluffed his answers when anyone asked him a question. Eventually, he worked his way towards Pedro's sister who was smiling as she laughed at something with AJ's wife, Kate. She glanced up, smiling as soon as she noticed him and nodding her acknowledgment. She dipped a hand in the bowl of pretzels he brought and placed one in her mouth. She had a huge, wide smile and her lips were a lovely shade of red tonight, making his heart clench while watching her.

She shifted her body towards him, seemingly to begin a conversation. "Caleb, it's so nice to see you here." Her eyes twinkled, and her mouth smirked at him. Anyone who challenged him like she did would have usually ticked him off, but he accepted the challenge and took it with a bowed head.

"Yeah. I came. First housewarming party. How could I miss it?"

"I hear you've been coming around quite often and for more than just this."

He shrugged. "Been trying to…"

"Keep your word, huh?"

"Yes." He cleared his throat, desperate for something to say. Something to chat about, flirt about, anything to justify keeping near her. Yet his brain went blank. He was usually drinking beer or another form of alcohol before he tried to pick up women. Yeah, he had no trouble then. Liquid courage. Of course, he never cared before if the women wanted his company or not, and he actually preferred not to talk to them. With Josefina, however, he hoped she wanted both tonight because he wanted to stay with her.

"Did you make that special salsa of yours?"

"I did. It's right over there." He turned and grinned before grabbing a plate and scooping the salsa on a tortilla chip. He shut his eyes and savored all the spicy, tangy, excellent taste of it on his mouth. "Best in the world. You should bottle this. You'd make millions."

She outright laughed. "Or I could just reserve it for clever housewarming gifts."

"Do you want a drink?" he asked before he fidgeted around again, unsure of what to say next.

"Sure. What are you having?"

He smiled and shrugged, slightly embarrassed to admit. "Iced tea."

"Oh," her face exploded into a huge grin. "You kept your other promise."

He nodded and shrugged and blushed. Damn. He lost the

edge he had. She kept him honest. He couldn't spin things or charm her. He used to smile and smirk and talk of nothing, saying as little as possible and still getting what he wanted at the end of the night. Josefina demanded respect. Honesty. Truth. And she ignored any attempts from him at charm. It left him feeling like he was treading water and barely keeping his head up. "Trying."

She tilted her head, her eyes scanning over him. "I think you are, Caleb. And I'll have a glass of wine." Her mouth looked so soft, and her voice was sincere, holding his attention far longer than he should have stared.

He shook off the trance she seemed to put him under and turned toward the table that was set up as a makeshift bar. He poured her a large glass of wine and brought it back to her. She smiled in thanks, and to his amazement, didn't just turn away from him. They were talking for an hour, maybe even longer. Moving back and to the side when people jostled around them to grab food or chairs near them, they smiled and talked, sometimes including others, but he was aware of how close she stayed to him. No touching, but it seemed like she was helping him face his fears.

Eventually, people filtered out to the back yard. A fire was built, and the descending darkness enveloped the valley. More booze flowed as people laughed louder at the humorous stories being told. It might have been the first time Caleb wasn't monopolizing everyone's attention by busting out with a wealth of stories from a decade-and-a-half of these late nights.

Except, half of this crowd was already married, and he was at a housewarming. He poured Josefina another glass of wine, and she got up and poured her third. It startled him when he realized he wasn't deliberately plying her with drinks. He shook his head, confused why he forgot to do that.

Would have made it easier to ignore his tension with her. The idea that he was conversing with someone who was way, way out of his league motivated him and he couldn't help but try even harder. She was definitely worth it. Even to his sober, newfound, clearer vision and standards.

He had to admit, however, that without a beer in his hand or several in his system, half of his confidence, swagger, arrogance, and ego were missing. He felt stilted. Unsure. Bumbling. But he wondered if, perhaps, he had become far more tolerable than he usually was when he drank.

His sister came over and talked for a long while to him, and he even spoke to Ian, casually. Caleb made no reference to that day when they took the horse ride. Or his work. Or the recent threats Ian gave him. Nothing. They kept it light and easy, as if there was nothing untoward to remember or care about. They could finally interact as freaking in-laws.

It was like what happened with Pedro. Caleb stiffened at the realization. He treated Ian and Pedro about the same tonight. Courteous hellos and small talk, peppered with a few conversations and... damn. He actually treated his siblings' spouses about the same. He was stunned because it was real. It didn't have to be forced. He straightened up.

He doubted anyone else noticed but it was life-changing to Caleb.

Maybe this was how one changed things. By acting differently. Decently. It wasn't even all that hard.

When the clock's hands moved towards 1:00 a.m., people began trickling out and leaving. Josefina sighed. "I think I drank too much. Would you give me a ride home, Caleb?"

Startled that she turned to him and asked, Caleb didn't answer at first but soon nodded eagerly. "Yeah, sure, of course."

"Even though it's out of your way?"

He lifted his half empty glass. "I'm also one of the few who drank strictly iced tea."

She giggled, her eyes glistening, and her skin color flushed. "True, that is so true and for that I must thank you."

She collected her now empty salsa bowl and kissed her brother and his husband on the cheek. She held Pedro's hand as she said, "I'm so happy to attend your first housewarming."

His eyes gleamed as he smirked back at her. "Me too, Josie." She teared up and he rolled his eyes. "You're so emotional. It's not that exciting. Just a party."

"At your own home. Hosted by you and your husband. Your husband, *Jordan.*"

Caleb winced at the awe in her voice when she said *Jordan.* Like neither of them ever believed this could become reality. Caleb now understood, for the first time that he had a distinct role in that event. Caleb heard the tacit message in her tone of voice. Like this was impossible to imagine. And she seemed almost reverent.

"Josie, you're so mushy when you drink."

She smiled and laughed. "I am."

"Let me take you home."

"No, your newly sober brother-in-law has offered to."

Pedro glanced his way and Caleb shrugged. "I have to leave anyway. So, it's fine."

"Okay. Thanks."

They exchanged a long look and Caleb wondered, for the first time, if he saw Pedro melting. The former icy disdain and distrust Pedro harbored towards him was not entirely gone, but now, he believed Pedro's heart was thawing, maybe only just a drop, but still, it was a start. And to Caleb, it meant more than ever before.

Josefina curled up against the door when they settled in his truck and rested her head against the window, her eyes fluttering shut. "I am so tired."

"And maybe a little tipsy."

She grinned, her eyes still closed. "Maybe that too."

It was a quiet drive, but pleasant because she trusted him. She relaxed and remained at ease in his presence and under his care. When she first met him, Caleb doubted that she would have trusted him. Once they arrived at her place, she stretched and woke up before glancing over at Caleb. "Will you stay just until I get inside?"

Surprise showed in his curious eyes. "Sure."

"Just… the night and all. You know."

"No, I don't know. Look at me. Who'd try and mess with this mean, old, crusty, horse's ass? Besides, I have a badass reputation."

"Yes, you do. Well, I don't."

He turned his truck off. "I'll do one better. I'll walk you to your door, like the gentleman I am."

She laughed, getting out. "Have you ever done that before?"

He ducked his head down, feeling chagrinned. "Nope. Never. Again, you are witnessing a wealth of changes happening here."

"Yeah, it seems so."

They stopped, and she unlocked her front door. She glanced up at him. "Thanks, Caleb. And for trying so hard to change. Now I can stand to be near you."

He flashed a wry smile. "I have a long way to go, don't I? Between you and my brothers. And my sister, but mostly with you."

"There's nowhere to go with me but friends."

"That's a lot farther than I hoped at first. So, I'll take it."

Her eyes glistened as she stepped back towards her door. "Me too."

She was about to go inside and the mutual warmth that sprang up tonight between them was about to end. About to be extinguished. It was probably false and encouraged by the large amount of booze in her system anyway. But it existed right here and now, and Caleb liked how it felt.

She turned to leave, and he said her name again, surprising himself when he said it out loud. "Hey, Josefina?"

She stopped and twirled around, leaning on the door handle. "Yes?"

He swiped his leg forward and back, making a scuttling sound on the concrete. "Do you… I mean, would you want to hang out sometime?"

"Hang out sometime?"

"Go out sometime. I mean, go out on a date? Us? You and me?"

She didn't expect him to ask her out, he knew by the way her head jutted back and her eyes widened. She tilted her head and said with a nod. "I would go out with you. But definitely not to have sex. I don't see you like that, Caleb. So, if you could accept that on a date, then yes."

He had to blame it on the wine or she'd have never uttered the word, *sex* to him. Of that, he was sure. But the honesty she displayed was helpful and clear, so he nodded.

"I could accept that. Yes. Okay." His smile grew huge as he stepped back. "I'll call you then, okay? Next weekend?"

She sucked in a breath. "Fine. Sure."

He grinned. "I'll take it!" he called out when he was halfway down the sidewalk. "You won't regret it, Josefina Ruiz. I swear. You'll be amazed how much you like me, the new and changed me, that is."

He waved as he turned to jump into his truck. A date with Josefina Ruiz. A no-sex date. But still, they would spend time together. And when did he ever want to just spend time with any woman? Or look forward to it more eagerly than any sex-date he'd ever made? Damn. Hell might be freezing over and he just might have been changing for real.

CHAPTER 7

*C*ALEB CALLED JOSEFINA AND asked her if she'd like to go out that Friday night to dinner. He was formal and curt over the phone. She accepted his invitation and now waited for seven o'clock to arrive, her nerves jumping in her stomach, which surprised her. Why did she care how this went? It was Caleb Hayes. But oddly enough, she was excited, not to mention, eager and willing to see him.

He came to her door and knocked, wearing clean, pressed jeans, a neatly tucked-in flannel shirt and a white cowboy hat. Seeing the clean, groomed version of him surprised her too since she didn't often see him like that in the few times they passed each other over the years.

She thought he never realized it since he didn't know about her brother. She sure as shit knew about his brother and him though.

The changes Josefina saw in him were startling, from his attitude, to his courtesy, and his formal, neat appearance, which she beheld now. He took his hat off and held it against his chest as he waited for her to answer his knock. She peeked from her window, taking a breath before she jerked the door open. He smiled and blinked as he lowered the hat into both his hands and spun it around in little circles. Was he nervous? About her? She saw Caleb as a ladies' man, a player, never settling down with a specific woman. To see him reacting to her now, felt odd.

"Wow, you look lovely, Josefina." His gaze, however, didn't slide down her body salaciously. It stayed right on her face. She lowered her brows. Was he okay? Nothing about him seemed anything like the brute she first met only a few weeks ago.

"Uh, thank you, Caleb. You clean up pretty well yourself."

She wore a casual dress made of blue denim with small flowers patterned on it and white-laced, cap sleeves, which she accessorized with a wide, white belt at her waist. Her long hair was free and flowing, ending just above her waist.

He swiped his hat as if to say *ladies first.* Startled by the gesture, she walked forward, her cowboy boots clicking on the concrete. She liked how they made her legs look when coupled with the flouncy skirt that skimmed her thighs. He strode around her and hurried to open her door. That stopped her dead. Huh. What the hell was going on here?

Nervousness started to bubble inside her. This wasn't anything like they'd experienced before. This was so formal. This was really something. This was Caleb obviously putting all of his effort into pleasing her. They were silent on the drive. There were only a few restaurants in Brewster. One chain fast food dive and not a lot of enticing choices.

Neither of them had the money to waste by going farther away. She genuinely hoped Caleb wouldn't bother, and it was on the tip of her tongue to say so. She wasn't looking for anything romantic with Caleb.

Just friendship. Companionship. Seeing him trying so hard with her brother was good, so naturally, she wanted to keep encouraging it. But anything further? No. Oh, hell no.

Therefore, she was not worth him spending a lot of his hard-earned money. She knew firsthand how tedious the work at the ranch was. Not to mention, physically demanding and tough. Perhaps that was why they acted the way they did about life's problems in general.

Caleb drove straight through Brewster. On the highway, Josefina asked, "Where are we going?"

"Lake Chelan. There are a lot better restaurant choices over there."

"You don't have to drive so far. It's pretty expensive up there, catering to all the tourists."

"I don't mind." He glanced her way and she saw a small, shy, smile. "I don't mind at all if it's for you, Josefina."

She repressed the urge to fidget. No. Oh, no. She wasn't looking for more dates with Caleb Hayes. He was the last type of guy she wanted to encourage or end up with. Her entire goal during her twenties was not only to improve her life and earning potential, but also to enhance her whole lifestyle. She wanted to do something real and meaningful with herself, to accomplish significant achievements.

Any man in her life had to be an integral part of her master plan. He could not hinder any of her goals. Having grown up dirt poor in an overcrowded trailer with too many kids, and not enough money to support them all, she was dedicated to her carefully crafted plan of financial security and independence.

She adored her father, who worked very hard, but couldn't ever cover the costs of raising five kids. She didn't begrudge him the childhood he provided for her. It was full of love and that extended to all of her siblings. But as far as lifestyles? Hers was tough. She decided long ago that she wanted more. So much more.

But she still felt obligated to help out her family, so it couldn't happen fast. She didn't waste her money on trivial

RIVER OF CHANGE

things like hobbies or eating out at fancy places. She hated to
make Caleb waste his money. But she didn't know how to
articulate it. *Gee, Caleb, since you stand no chance of having sex
with me, we might as well grab some McDonalds?* That sounded
pretty awful. She tried to think of a better explanation.

They turned off the highway and started up the hill until
the road crested before they entered the Chelan Valley. Lake
Chelan, a glacier-fed, clear, cold lake that traversed fifty
miles had recently become a beacon and hub for all the
preppy, middle-to-upper class tourists.

All summer long, this end of the lake was constantly
bombarded with traffic from jet skis and ski boats. Most of
the water skiers got up in the wee hours of the morning to
seek the most remote and calm waters. The wakes of passing
boats kept the lake bumpy and the traffic only increased as
the day progressed. Swimmers used the public pool at the
city park along with the campers in the RV parks. A multi-
tude of resorts hugged the beaches overlooking the sparkling
water.

Serious money flowed through there too, which was so
opposite when compared to her side of town. Or Caleb's.

He stopped and parked along one of the side streets and
waited for her before they started towards the waterfront.
"So, are you in the mood for anything in particular?"

She scanned the area, observing the throngs of vacation-
ers, many still in their swimsuits, walking all around the
beaches. "Um... ice cream. I'd love to have an ice cream
cone." She saw the sign for waffle cones and hoped she could
avoid eating an expensive meal. She tried to discourage
Caleb from spending too much money on her. She had a
good inkling she wouldn't be paying for her order, even if
she were prepared.

"Well, okay. But don't you want something like dinner
first?"

She kept scanning the fancy restaurants, growing more desperate until she spotted a sandwich shop. "What about that over there?"

He glanced at it with real surprise on his face. "I was thinking somewhere that we could sit down together."

Right. She scanned some more. "We could get something to go and take it down to the waterfront and watch the sunset."

The sun was already lowering, a golden ball catching the rim of the mountains, its rays bouncing and swirling on the surface of the water. "Okay. Yeah. That sounds nice." *And romantic.* But it was half the price of anywhere else to eat around there.

They walked in and ordered two sandwiches with chips and drinks, then carried their meals towards the grassy edge of the public waterfront area. People milled around everywhere. Sunbathers, kids playing down on the sandy beach and others braving the cold water. They sat down, and she crossed her legs, sedately hiding them under her skirt. They ate in amicable silence but there was a definite air of tension, as if the universe were confirming, *this is a date.*

The nice setting gave her pause and Josefina relaxed and began enjoying it. Watching people, from families to couples, old and young, it was amusing and busy. Conversation was easy and several small comments about this and that went unnoticed. They finished, and Caleb nodded down toward the grassy area. "You ever go on the bumper boats? Or the go-carts?"

No. There were rarely family trips to Chelan, not for the Ruiz family. There wasn't enough money for frivolous things like that. "Not really. There were seven of us and not a lot of extra money or even the time to go off and do stuff like that."

"Yeah, us too. Not as many as seven, but also not a lot of

money to spend on useless things like that. You want to now?"

"Right now? Us?"

"Sure," he shrugged and grinned. "Why not? We can afford it now since there aren't seven of us, only two."

She still didn't want to owe Caleb anything. As a cheap date, she wouldn't have to feel guilty, but she had to admit being lulled by the picnickers and loud laughter and voices all around them, especially from the few rides that were featured at the city park. It did sound fun. Hell, why not? "Okay."

He grinned like a little boy and jumped onto his feet, balling up the wrap his meal came in. "Let's do it."

She had a hard time not smiling back at his child-like enthusiasm. They found a garbage can, and threw away all the sandwich packaging before heading over towards the go-cart track. "Which would you like to do first?"

"The go-carts. People come off those boats looking pretty wet."

They patiently waited in line until they reached the front and paid the fee. Josefina ducked into a royal blue go-cart and Caleb was right behind her in a red one. The mini-track had a stoplight that changed from red to green before the small herd of tiny cars took off. The one Josefina drove turned on a dime and it took her a lap or more to get the stop-and-go as well as her steering coordinated.

Meanwhile, Caleb kept bumping into her and making her jerk forward. He passed her with a laugh and got in front of her. She managed to edge in closer to him and push him out on a turn, after being neck-and-neck, and all the while, she was screaming and laughing out loud, which surprised her a lot. He yelled back, and their good-natured taunts and jeers continued until the caution flag came up for the last lap. Flooring the little carts' accelerators, they raced to the end and Josefina completely cut Caleb off before another cart bumped into him, pushing him off to the side and beating him.

Cheering, all the carts died out completely and she climbed out of hers with a huge smile on her face. "Ha. Got you. I totally beat the pants off you."

He threw his head back and laughed as he nodded. "Fine. You beat me silly in a go-cart, Josefina Ruiz. Now, let's see who's got it on the water. Boats, you know, are a whole different deal."

Grinning and laughing still, they kept ribbing each other over the small race until they were next up for the boats. People got off in front of them, many with big, damp circles on various parts of their clothing. They exchanged happy grins before each chose their spot in front of a boat. Josefina insisted on paying this time, so Caleb waved at her to go ahead. Permission granted, they both climbed into their bumper boats. The attendants came by and adjusted the safety bars, unhooking them from the ramp. Off they floated until the signal sounded, informing the riders that the steering was now engaged. It was pretty simple: a lever moved right and left to control the circular, little boats.

She didn't have a free moment before Caleb plowed into her from her left and his pontoon caused a huge splash of the pool water to drench her thigh and butt. "Oh. That's so cold!" She called out, scowling at him. She spun her boat around and tried to chug off but he followed.

Then it was all-out boat warfare. Other boats bumped them, dodging around and slipping in between them. For some reason, she was everyone's favorite target, it seemed, getting drenched with large water spots on her dress and boots, as well as her legs and entire right side.

The round ended and they docked the boats. Laughing harder than they did after the go-carts, they were comparing wet marks and he conceded she won for being soaked more thoroughly. They couldn't stop laughing while ruminating over it as they wandered back towards the park.

"How about that ice cream now?"

She nodded. "Okay, now." This time, she meant it and looked forward to it. He ordered a double scoop of bubble gum and birthday cake hard ice cream. She gave him a quizzical look. "What are you, thirteen?"

He shrugged and laughed. "I never said I developed adult taste buds. Let's just call it boyish enthusiasm," he added while licking the top scoop of ice cream. Josefina got a single scoop of mint chocolate chip.

She licked hers delicately as they wandered towards the lake and this time, strolled along the edge of it. She slipped her boots off and let her bare feet sink into the sand and between her toes. She was cool from her damp clothes when the evening breeze just barely touched her. After the extreme heat from earlier, it felt lovely. She was comfortable and thought it was quite fun when they relived their recent races and challenges.

She licked the cone where some mint ice cream started to drip. "People should do this as kids." She sighed. "That sounds so selfish. I had a full childhood. And a few carnival rides wouldn't have made any difference."

Caleb was staring out at the lake and he turned towards her, licking his ice cream. Then he said softly, "No. Love makes all the difference."

The soft tone of his voice surprised her. It sounded so serious and so unlike Caleb. "Were you not loved?"

He sat down in the sand, and so did she, next to him. Fewer people were around now and they had most of the beach to themselves. He licked his ice cream again. His tongue turning the same shade of blue as his puerile, candy-flavored ice cream.

But his tone of voice was not childish, and there was nothing juvenile about the size of his tongue or the way his dark lashes grazed over his cheeks when he blinked. Despite shaving, his whiskers still colored his cheeks and neck. Caleb was a very big man.

But his voice sounded very sad.

"I was loved, sure. By my dad. He loved us. He just didn't know that kids like to do things that are different than adults. He didn't like to do anything, you know? He didn't see the value of going to town or out to lakes or even taking us kids for an outing down to the river. I'm sure he never supervised us doing anything. Jordan, Kailynn, and I were left completely to our own devices. He worked like a fiend until he got injured in a tractor accident and then he refused to leave his bedroom. Sure, he loved us, but not in a fun, involved kind of way. You know? I don't think I knew the difference until I started working at the Rydells, when I saw Jack interacting with his two boys. I mean, no one is more accomplished than Jack Rydell, yet he was all about his kids. It looked… nice. I think… if I ever had a kid or two, I'd like to do lots of things with them. Show them some fun. Maybe just play at the lake or the city park. Still, it would be something. That makes it special."

She kept licking her ice cream while her brain was spinning. She didn't expect anything like that from Caleb. At all. Much less, for him to vocalize something she herself had thought of many times. "I… me too. I mean, our dad loved us, but he was never involved with us. We were on our own, finding ways to entertain ourselves all the time. There was never anything to break up the summer. Nobody ever monitored us. God, our safety? I cringe at all the dangerous things we did on our own and wonder how we all managed to survive to adulthood."

His teeth flashed. "I know. Jordan and I should have died

or at least, lost a limb or two on about a dozen occasions I could spout off without even thinking on it. Like one time when we decided to race two old, nonworking tractors down the hill where our trailer used to be... No brakes, no helmets. Just straight down." He shook his head.

"Who won?"

He jerked his head up and let out a husky laugh. "I did of course. I won. I was a lot heavier so mine went a lot faster. Jordan was always a skinny skeleton, much like he is now."

"We used to play in that old junkyard across from Harvey's Fruit Packing. Do you know it?"

"'Course I do."

"Well, the fence had a hole in it down on the south end. We'd sneak in there, usually close to dark and we'd stay well after. Playing in all the wreckage and taking home any parts we wanted to build our own weird things from. Surprised Dad never asked or even wondered where we got the parts. We'd finally get so exhausted that we would fall asleep but there was no curfew. It was not safe, I see that now... but damn. We sure had fun." She smiled, remembering the long summer nights they scampered all around, making up games, anything from hunting for treasure to hide-and-seek or Green Goblin. Sometimes they did scavenger hunts. Night-time meant it was cooler and their energy automatically perked up. God, for years they did that.

Caleb smiled too. "I know what you mean. It was always Jordan, me, and Shane Rydell. The shit we did—I see now as an adult that it was pretty stupid shit. We're lucky to be here today, but damn, was it fun. Kids don't grow up as free as that anymore."

She slipped him a smile to show she agreed. "As they probably shouldn't."

Stuffing the end of her waffle cone into her mouth, she crunched it down along with the last of the ice cream. It dribbled all around her mouth and she groaned, "I love the last bite. Makes the entire, fat-causing event worth every mouthful."

"With the ice cream melted in there for more flavor. Yeah, it is," he agreed, taking his last bite and grinning at her as he did. He even moaned with the same little sound she made. She swatted at his bicep, which was close to her.

"Okay, I sounded stupid. You don't need to do it or rub it in."

"Oh, not stupid. Just satisfied."

She rolled her eyes at his obvious innuendo. But he grinned and shoulder-bumped hers with his. "But hopefully, in a good way."

Her eyebrows rose upwards. "Probably more satisfied by it than most other things."

He turned his gaze towards the now twilight sky, and different shades of pink and gold streaked across the heavens. "Yeah, every kid should have some fun and love."

"What happened to your mom?"

"She left. She hated the trailer and River's End. She lives in Yakima, last I heard, with her boyfriend-turned-husband. She never really liked us, least of all, me."

"Do you still have contact with her?"

"No. She walked out when I was a teenager and I never wanted to see her again. Kailynn saw her a few times, but even that waned. Mom wasn't motherly, not even to her. Especially, as I look back now, when Kailynn most needed her. She got stuck with us Neanderthals and all of our jerky friends. Dad never cared much, so some of our friends lived with us on and off. I loved it. Drinking and partying and gaming and ribbing each other. But Kailynn became a frequent target. She struggled for her privacy and I only realize now, how hard it must have been on her. She was reserved and quiet and then there we were..." He slid his gaze to her. "What about you? You don't mention your mom."

"She died when I was young from adverse complications of diabetes. I never knew her. Then Dad married Izzy. She died two years ago. They had five kids between the two of them. Dad had me and Izzy had two girls, and then they had Pedro and another girl. Dad considers her two kids his kids. She and I always got along... just fine."

"But not like a real mother to you?"

"No. My mom was white, so Izzy felt intimidated by me. Yet, my mom was dead. It shouldn't haven't mattered. I needed her."

"I didn't know that."

"Yeah, Pedro and I are just half siblings. But he's my favorite."

"Complicated."

"Stupid and complicated. If I ever do it, I vow to do it right, and if I don't, to freaking stop. No more marriages or kids or boyfriends. Figure it out. You know?"

"I do, actually. I don't want any kids of mine to lose a parent. It's too painful. Ends their childhoods way too early."

She tilted her head, considering him in a completely different light. "Is that what it did to you?"

His eyebrows furrowed. "Yeah. I think it did. Maybe that's why I acted like an overgrown adolescent for at least a decade too long until about...now."

"And now you're not?"

"Now, I'm trying not to be that person. Except after a date with bumper boats and ice cream, maybe I'm still just a stupid, cocky adolescent, someone who's so insecure I can't do anything, so I childishly try to cover it up with a lot of bluster and rudeness."

She tilted her head, evaluating him. "First of all, I asked

you for the ice cream and I thought the rides were fun. But do you think you're that person still, Caleb?"

He shrugged, squeezing his eyes shut. "Unfortunately, I do think I am." He glanced her way. "But after both of my siblings just informed me how miserable their life with me was, I prefer not to be that stupid jerk. I'd like to grow up and be better now. I'm just not sure I know how."

His tone was so heartfelt. So vulnerable. So real. She touched his arm, unable to resist his sincerity. "You do know how, Caleb. You've been doing it. That's the only reason I'm here."

He stared down at her hand on his arm and his expression seemed oddly stricken. She was so candid with him now. Even she was surprised by her own truthfulness. He touched her hand with his and squeezed her fingers, saying, "I'd like to think so. But there's still a lot to undo."

She held her breath and their gazes locked, like a shared whisper between them. She let his arm go and he clutched her hand as they dropped onto the sand below them. Her heart beat erratically and much harder. It was interrupting her usually cool thoughts. Damn. She was all jumbled up. Surprised at how serious Caleb had become and recalling all the fun they had, her understanding of his childhood and dreams reflected her own and were nothing like what she originally imagined.

She couldn't look at him as a flush of confusion swept over her. Luckily, it was growing dusky and the sun's glare had already vanished. Silence descended between them while they held hands. But it wasn't anything like before. This time, it was comfortable.

Their hands were joined. Caleb cared about what Josefina thought. They shared intimate revelations and somehow, still connected. She shuddered at the thought. God. No.

She could not bond with Caleb. She adamantly refused to

be drawn into a sob story and a little boy desire to change and grow up. She saw no proof he was even capable of doing that. How easily he could turn out to be a disaster. Someone who seduced her into a futile, immature relationship. No. Hell no.

She had plans, and goals and unflappable ideals. And they didn't include a guy.

Not a damn Caleb Hayes from River's End.

His big, warm hand felt nice, however, so she did not withdraw hers. Not yet.

"We should go," she said, but her tone sounded weak and soft.

He shifted and released her hand, rising up to stand and she followed. They stood together, and he nodded. Still quiet, they turned and walked to his truck. Halfway there, he took her hand in his again and held it tightly. His thumb rubbed the outside of hers. Damn, it felt good. Soft. Sensuous. Strange, little feelings tugged inside her stomach. No.

She was grateful when she ducked into his truck and stayed quiet as they drove homewards. More silence. He pulled into the front of her place. Darkness obscured the land. Moonlight shone, all silvery and bright, enhancing the few streetlights and house lights scattered over the mountains around town and across the river.

Was this a good date? It was fun. Definitely honest. Most surprising of all, they were connecting. She looked at him, but he just turned his truck off. Alarmed, she jerked upright, and he glanced over at her.

"Just walking you to the door. Remember? Like last time? Being a gentleman?"

She let out a breath. Okay, she was jumpy. That was because she was worried. Worried that she liked the date, and worse still, she kind of liked Caleb. And seriously. Sure, of course she was attracted to the big, hot, strong man.

Ignoring her concerns, she slipped out of the vehicle and hastily walked up the sidewalk to unlock her door. He stood back, hulking, which made her hands shake. No. They were done. Nothing could happen. He had his hands in his pockets and she looked closely at him, but his gaze scanned all around, avoiding her. Was he... nervous? Because of the moment? That shocked her. It melted something previously frozen about her attitude toward him.

"It was fun. Thanks."

His blue eyes returned to hers. He smiled, and her stupid, weak heart fluttered when she saw the shyness in his smile. What happened to the cocky, arrogant jerk who stared at her big boobs and called her "señorita?" Where did this *gentleman* come from? This man who behaved like a real man, not an obnoxious lout whom she wanted to knee in the groin. She found him so confusing, she wasn't sure what to say.

"It was fun. I'm glad you liked it."

His hand rubbed the back of his neck and he looked at her. Then he turned away. Eventually, he stepped closer, but only half a step. "Can I... I mean... should we...?"

"I need to go inside now." She cut him off, clean and quick.

He nodded. "Right. I meant, would you want to go out with me again? Maybe tomorrow night? Or if that's too soon, how about next weekend? We could... I don't know yet, but I'll think of something. Something fun. Something worth your time."

She couldn't help it, she just had to ask. "Why are you trying so hard with me? This isn't your normal way."

"Because I don't consider you to be like anyone else. I guess I'm not very good when I'm not doing my norm."

"I don't know if we should."

His gaze snapped to hers. "You had fun, didn't you? You seemed to."

"I did but…"

"But what? Just tell me? Let me know so I can fix it."

She bit her lip. "You don't need to fix anything. I mean, I guess you should keep fixing yourself and moving towards the new you, but you don't have to do that with me. It's not anything like that. I'm not looking for anything. Remember? Friends. That's all I want."

His mouth twisted. "Okay, but it's not all I want. However, in the interest of self-improvement, I'm willing to take it, Josefina. Besides, I really like you."

"You want to have sex with me."

"I do." He shrugged. It surprised her when he didn't squirm and shift around, like every other subject they discussed. Sex, however, seemed to be an area well within Caleb's comfort zone. "I want to. But that's okay if you don't want to. I just like being with you."

"Is that… a new experience for you?"

"So new." He grinned brightly, and she couldn't help returning it with her own. She shrugged.

"I guess next weekend will work, as long as you under-stand what this is between us and what I expect. I'm not playing games or being coy, so you can't blame me for not putting out."

"I don't want you to put out. Not for anyone."

"Anyone?" her eyebrows rose.

His cocky, self-assured grin returned. "I didn't mean anyone. I meant me. But I don't want it to be anything that is common or usual. I want it to be… longed for. And different."

"You do?" Her eyebrows scrunched together in surprise.

"I do. For some reason, it's different with you. That's all I can articulate."

"But that's exactly what I'm saying. I'm flattered, honestly, I am. But I'm not the girl for you. I mean that, Caleb."

"I get it and I know you mean it. But maybe I could change enough for you to change your mind."

"I can't be the one to change you. Don't put that burden on me."

He nodded. "I know. I gotta do it. Just... I had fun with you. I'd like to do it again. I understand your position clearly and unless you want to end it, I'm willing to abide by your rules. So, do you want to do something next weekend?"

She sighed. "Fine. Okay. As long as you understand—"

"I don't understand anything. But I'm ready and willing to learn now."

She shut the door as he winked and waved but her stupid heart fluttered at his flirtatious smile when he left. She locked her door, falling against it, and realized her heart was racing. Her reaction to him wasn't just friendly and platonic. Duh. Of course not. She was flattered and attracted to him. But that didn't mean she would do anything to encourage it. Nor should she have. She was very firm that she should not.

Nodding, she marched towards her bed, feeling proud she was all alone and unkissed. Okay, she was a little bit turned on and slightly unsatisfied and foolishly flattered at his undying interest in wanting to have something more and something different with her. But could he be serious? NO. He was Caleb Hayes. She may have appealed to his impulsive, short attention span and may have captured his interest for now, but it would never last or mean anything. And it could never survive in the long term.

But that didn't mean she couldn't have short-term fantasies of her own and pursue some of her irresistible attractions, now did it?

CHAPTER 8

ALEB HOPED THAT JOSEFINA would not cancel when he called her the next week to ask if she still wanted to go out. Yes. Saturday night this time. He walked on air for the rest of the week. A reaction he never once experienced before with anyone. No woman or even a past sexual encounter could have made him more excited or so full of anticipation. He fairly glowed and smiled at Pedro and Jordan, the air now cleared with them, and it was like a new beginning, which so far, was a good one. Why had he wasted so much of his time with hatred and bitterness? And Josefina? She was never a waste of his time.

Caleb hadn't told his dad about his new epiphany and sometimes he got claustrophobic at being stuck in the same house as his dad, so he started working longer days. He flagged Ian down and asked for extra work at overtime wages. Ian complied with a startled look on his face. Caleb chose to ignore it even if Ian seemed surprised by his request. Jordan noticed and stayed late to work with him one evening.

"Anything going on with you?"

"What do you mean? No. I thought I was getting better. Or at least, I'm trying to."

Jordan and he were lifting old crates, which they had to break down and flatten. They would be stacked to burn later in the fall after the fire season had passed. It was hot, back-breaking work but they tackled it together. "Yes. That's just it, you're not acting at all like yourself anymore."

"Well, my old self wasn't very nice, Jordan. Weren't you first to suffer from it? I'm trying to learn how to be better. Everyone always said I was a lazy SOB. So that seemed the obvious thing to fix first. The opposite of being lazy is working. And it's not so bad. I mean, it stops me from getting bored, which keeps me out of trouble. So maybe I'll have a domino effect, you know? By changing one thing in my life, other things will follow. I don't have a clue how, but I'm trying to be different. And Kailynn told me that all the time over the years but I ignored her, so now I'm trying to do it right."

Jordan's eyes brightened. "Are you saying this is because of me?"

Caleb stopped busting the boards of the old box in his hands. "Yeah. It's completely because of you. I was calling you names for a decade and I didn't even know it was so cruel. That's... yeah, it's because of what I did to you in the past."

Jordan nodded casually but his eyes glistened. "Pedro said so too, but I had hard time believing it. He said you apologized to him and have been acting completely different."

"I'm trying to every day. It still startles me sometimes when you two touch each other affectionately. Like when he kissed your cheek before he went off to lunch. Well, honestly, it still startles me. I automatically feel weird before I remind myself that it's okay. I don't know how else to word it. I'm not used to it yet, but I'm trying hard to get used to it."

Jordan smiled and dropped his head, blushing in what seemed like shame. "Can I tell you something?"

"Of course. But you haven't talked to me in what? Years? I didn't even realize it until this month how far we've drifted apart."

"We did. Because I had to in order to hide this stuff. I *had to*. No other choice. But it's okay if you get startled by us and confused even. To be honest?"

"What?" Caleb was breathless in his hope that his brother was talking to him because he trusted him.

"I'm not used to it yet either."

"You're not?"

"No. That's what broke us up the first time. But every time he touches me in public, I resist the urge to look around and see who's watching us. I'm not used PDA. That was something disdained for us. I grew up with Dad too. So—"

"So, we gave you a terrible complex." Caleb faltered but forced himself to power on; he had to be different. He heard his brother now loud and clear and it shamed him that his brother felt so bad over what Caleb did to him.

Jordan's entire body straightened and stilled. "That... that... yes. That's what it feels like. I hurt him all the time with that reflexive action. He feels rejected, or thinks I'm embarrassed by him... and us. It's the last thing I would ever want to do to him, but it's what I do despite all of my effort not to."

Caleb fidgeted. Discussing a man's feelings was as new for him. But this was his little brother. "But in your defense, remember that you grew up listening to Chuck Hayes. Dad was *wrong*. I know what a loud voice he has. It echoes inside my head too. But we have to realize he was all wrong. If I can see that now... I mean, come on, Jordan, you have to realize it too."

Jordan's eyes flashed with hope. He also sensed some

127

insecurity and Caleb was astonished at the level of it he saw from his brother. How the fuck did he never notice that before? How much his brother admired him and his opinions? Caleb cringed because he was the last person anyone should admire. He felt so undeserving of Jordan's loyalty and forgiveness and respect despite what he had to say. Caleb shifted his shoulders back in a silent vow: *he had to do better.* For Jordan, his brother.

"I'm not anymore," he confirmed in a solid tone with an unwavering gaze. "But I am still learning, so I'll screw up. I have no idea what I'm doing but I want to do this, and I plan to keep trying."

"Thank you." Jordan bent down and grabbed some more boards. But he fumbled with them and Caleb knew he was trying to hide his emotions.

Caleb shook his head and marched over to Jordan. Leaning close, he put his arm around Jordan's shoulders. "You should be proud of your relationship with Pedro. It's far more than Dad ever had with Mom and I've sure never come close to anything like it."

Jordan's shoulders tightened, and he was quiet for a long moment. "You've never talked like that before."

"No. I haven't. But hell, even old asswipes like me are wrong sometimes. I was wrong, Jordan. I was dead wrong. So is Dad."

"Dad won't—"

"No. Dad won't. But I will. And don't forget, you always have Ian and Kailynn. Along with Pedro and Josefina, and from what it sounds like, the rest of the Ruiz family. You're not alone anymore, Jordan. So, there's no need for you to glance around when you want to hug or kiss Pedro."

"I'll try and remember that."

Me too, Caleb thought to himself, squeezing his brother before letting him go. They both cleared their throats and glanced at each other, sharing an awkward smile before they started to crack up. They were laughing at themselves and how far this interaction was from anything either one had ever experienced before with anyone, much less with each other. They continued stacking the crate boards well into the evening. When they finished, both felt a sense of togetherness that had been lacking for years. Comradery. How could Caleb fail to realize how far they had drifted apart? He erroneously thought since they lived and worked together all the time, they were close. Turns out they were only occupying the same small space.

CALEB SHOWED up the next weekend at Josefina's house and this time, they went out to dinner and a movie. It was a more traditional date, and they talked and laughed easily. There was not one single highlight because the entire evening was exemplary. He again walked her to the front door and... and did nothing. No kiss. No "come hither" look. No asking to come inside. But she did smile, and Caleb knew it was genuine; he was sure of it. He left there light on his feet, excited and very pleased from their time together. He felt far more satisfied than he ever did before, even after great sex.

He really liked Josefina. There were no words he could think of to describe how he felt. No one had ever captured his attention like Josefina did. She was pretty, sure. There was no denying his physical attraction to her. But for the first time in his life, it felt like so much more. He seemed lighter whenever she was nearby. Just being quiet while he drove with her, his entire body felt calmer and brighter and full of hope, simply because she was with him.

But Josefina did not feel the same way about him. He understood that clearly. She wasn't kidding or being coy when she told him it was strictly friends only. He realized he had a lot of improvements to make before someone of high caliber like Josefina would even contemplate being with a guy like him.

They went out each weekend for the next several weeks. They spent time at the beach, up at the lake again and ate lots of ice cream. Turns out they both loved it and got it many times they were together.

Caleb never once made a move on her. The *friend line* was never crossed. Considerate, platonic and one hundred percent courteous. He opened doors for her and waited for her to proceed before he did. He let her speak first and he listened. That was a new experience for him. He walked her to the door and didn't stay when it was obvious she wasn't inviting him for anything physical.

But there were times, only a handful perhaps, when they shared a real conversation. Like the first date when they talked about growing up without much fun in their childhoods and their absentee mothers. They held hands after that and when those occasions happened again, that was the only physical contact they had. But for Caleb, it was the most profoundly intimate encounter he'd ever indulged.

"I just thought of something."

"What?" Josefina asked. The coming weekend was the start of July.

"Waterslides. We should spend the entire day at the waterslides."

"Waterslides?"

"Have you ever been there?" he inquired.

"Well… no. You probably already knew that."

"I did. That's why we should go. I never went either until I entered my twenties, and on my own dime. But every kid should go, although as adults, it's pretty fun too."

"For you in your twenties. Weren't you still just an over-grown kid about then too?"

Until then, he knew she was thinking about it. He let it go. "Come on, Josie, come with me," he goaded her until she let out a sigh, mixed with a laugh, one he often heard when she surrendered her argument to him.

"Okay. Fine. What time?"

"Open at ten, pick you up at nine-thirty and be ready. All day. Until they close."

"All day until they close," she relented as she laughed and agreed.

He picked her up and she wore a lace cover-up, so he could easily make out the outline of a modest bikini. Once there, he kept sneaking peeks at the rise and fall of her breasts in the skimpy top and black bottom. They spent the day frolicking. That's what it felt like too. Frolicking. Up and down the slides they went. Laughing on the inner tube rides together, as they bounced and splashed through the pools and rapids and sprays and bumps. On single slides, they raced and compared speeds while the winner waited at the bottom. They had snow cones in the midday heat, scooping up the flavored ice while basking in the sun. Still soaking wet, they dripped water all over the poolside as they ate. Josefina smiled as often as Caleb did. When he dropped her off at home, she laughed and said she loved their day.

He left, and his heart was hammering with excitement. Since meeting Josefina, his entire week was obsessed with thoughts of the coming weekends. A few times, it didn't work out because she had a family get-together, and those were crushing blows to Caleb. His disappointment embarrassed him. His heart sank, his mood plummeted and a yawning, hollow abyss seemed to form, representing a whole week before he saw her again.

Friends? Were they just friends? Maybe. The best of

friends, in his mind. He'd never been that way with a woman before. It was time he had a female friend. Bonding. Connection. He never failed to notice her beauty, but her mind, sense of humor, intelligence, quick wit, and scathing tongue were the things that kept him engaged, interested, and obsessed with her. Of course, he knew he couldn't possibly provide her with the joy and fulfillment she gave to him.

He often went quiet when the topics she discussed were over his head and beyond his knowledge, which included most things. She was so well read and informed that he just listened and trusted her opinions because he so rarely had any of his own. He would grow quiet until she nudged him for a response. He tried, he really did, to sound like he wasn't completely an ignorant moron, but he couldn't fake it. He was always a little surprised when she agreed to see him again after such a fiasco. He clearly understood his shortcomings as a person.

He just liked her so much, he greedily lapped up as much time as he could get with her. It made his life happier than ever before. He felt better too. Like he was becoming a better person. He found depth and understanding in Josefina, which made him realize that he'd floated over the surface of his life without even once dipping down deeper. He wanted to feel something much more meaningful and deep and truthful and enlightening now. He was ashamed to realize how shallow he was.

But changing that was hard to do. He seemed to be swimming over his head without a lifejacket or swim lessons. He was always out of his comfort zone lately and didn't know how to deal with it. After seeing the way his brother responded to him, however, well, yeah, he knew he was on the right path. He had to be.

Caleb and Josefina grew even closer over the summer, and in new ways, like they'd never experienced before in their entire lives.

His sister noticed his progress and never hesitated to comment and compliment him.

"I wondered…"

"What, Caleb?" she asked, nudging him one morning as they were alone in the house.

"If I should move out."

"You definitely should."

"I've never lived alone. I don't know how to."

"I know. For all your blustering and macho, you're completely dependent on those you love with a sense of loyalty most people miss about you. Your entire focus is centered on your loved ones. Family is all that you live for. You're the most family-oriented person I've ever met."

"You… you really think that of me?"

She smiled softly and leaned across the counter to touch the top of his hand with hers.

"Oh, Caleb, I really do. I've been dismissive toward you, haven't I? I got so mad when I realized Jordan was gay and why he was so ashamed to admit it. But that's the past. I let it obscure all the positives of your personality. You don't say much, Caleb, but you show it. Your intense love of our family, me included, wasn't always deserved by us, to be honest. I was always trying to get away and usually turned my nose up at what we had and who we were. I admit that now because I realize the value too. I was just too unhappy then to understand or see it. I didn't want to see it. And so was Jordan, but for different reasons."

"I was an ass, Lynnie. That's why you didn't see it in me."

Her lips curled upwards. "Okay, maybe so. But you were a loving ass. You always had my back. But I think I didn't give you the credit you deserved. I am now because I'm noticing now."

"Thanks, Lynnie. It's nice to hear that from you and Jordan. You know, you both mean the world to me."

"And that's what I tried to forget when I left here."

"I didn't accept Jordan, however."

"But you rolled with everything and everyone else. Loyalty is your finest quality. Don't lose that or forget that about yourself. Not like I did."

"Thanks, Lynnie," he said softly, dipping his head down, seemingly embarrassed by her unbridled praise. She was his beacon, his North Star. He admired his sister more than anyone else and knew she was light years beyond him in her intelligence, skills, and capabilities.

Kind of like Josefina.

"You know the home site, it's all yours as far as I'm concerned. Dad will never leave here. He loves it too much. Turns out our dad is a bit of a snob too. Apparently, he loves having his own hot tub and media room. Ian's family's money appeals to him, so he's staying here."

"Do you mind?" He tilted his head. Caleb never asked or considered what Kailynn thought about her family mooching off her and her husband. Thinking of himself. He winced. "Shit, that includes me, huh?"

"I know. It didn't occur to you. And if things were reversed, I know you'd take me and Ian, along with his entire family into your dwelling, no matter how small it was. That's what I mean about you, Caleb. You'd give the shirt off your back to your family and your friends. No matter what it cost you in resources or time or having to live in a crowded house even. Me? Not so noble. But this time, it was easier because there was no choice. Last summer... there was so much devastation, it was surreal and no, I didn't mind. I was relieved we didn't lose this place and that we all still had a place to live together. It could have burned us all out."

"But I never had the resources to help anyone."

"I do, but only because of Ian. Not me. So..." She shrugged.

"You'd do it on your own too. I don't doubt that, Lynnie. You were always destined for more than that single-wide trailer on the hillside." He grinned, crookedly. "But I'm not. It's where I belong."

"There's nothing wrong with that. Not after the way you've changed and begun to accept Jordan and Pedro. So... yeah, if you want the home site, as far as I'm concerned, my third of it is all yours. Dad doesn't care. And Jordan? He feels like I do. Lots of memories but he wants to live in a new place to make new ones. But you? It would be fitting and justified if you chose to rebuild your life there, Caleb."

His head swam with indecision and emotion. But he sat up straighter. *Rebuild your life, Caleb.* Those unique words had never been addressed to him before. No one believed he'd do much in life except drink beer, swear, and piss away his days. Now, that wasn't enough for him.

After work that day, Caleb drove up to the home site. He got out, the heat overcoming him. The first thing to do was collect all the wreckage and pile it up. As it looked now, it was widely strewn all over the acre lot. All the outbuildings were filled with old, metal relics from tractors to cars to trailers and mowers and the tanks they used for propane, along with tons of endless refuse. All of it was burnt, leaving only twisted metal haphazardly peppering the land along with the weeds, sagebrush and sticker bushes that were now taking over.

He grabbed a pair of leather gloves from the inside of his truck console and started gathering up the rubble. He jumped back when a rattlesnake started hissing and tried to strike at him after a distinct rattle. Grabbing a shovel from the back of his truck, he scooped up the hissing, coiled, rattling snake, carrying it far enough to safely fling away.

Then he went back to work. He wiped the sweat that streaked his face with dust and black ash.

He was making decent progress. By nighttime, he nodded as if someone spoke to him. Good work for a day. He smiled slightly. Who knew he could enjoy the satisfaction of a difficult job well done? He didn't enjoy the work particularly, but he lapped up the results. He guessed that's how other people forced themselves to face tedious jobs they hated for forty hours a week.

He came back the next evening and the next until he cleared the far edge of the lot. Naturally, someday he would physically need to haul out the debris, but gathering all of it into one spot opened the land up for so much possibility. Caleb thought it was a damn shame that all the biggest, oldest pines burned. Two were bent nearly in half. Only the blackened, charred remains were left. Others were singed and black primarily on the bottom halves; however, they looked so ugly and half dead, they also had to go.

Caleb took a chainsaw to the ones he couldn't salvage and started clearing them. He cut the trees into rounds and carried them too, separating them to the side by the debris pile. Maybe he'd cut all of that into firewood. And someday, perhaps he'd even have his own damn fireplace to burn it in. That would be nice. He recalled the old, rickety trailer they grew up in and its crappy insulation. They froze all winter and sweated all summer.

Caleb cleared enough that he figured he might be able to use a mower to cut all the brambles out. They were sticky and hurt whenever he brushed past them. Plus, the snakes liked to hide in it. He uncovered two rattlers and three bull snakes as well as a half dozen harmless blue racers. Up on the hill like he was, in the extreme heat, snakes were usually more prevalent.

One day in the middle of July, he wandered down to

Shane Rydell's shop. It occupied a small parcel of land near the river on the Rydell River Ranch. He walked in there after work one day and blinked before his pupils adjusted from the bright sunlight to the florescent lighting of the shop interior. The air conditioner rattled away, making a cool, refreshing breeze. Shane had a chopper up on a lift, installing a new engine.

He waited until Shane glanced up and noticed him. Then he stopped dead. Caleb nodded. "Hey."

Shane slowly lowered his hand and ducked out from under the motorcycle as he cleared his throat. "Hey."

Yeah, they were once best friends. For twenty-plus years, he and Shane were inseparable. Now, it had been three years or more since they last hung out together. In the snap of two fingers, Shane fell in love with the damn local schoolteacher. Then he was suddenly married and having his own babies and working in his own shop.

There were never any fights or nasty conversations to end their friendship. Caleb knew and understood that Shane had suddenly become like *them*, the ones he and Shane used to criticize so harshly. People like Shane's responsible, hardworking, got-their-shit-together, older brothers Jack and Ian.

Now Shane had turned into one of those too. And Caleb didn't. So, Shane no longer had time to shoot the shit over a few beers or spend all night on the road for no reason other than to see how far they could drive in one night.

Caleb loved motorcycles and Shane had plenty of access to them, so he'd often go with Shane, borrowing one of the bikes Shane was working on for other people. They never told anyone they borrowed the finished ones for joyrides. Yeah, Shane no longer took joyrides or seemed to do anything for fun anymore. Caleb realized that Shane had become another Rydell in the mold that Ian was.

People had expectations of him now. Big ones. And odder still, Shane seemed to enjoy meeting those expectations and planned to do everything he could to surpass them. He even expected Caleb to do the same, especially in Caleb's capacity now as one of Shane's employees.

It was shit. When Caleb first started working there, it never came between him and his friends, never at all, but as the years passed, Shane conformed to his legacy and suddenly, they were on two different levels. And two very different kinds of people.

The worst part was: they were no longer friends.

"Caleb. What can I do for you?" Shane still didn't look like the rest of the Rydells. He was a monstrous guy, bigger and taller than Caleb by inches and sheer brawn. He had several huge tattoos and (so it was rumored) a piercing, although Caleb didn't know anything about that.

"You... do you have time for a beer? At the tavern? Or... I mean..."

Shane nodded, setting down the tool he was using. "Yeah. Yeah, sure, I have time. Let me just call Allison and let her know. Iris isn't sleeping great lately so let me check and make sure she's good."

That was why they stopped being friends. Shane had two little girls now and he loved being a father. He quickly called his wife and got her permission. A year ago, Caleb would have sneered at Shane over having to obtain the permission from some chick.

But after the fire last summer and the consequences of being homeless, not to mention, Jordan almost banning him from his life, and his introduction to Josefina, Caleb appreciated knowing that Shane had someone to check in with. Someone who cared very much if he came home at night, someone who wanted him home safely.

Shane had a loving home, even if it burned last year too.

No amount of money could have stopped the inferno of the previous summer. It did not discriminate between anyone or anything in its path of destruction. But Shane still had a home with his wife and kids, even if it were temporarily gone now, since it was being rebuilt.

"Meet you there?" Shane asked. Caleb nodded. Ten minutes later, they both took a seat at one of the small tables in the tavern. Shane asked for a beer. Caleb ordered a Sprite and sat down.

"Simple drinks..." Shane stated, staring at the foamy liquid.

"For simple men." Caleb finished quietly. That was what they used to say. He added, "Not so simple anymore, huh?"

"No. Not so much anymore. You didn't like me for a while. Everyone else approved when I grew up except you. You didn't even talk to me anymore."

"No, I had years to go before I could appreciate it."

Shane grinned. "And now?"

"I'm slowly bumbling through it."

"There's a girl?"

"Actually, it started with a brother."

Shane nodded. "Jordan. Choosing Ian to be his best man must have pissed you off."

"It did. But I guess he had no other choice at the time. I'm trying to correct that."

"That's good, man."

Caleb smiled and stared around, softly adding, "But there is a girl..."

Shane laughed and shoved his shoulder. "Always. There's *always* a girl."

"Unless you're Jordan, in which case, there's always a guy. You know what's funny? He has as much trouble as I do trying to understand his relationship. Who'd have guessed? Is it that way for you too?"

"It can be. I think romantic relationships are inherently complicated and bring out intricacies and difficulties that no other entity can mimic. So yeah, it's that way for me, as much as it is true for Jordan."

"I can't say we've ever once talked about it."

"No. We haven't spoken too much lately."

"No," Caleb agreed, staring down. "I didn't like it when you grew up."

Shane let out a laugh. "Yeah, I did finally do that. What's changed?"

"I guess only me. I'm trying to change now."

Shane lifted his glass in a mock toast. "Damn. That's great. Really." Shane nodded at his drink. "What the hell you drinking? That isn't beer."

"I've been avoiding liquor. Seems to be working for me so far."

"You think you had a problem?" Shane's eyebrows jutted up in surprise.

"You were there more often than most. What would you say?"

He nodded and stared at his drink. "Maybe. Yeah, I could see where it could hinder you. Has it been hard? Quitting, that is?"

"Not as bad I thought or heard it could be. So far, it's been pretty good."

"That's great, Caleb, really." A stifled awkwardness descended between them.

Caleb asked, "How's that baby?"

"Iris is great."

"I should get your family a baby gift, shouldn't I? I mean, isn't that what people do for new babies?"

"That would be weird as shit. But... yeah, that's what people often do." Shane grinned, lifting his drink in another mock toast.

"Well, I attended my brother's damn housewarming party, so I guess it isn't so far off from that. Respectable person that I now choose to become." He lifted the glass of pop.

Shane nodded and said quietly. "I think it's great, all of it, Caleb."

Caleb scooched around and cleared his throat. "I've been clearing the old home site, thinking of moving something up there or building something kinda small. Can't afford too much, but anyway, I wondered if I could borrow a tractor and mower deck? I'll pay for the gas, of course, it'll just be a lot less work than doing it by hand."

"'Course, Caleb. We can load it on the trailer tomorrow and you can haul it up there." Shane tilted his head. "But you know, Ian handles all that shit, and you see him on a daily basis. Why did you ask me?"

"Because I wanted to borrow it as a friend and a neighbor. Not as an employee."

Shane held his gaze, and nodded slowly, putting his hand out. Caleb seemed startled as he stared at the outstretched limb. "Okay, my friend and neighbor, I'd be glad to let you borrow a tractor."

Caleb smiled and shook his hand as the formerly odd, weird ice between them started to thaw. It was like they suddenly recognized each other again. A few hours later, they were cracking each other up over the old times with anecdotes and stories, things they might not have remembered or dared to repeat to anyone else.

Caleb nodded at the lineup of beer glasses before Shane, who most definitely wasn't sober now. "Didn't think you'd still do this. Drink like that."

"Hell, not every night. Can't do it like the old days. This old body would fall apart, but yeah, sure, sometimes it's fun."

"But not too often. You've got a wife and kids waiting at home."

"Sound lame to you?"

"It was before. Now I think I might be a little envious. Of all couples. When I find myself feeling jealous of Pedro and Jordan, I have to think, wow, how shit has changed."

Shane grinned and nodded. "Damn, shit *has changed*. But you know what I've come to learn from Allison? Change can be a damn good thing, and you don't have to hate or banish your past. You can change and still count your former friends and acquaintances as important."

"I'm sorry I ignored you."

"Me too, but it can be the way it used to be now, right?"

"Yeah," Caleb said as he turned away. What the hell was wrong with him lately? Twice now, he teared up while talking with other men. Bonding. Talking. Admitting his feelings. He shuddered with regret, but a sense of relief soothed him.

Caleb borrowed the tractor and mower deck and promptly spent two weeks clearing, mowing, leveling, and grading. He put a new driveway in and ordered a huge dump truck to spread fresh gravel. He got large, round rocks from the river and hauled them up to remake the old fire pit much safer. When it was all cleared, Caleb looked around and thought it turned out to be a rather attractive spot. Staring out over the valley, he looked at the wood shed he built so he could invite his family and friends up there to enjoy an evening with him.

Yeah. That sounded about right.

And maybe someday, he'd show Josefina what he'd done with himself all summer... Maybe.

GLANCING up from the home site one weekday, Caleb was shocked to see his dad. He'd been working on leveling a nice, flat pad to build a house or hook up a trailer. He hadn't decided yet, and he stopped dead when his dad's truck parked at the site and he stared out at Caleb. His dad didn't get out or move for a long, profound moment.

Caleb set down his tools and crossed the decent looking plot of cleared and mowed land. It needed some damn water, that was for sure. The well was still potable luckily and irrigation was a must, as well as the next item on Caleb's list.

"Hey, Dad."

Chuck hobbled out, slamming his truck door. He only scowled and glared, offering no answer as he observed the location.

"It's… I mean, Kailynn and Jordan didn't want it and you…" *Can't work on it,* was perched on the tip of Caleb's tongue, which he bit down on to shut up. His dad hobbled closer, and the silence isolated him. His disdain was crystal clear. Caleb wasn't quite sure why.

"Well, I s'pose it's better than a couple of men movin' up here."

Caleb winced as he stared at the back of his dad's white head and sagging shoulders. He swallowed. No one was around. No one would know how he responded and what he did or did not do in that moment. No one would ever have to know about his father's visit. What was said or purposely not said. Only his father would be the one to judge Caleb on it.

But oddly and for the first time, something pricked Caleb's conscience. He'd know how he responded. He'd know if he let his dad talk that way about Jordan. "You can't talk about Jordan like that to me anymore." Okay, it was a weak, sad defense, but the most he'd ever protested.

Chuck whipped around. "What did you say? Are you correcting me?"

Caleb instantly weakened, but held his ground. His old man was tough as nails despite being handicapped and disabled. Only Kailynn received a softer, kinder version of their father than the man Caleb and Jordan encountered. Jordan usually withered in front of him. Growing silent, keeping eyes down, he would usually mumble to himself. Caleb was always respectful of Chuck, far more than his other two siblings.

"Yeah. I am," Caleb answered, his chest tightening as he raised his gaze higher. "I am. And Ian and Kailynn will kick you out if they ever hear you spouting off more of that shit."

He spat and turned around, putting his back to Caleb. "I know, you stupid, little shit. I don't say nothin' there. I keep it quiet. But here? Oh, no. This is my fucking land, Caleb Hayes. I gave you life, and I provided for all your care, did I not? This is *my land*. And here I'll say whatever the fuck I want. I ain't in the ground yet, am I?"

"No."

"Sir. Since when have you stopped giving me the respect you owe me and I deserve?"

"Since I don't like how you treat Jordan.When I'm done, if you wanna move back here, I'll always have a room for you, but you can't say that shit about Jordan anymore or Pedro, either."

"What the fuck? Who are you to give me orders?"

He shrugged. "Jordan's still family. And I'll never turn my back on any family member, no matter what. Even you. You bigoted, sour, old asshole. Do you want to lose your son? Jordan is a decent, hardworking, good person—"

"Who fucks a dude."

Caleb's anger stirred up his stomach acid, which, in turn, climbed up his throat. "Watch it. Pedro's my friend. Long before I knew any of this. And Jordan is my brother. You can't… you just can't be like that anymore."

"Yes, I can. Again, this is my damn land. I bought and paid

for it with my sweat, paying taxes that were gouged out of me every fucking year, so, yes, I can."

"Don't be like that." His politeness had no effect. Caleb didn't want that to be his dad's personality. He felt his entire world beginning to erode. The man to whom he'd listened and revered for his entire life was nothing but a homophobic, small-minded, self-entitled asshole. He believed his poverty was better than anything Pedro's family had to offer. Caleb felt like he'd been punched in the gut when he realized that, as if it weren't always right there for him to see.

"Please don't..." Hearing his dad's nasty imitation of him struck him hard, which, he was sure, was just as his dad wanted. Then Chuck sneered, "God, are you turning into a dick muncher too, Caleb?"

Caleb was ready to immediately deny such an accusation. That was how he used to react in the past. Now he had to be better. All of his adamant denials to his dad's incessant goading were exactly what his dad wanted to hear. He just didn't think about why his dad goaded him before now. This time, he did and remained quiet.

"Leave, now. I have a lot of work to do." Caleb passed his old man, and his cold tone and neutral expression said it all. Caleb didn't turn back around. He returned to his work, trying to level out the house site, scraping all the dirt he uncovered. He picked out the larger rocks and sticks and flung them off the site. He worked harder, his face glowing red in anger as well as embarrassment.

It was hard for him to turn his back on his dad, ignoring his accusations and insults. It was hard to pretend he didn't care. He did now. But he also began to realize he had to be different. The world was a different place, and after meeting the Ruiz family and experiencing his own brother's relationship, maybe that was okay. All the changes he was seeing.

Maybe it was a good thing for him to try and understand a lot of things he never cared about before.

But it still fucking hurt.

His dad's truck roared down his gravel driveway without another word. Caleb blew out a sigh, he was ashamed of his regret as well as relieved that his dad was gone but he still he felt no better.

He needed and wanted... Damn, he just would have liked to talk to someone. He sat back on his heels, stunned.

Talk to someone?

He'd never been like that before. He felt an irresistible urge, that started deep inside him, and he longed to describe his feelings over what just happened. He wanted to share his experience with someone. He never felt such an irrepressible urge before. But to whom? He could never repeat what his father said to Jordan. It was too mean. It could only hurt Jordan and set him back. He'd never burden his brother again with his dad's vile statements.

Kailynn? Ian? Shane? They'd feel compelled to kick his dad out. As he was sure even Shane would. No. Not the Rydells.

His friends? Hell, all of them had ignored him lately, not understanding his metamorphosis, and quite honestly, neither did he. How could they? But he couldn't talk to them.

Josefina.

She was the one he needed, wanted, and longed to talk to. *Josefina.* He never saw her on the weekdays because he never showed up. But what about a phone call? No. Not enough. Just once, maybe she'd forgive him if he saw her just this one time.

Josefina. Yes. She was the only person Caleb wanted to talk to.

CHAPTER 9

ALEB SHOWED UP IN Josefina's driveway barely twenty-five minutes later and swore when he glanced down and looked at himself. He forgot how he appeared. He was filthy. Covered in dirt, dust, ash, soot, and all of it streaming over his skin after mixing with the dripping sweat that poured off him. His clothes, his skin, his face and his hair were covered in a mess. He sighed, wilting. Damn. Just as he tried so hard to show Josefina he wasn't a mess, here he was.

But remembering the spiteful things his dad said churned his gut all over again. He was so confused. So upset. It was all new for him to feel so uncomfortable, but he did.

Maybe change wasn't worth all the fucking work or the gut-twisting harm it caused him to feel.

He waited, and was about to leave when her front door swung open. Her expression was serious as she waved at him, but it turned puzzled and curious.

He sighed, getting out of the truck, dropping his boot onto the concrete. She stepped forward as he crossed past the door. "I—"

"What's wrong?"

"I came from working on my family's place... I just, wondered, I mean, I wanted..."

"Caleb, what is it?" Her head tilted with visible concern. He glanced up and the hot sun beat down.

"Wanna go to the park? Maybe talk awhile? I mean, if that's okay. You said you're okay with being friends with me and, well, I could use one right now, big time." He winced. *Big time.* Oh, real articulate. He stared down. Damn. He was an incorrigible hick.

Her expression eased. "Yes, of course we can talk. Let's go to the boat launch and put our feet in the water. At least we can cool down for a while."

Clean off maybe too? He had to stink. But it was too late to address that. They got into his truck. In a matter of minutes, they were parked and walking to the docks, which were empty. They slipped their shoes off and dipped their toes before immersing their calves in the cool depths of the clear Columbia River.

"Did I pull you away from anything?"

"Nah. Just got home. Doing the usual, evening stuff. It's fine. This is nice."

She leaned back, tilting her head to let her face feel the sun. She looked so beautiful with her black hair skimming the dock and her face tilted up towards the sky. She was here for him. Caring and supportive and genuine and... His father was so wrong. Wrong to speak as he had. Now he didn't want to repeat his father's nasty words, none of them to Josefina. It would ruin her day as it had his.

He sighed. There was no one to talk to. Then she set her hand on his forearm, and it felt soft and cool, making his heart twist. "What's going on? What happened today? I've never seen you this upset."

"My dad paid me a visit."

"So? What does that mean? From the look on your face, I have to assume it isn't good."

"That's just it. It used to be okay with me." Caleb paddled his foot against the water, making it splash and sprinkling drops onto the surface. He ducked his foot back underneath, sighing at the cool refreshment on his sweaty, hot skin. "It used to be fine with me. He and I saw eye-to-eye on everything. We'd swig down some alcohol and if we spoke at all, it was just to be crude and rude. I see that now, but I didn't realize it then."

"In these conversations over the years, did he do most of the talking, or did you?"

Caleb whipped his head to look at her. Frowning, he tried to think back. He never considered that before. But it wasn't like he was ever a quiet man. No, he was mouthy, crude, rude, and lewd. Wasn't that what he was known for? And what Josefina didn't like about him? All she heard about him was based on facts. But was it all him? Or his dad?

"I think in my lifetime I've said as much as whatever Dad said. Yeah, maybe he does most of the talking around us. That was just how it was. But you know, my history of being less than stellar in how I behaved, talked, and treated others is pretty well known around here."

"But not now, huh, Caleb? Otherwise, I wouldn't be here now, would I? I only hope you realize that much about me. Do you?"

He smiled. "I do."

"I believe you're doing something entirely new as you work on yourself this summer and that's the only reason why I'm here now."

He stared out over the water before them and she nudged him with her shoulder. "What happened this evening?"

"I've been clearing our homestead. Did you know where we lived before the fire?"

"I know of the location, but I've never been up in the Gunderson Hills."

He smiled softly, and his tone was hollow when he said, "God, my sister hated living there, or even being from there. I truly never understood why. What was there to hate? For me, it was home. Now, I'm seeing it for what it wasn't for them."

"And now you're seeing it from your brother's and sister's points of view?"

"Yes."

"Nothing wrong with that."

"It should have happened sooner."

"But it happened. They're both listening to you and you're listening to them now. Nothing wrong with that. It's definitely never too late."

"No." He sighed. "But what if it's too late with my dad? What if he's too old and stubborn to change?"

She shrugged. "Yeah, so what if he can't change?"

"He's still calling Jordan and Pedro names. And I... holy shit. I hated listening to him. I never knew I felt so strongly before. But I realize now, I hated when my dad talked like that. Then... then I turn around—"

"And did the very thing you hated? I don't think that's so uncommon in kids."

"But I wasn't a kid."

"Maybe you were kid a little longer than you should have been."

He nodded, looking glum. "I was."

"What are you doing at your homestead?" she asked after he fell into a moody silence.

"I already cleared and mowed it and now I'm working on grading a new home site."

"For your dad?"

"No. Not really. I think... I think it's entirely for me."

She jerked up straighter. "For you? I had no idea you wanted to do that."

"I live with my sister and her husband and Dad. I'm thirty-one years old. Believe me, I see now, it's beyond time that I move out."

"You're lucky to have access to land that you already own. That's pure gold."

He glanced her way, never having considered himself the recipient of much financial luck in life. But looking at it now, he owned a plot of land. Owned it free and clear but for the property taxes and insurance.

"It is and that didn't even occur to me until about now."

"You're changing so fast, you can't adjust yet. You can't undo your entire past, along with all your basic beliefs and values in a single summer. That you're even attempting to, however, is rather impressive."

"I have to. I can't sound like my old man anymore."

She touched his hand, resting it on the dock, between her thigh and his. He closed his eyes at her gentle touch, wishing he could sink into her comfortable lap.

"You're not your dad. Even if you once were, you aren't now."

"I said shit like that. I'm... I'm really sorry," he whispered, shutting his eyes, and sounding horrified at his own short-sightedness. "I didn't like Pedro doing my job. I got all jealous when he earned a pay raise, and I didn't and so I... said mean stuff, stuff like my dad did."

"I can just imagine."

"No, you can't. It was so bad. So wrong—"

"Caleb, I've listened to that vitriol for my entire life. There are just some people who will base their reactions to me based on stereotypes they believe no matter what. I never know who to expect to it from."

"You don't recognize who or what or when it will pop up?"

"No."

He shook his head. His insides were clenching at her description of a reality he never considered. "I never once had to worry about that."

"I'm not always presumed to be an American. I'll bet no one's ever questioned you. Or told you to go back to where you came from… and never in a nice way."

He winced. "That must be hard to get questioned when other groups of people aren't."

She shrugged. "It's those damn stereotypes." She bumped him again, smiling now and obviously trying to get him to smile. "I can forgive you because you're not like that now. I've never seen anyone try so hard to right his past wrongs."

He gripped her hand. "Yes, considering. But Josie?"

She glanced at him since he rarely called her that. "What?"

"Will you promise to tell me if someone ever bugs you like I did again?"

"No. I won't. I'll handle it myself. As I always have. I had to learn how to pretty early on."

He blew out a breath, shaking his head. "I was so fucking arrogant and stupid all these years. I never even considered how much you had on your own plate. Look at me. Just once I get offended, and I can't even handle that."

"Maybe no one should be able to feel comfortable handling it? You know? It's wrong. It really is."

"Yeah, it really is."

She leaned her head gently on his shoulder and his entire body stilled. He dared not breathe, or turn his head or even flinch. He was so thrilled by the tiny bit of pressure she exerted against his shoulder, he felt his heart skip and the blood rushing through it.

She leaned her head on him. She'd never touched him like

that. Only their hands touched before. This was exciting and new. It was huge. He couldn't breathe, becoming so nervous that she'd move away if he moved. So he stayed stock-still. He kept trying to regulate his breathing so she didn't realize he was frozen in shock that she was pressed against him.

"You give me hope for all people. If you can change this much, then anyone can. If that sounds a bit rude and condescending, it's only coming from what I knew and heard about you."

She lifted her head and splashed her feet back and forth, ending the moment.

"No one's ever said such a nice thing about me. That's giving me way too much credit."

"I don't think so. It's becoming a pleasure to know you, and I sure didn't feel that way at first."

He grunted. "Clearly not."

She smiled, looking a bit chagrinned. "Yes. Clearly not. But now? It is a pleasure whenever I see or talk to you."

"Thank you. I can't tell you how much that means to me coming from you." So much, he couldn't breathe being so near her. Could he have slightly cracked her original opinion of him? No. It didn't even matter. As long as she still wanted to be his friend, that was enough. Although he had to acknowledge she was the only highlight that made his day tolerable.

"Thank you. For being here with me today. I've never felt the need to talk to someone so badly before. It's all pretty new for me."

"Doing that doesn't make you weak and certainly, no less masculine. I think you tend to struggle with that. Know what I mean?"

"I didn't before. I do now. Does that mean, you might consider this new me... sexy?"

She cracked up laughing and he loved the sound she

made and the way her head tilted back, letting her white teeth flash. It made the entire evening worth it for that moment. "You were always sexy. I assumed you knew that. You used it often enough. Way too often because for you, it worked. I had to give my brain a mental lecture not to let it work on me. However, I like this new Caleb Hayes much better."

Hearing such a treasure trove of information that Josefina never gave out before, Caleb sucked in a deep breath. *Hope.* Josefina was giving him hope. But for now, he was content only to be with her, having her beside him, enjoying the sunset, soaking in the cool water and breathing the pleasant, warm air that hummed around them. "Thank you, Josefina. For being my friend."

"It's a pleasure for us to be getting so close now."

They shared a smile and to Caleb, it felt like she reached inside his chest and touched his heart with warm sunlight. He had no idea how to respond to the feeling that lifted him up so high. Hope. Caleb saw a beacon of hope.

CHAPTER 10

*J*OSEFINA DIDN'T KNOW WHAT to with the confusing feelings clashing inside her about Caleb Hayes. As the summer progressed, so did Caleb. He called her consistently every single Wednesday evening, always well in advance of the weekend before he asked her to do something. She knew he called it a date, but she referred to it as "doing something."

The surprising thing was how well thought out the things they did were. They never just hung out or did whatever was easy. He put time and thought into each encounter and often, they were special things that neither one had ever done before in their lives.

She always had fun with Caleb. Smiling, grinning, chuckling, cracking jokes, and gut-splitting, helpless laughter made for easy camaraderie. It surprised her more than anyone how easily and happily they got along with one another.

So, in a real sense, Caleb became her true friend.

Today's visit, detailing how upset Caleb was after what his father said to him, left her nearly speechless. She hoped she handled it right. Caleb was sick at times from his regret over his past actions, words, insults, and assumptions. Of course, she wasn't thrilled about his past either. But she also never witnessed a grown man listening to the advice of others, and taking in the information before applying it to himself.

A man who so thoroughly was ashamed of his past that he apologized for it—profusely—working even harder to change his future. He wasn't afraid to ask questions whenever he was stumped in his reaction, and he never failed to listen to the answers and apply them to himself.

His determination to change and become a better man, albeit, one full of regret, reminded her of a little boy realizing his best friend was a bully who responds by dedicating his life's work to atoning for the bullying and trying to assist the victims.

Last night seemed as if a mirror were being held to Caleb's face. Josefina empathized with what he experienced, but saw a pivotal changing point in Caleb. It solidified her hunch that he wasn't like his dad or a believer of anything his dad spewed or tried to get him to believe. It showed in his horror and offended reaction that all the prejudice and intolerance Chuck tried to instill in Caleb never took root.

It was the honest to God truth that Caleb's example was the very first time she'd ever witnessed a grown man changing so quickly and adopting formerly polarized notions he tried to ignore. No one could have excelled to his extent so rapidly. Caleb was a veritable metamorphosis.

Each week, the inevitable call came. Not a text, but a physical phone call, and always a few days in advance. She had even started to look forward to his calls with eager anticipation and would have been sorely disappointed if he didn't call.

This week's outing was an invitation for her to come up and see his family's homestead and all the work he'd done. After picking her up, Caleb drove through River's End and began to ascend the hills above the ranch. When they hit a long streak of gravel, he brought his truck to a standstill.

The view was sweeping, going on forever and breathtaking. The panoramic expanse must have encompassed a good ten miles, revealing the unobstructed horizon for as far as the eye could see. The valley was narrow, clustered around the bright, cool colors of the river. She moved away from the vehicle and shut the door. From the edge of the cliff, the sprawling ranch rambled down one side of the river and River's End occupied the other side. It looked so small and neat as an artificial landscape around a doll house. It seemed so clean from this altitude, complete with horses and rolling, green pastures. Lovely. She glanced back at Caleb.

"This is stunning."

"Yes. The view is its only real worth. It's too hot in the summer and snowbound in the winter. It's pretty far from anything and there are no real neighbors. But this view is so awe-inspiring, it's almost holy. It always makes me feel like I am the king, ruling the kingdom from up on his hill. Except, all I had to do was turn around and see what a pauper I was, clinging to a piece of land on a hot, arid-as-a-desert hill. The view was even better, if you can believe it, before last year's fire. Most of the old, tall pines burned up and all that is left in its wake now is the barren land and the black, charred reminders of everything we all lost."

"Most, but not all lost. We were lucky that time. The fire followed the fringes of Brewster but never got to downtown or along the river where we were. I know from Jordan's descriptions how devastating it was for your family."

"It was that."

"But look at all the work you've done." She pointed toward the growing mound of discarded metal and wood on the opposite side of the land.

"Yeah. It's kept me busy and out of trouble, for once."

Her lips lifted. "Is that why? Not one cop ride this summer?"

A blush crossed his face. "Yeah. There were a few of those. Jordan, again? Tell me how you knew about them."

"Mostly drunk and disorderly. A few fights. Trespassing. Shooting grouse out of season, shooting on other people's private land, one fight with a woman and disturbing the peace... should I go on?"

He winced. "You know all about my record?"

"Yes. What was the woman upset about? I can't imagine you getting physical with a woman against her will—"

"No. Never." He beamed at her. "I'm glad you assumed that."

"I do. What did happen then?"

"Well, see, there was this woman and we'd been, you know, *together*. We were not exclusively seeing each other, however. It was for fun until she got a little too possessive and failed to understand why I was enjoying someone else's kind affections. She might have even come to wherever I was at the time and caught us. Maybe she went after me—"

"Weren't you seen running down the neighborhood half-dressed and trying to hold your pants up while she screamed and threw stuff at you?"

"See? You already know the story."

"It's pretty well known."

"I know, but no more. I won't ever make that mistake again. One thing, I can usually learn from my mistakes. I just make lots more of them than most people. Especially when it comes to variety."

She laughed at him. "Well, maintaining a variety of them means, at some point, you expect to run out, correct?"

"Correct."

She turned back to the setting sun, now tipping golden hues over the valley. "I see you here. Man of the mountain. Country boy."

"Yeah." He came along beside her. "Yeah, that's me."

She peeked up at him. "It's nothing to be ashamed of. You should be very proud of the work you've done here and are continuing to do. I have to admire your plans to settle here."

Her words boosted his entire posture and he seemed to relax as he rose upwards. It startled her how seriously he took whatever she said. There was something so sincere and sweet about him now. She could barely remember the cocky, assured, rude man he used to be.

The view was undeniably beautiful and a good place for him to live. Far more than Josefina had now and would probably ever have. A pang of jealousy stabbed her gut; even Caleb had something to start with.

She had nothing, zero, everything was at ground zero for her and it was taking too long for her to even get where she wanted to start. She would not be there in the decade she hoped to be, despite tackling her goal the decade before.

From the age of seventeen, the summer before her senior year, she never quit working. She never had the luxury of spending a decade going wild, being careless and fruitless and doing whatever she felt like because she would have starved to death if she had. There was no opportunity for Josefina to do anything like that.

Although Caleb certainly didn't live in any kind of luxurious manner or flaunt his ownership of anything, he was still half again as wealthy as Josefina and far beyond the hardscrabble life where she came from. There was no chance to make a mistake for Josefina, let alone, several years' worth.

But look at what he was doing now.

She glanced up as she watched him with curiosity. He started a fire as night fell.

"There's still a burn ban."

"Ahh, hell, I know that. I've still got some of the old me inside here. I'm doing it anyway. I guess if this is the worst I do, well, then, maybe you could forgive the minor lapse."

"I guess so…" She grinned. But the fire was burning in a big, safe fire pit and Caleb had a water hose attached to the water faucet he salvaged from the existing well close by.

He carried out two lawn chairs and a picnic dinner he made for them. She appreciated the simple sandwiches and snacks with grapes as they dined and watched the view. The colorful sunset played out in a vivid array of hues and the orange flames from the fire encouraged them to talk in low murmurs. The idle thoughts were relaxing. Though the fire's heat was not needed, the atmosphere it imbued and the ambience lulled Josefina into another wonderful, easy, thrilling evening spent with Caleb Hayes.

CALEB GLANCED up to find Jordan and Pedro standing before him. He and Josefina were sitting at a booth enjoying a casual deli dinner when they popped in. She waved at them and Caleb turned towards them. Initially startled at their hand-holding, Caleb knocked his surprise right out of his head and lifted his hand in a warm greeting too. They came over, and there was no mistaking their shock at seeing Josefina and him together.

He didn't miss the scowl that Pedro gave him and Josefina. Oh, no. Pedro did not like seeing the two of them sitting in a booth together. But Josefina invited them to sit down and Jordan agreed without glancing at Pedro first.

Jordan seemed oblivious to Pedro's not-so-subtle, dour expression about the invitation. Caleb was shocked to see Pedro's reaction and wondered why the other two didn't seem to notice. They both ordered a dinner and conversation traversed between news of the ranch to Josefina's job and clients, along with idle comments about the heat and the occasional smoke drifting from a neighboring wildfire.

Jordan invited them back to the ranch where Kailynn had asked them over for dessert and Jordan was sure she would have wanted Caleb and Josefina to also come. So they did. There they all were, all of his siblings together, with other people. Caleb refused to show any romantic interest in Josefina, even if it were all he dreamed and longed for.

They talked and laughed, sharing heaps of pie and ice cream until it drifted late into the evening. It reminded Caleb of past evenings at the mobile home before Kailynn left for college and their entire life blew up in flames. It was nice to relax and listen to them relive old stories and rib each other.

There were some things that only some siblings knew and only they could press the other sibling's buttons. And damn, if Caleb wasn't missing exactly that. The sensation of having it again validated all the changes he tried to accomplish completely, and made his efforts well worth it.

He got up and wandered towards his bedroom to grab a sweatshirt, stopping dead when he heard Pedro's voice in a near hiss. "What the hell are you doing hanging out with him?"

Caleb stepped back into his room. Josefina and Pedro were standing in the hallway, obviously unaware Caleb came down the very same way. "What? Why are you yelling at me?"

"Caleb Hayes? You can't be serious, Josie. You know what he's like. What he's all about. How could you fall for his transparent shit?"

161

"First off, I know what he *was*, and he isn't now. I didn't fall for anything. Even you must realize he's different now."

"You sound like every other bamboozled woman in the world claiming some asshole guy really isn't 'like that.' When duh, yeah, he really is."

She bristled. "Sure, it's okay for you to have a redneck, but not me?"

"Yeah. It is. Jordan isn't Caleb and Caleb is not half the damn man that Jordan is."

"Jordan still cringes when you touch him in public."

"He's had some adjustment problems, I admit, but loving me isn't included."

"Showing his love for you in public is."

"You know what I mean. You can't do this. You can't waste yourself on some loser going nowhere who will never give you the life or the respect you're owed. You're so much better than that and destined for much bigger things."

"First off, Pedro, I'm not sleeping with him, and if I ever did, it's none of your damn business. And sleeping with doesn't mean ending up with. I'm enjoying my summer so far and I've barely ever had a lot of time to enjoy myself and I want to keep on doing it for as long as I can."

Caleb stepped farther back in his room and his heart hammered in his chest. Damn it. He knew, right? That she was too good for him. As always. That was no surprise. It was obvious.

Of course they could not end up together. She even said so from the start. So why were his suddenly fragile, damn feelings hurting so much?

Crap. That was stupid. So short-sighted of him. Of course Pedro had that opinion of him, since Caleb also thought that of himself. Why did it hurt so much when others noticed and spoke the truth? Why did it feel like such a punch to the gut?

Fine. Duh. He'd stick to reality and ignore anymore

dumbass fantasies about something happening. No more wishing for anything more. He had to accept what it was and work on getting over his crush on Josefina. One destined to go nowhere.

No. How could it? She was everything he wasn't. It was good for him to hear that. And be reminded of reality. When did he forget how to live one hundred percent in complete reality? He always erred on the side of the starkest, clearest reality. There were no illusions in his life about his place in the world, lowly and base though it may be.

His dad never inspired him to hope for any dreams of what he could and should try to make come true. Never.

They quit talking and he walked away before he dared start to breathe again. There was a deep band of pain around his middle and he had to consciously exhale. Damn. Reality kicked him in the guts once more.

So what? He knew this, right? Josefina made her opinion very clear from the get-go. She was out of his league. Simple as that.

But goddamn. It pissed him off. Not toward Josefina. But at himself. For being so much less than she was and not good enough. Not nearly good enough for the likes of Josefina Ruiz. How did he manage to forget that? He deserved the humiliating description of himself he just overheard. Of course he didn't deserve her, and Pedro was right. Caleb was the big asshole. Always had been. Apparently, always would be too.

In many ways, Caleb was grateful for the unintended reminder. He took Josefina home later and she asked if anything were wrong. He denied it, while trying to act normal. He avoided her for the next few days and didn't call her on Wednesday like he usually did.

What shocked him was when she called him on Thursday because she was worried something happened to him. He agreed to see her, but was determined never to forget again. This was all just a temporary pastime. A good pastime. Maybe at most, a chance to sleep with her eventually. Right? Of course. That was always his main goal.

But the longer he stayed with Josefina, the less true that rang.

CHAPTER 11

*C*ALEB WAS SOUND ASLEEP when his phone on the nightstand awoke him. Picking it up, he recognized Jordan's number.

"Caleb? I need your help." Caleb sat straight up in bed. *Help? What?* His brain was addled and foggy.

"What is it? Where are you?" He jerked the covers off and rushed to his feet, finding jeans and a pair of socks before putting them on.

"We went out... with friends, drank late at the tavern. We were walking home... It's only a couple of blocks... and we were jumped and attacked."

Caleb stilled and shut his eyes. "Are you hurt?" Alarm tinged his voice.

"Yes. No. Kind of. They hurt Pedro worse than me. A neighbor heard the commotion and shooed them off. We're at their house now and we just called the police—"

"Text me the address. I'll be right there."

With his keys in hand, Caleb went out his bedroom door and ran up towards the master bedroom.

"Ian? Lynnie?" He banged hard on their door. In a matter of seconds, Ian jerked it open with Kailynn right behind him.

He didn't waste time with a preamble. "Jordan and Pedro were jumped in town. I'm going out to get them."

Ian nodded as he turned without a word and Caleb could see him grabbing some clothes to put on. Kailynn started to cry, using her hand to cover her mouth. "No! Oh, my God!"

Ian barely stopped for a moment to kiss her head before he followed Caleb without a single word. He was already out the front door when the neighbor's address came through.

They didn't say anything to each other and Caleb drove hastily in silence. They pulled into the driveway and found an ambulance and two police cars already there. Jumping out in tandem, they approached the ambulance.

Caleb's heart finally registered the words his brother said. Until that moment, he felt nothing. Numb. Like none of it was real. It couldn't be real.

Jordan was outside the ambulance and Pedro was inside, being attended to. Two cops spoke to Jordan, who noticed Caleb and stopped talking. "Caleb?" His voice was strained as well as relieved to see him. Caleb saw how tightly strung Jordan was with anxiety and emotions. He turned to the cops and announced, "These are my brother and my brother-in-law."

They stepped back, allowing Caleb to embrace Jordan. "What happened?" he asked as he let his brother go.

"We were drinking with friends at the tavern. You know? Just shooting the shit. It got late, we decided to walk home as we kicked back a few, well, a lot. Anyway, halfway home, these guys surrounded us. Three of them."

"Three on two?" Caleb questioned, his voice deadly serious.

"Yeah. They grabbed us from behind. I didn't hear a damn thing."

"Not a crime to enjoy a Saturday night out drinking," Caleb's voice broke in.

Jordan scoffed. "One fucker got my arms behind my back. They managed to get a few hits in before I was able to get free. Meanwhile, Pedro was holding his own. We managed to give almost as much as we got, but with the third person, they were tiring us. They pushed Pedro down, and when he fell his arm got pinned. I—I think it might be sprained for broke."

Caleb sucked in a breath as his emotions overcame him again, even more horrifying and appalling.

"How badly hurt is Pedro? You? Have they checked you out?" Caleb was panicking with his litany of questions. He needed the answers fast. He was so eager to do something about it. Action had to be taken. Caleb intended to do something to avenge this wrong. He wished he could make it disappear, like it never happened. He wished it were not happening.

"I'm fine. Just a few blows, mainly to my face. It's Pedro—"

"I'm gonna live," Pedro yelled from the bed inside the ambulance.

"He's refusing medical care. Says he doesn't want to go to the hospital." Jordan ran his hand through his hair, messing it up while shaking his head and sighing, "I don't know what to do."

"You should go to the hospital and get checked out," Caleb called out to Pedro.

"I know what's wrong with me. Couple of bruises and sprained wrist. All of it will heal in time. Just let me go."

Jordan shrugged. Then Pedro's head appeared over his shoulder from inside the ambulance. "I don't want to go to the hospital."

"Sir, you'll have to sign a waiver—"

"Fine, I'll sign whatever is necessary." Pedro glared at those around him. "I decide when I need help or not. And I don't. Fuckers only got away because I fell. Otherwise we'd have had them. Pussies. Three on two with them having the element of surprise, and yet, we almost had them."

Caleb stepped back, giving his brother and Pedro space to talk to the ambulance crew and police. They led Jordan over to their car. Another man spoke to Pedro after he dealt with the ambulance.

Ian stood nearby, his jaw set. After what felt like an hour although Caleb didn't know, since time seemed to stop altogether, Jordan went over to Pedro, ducking under his shoulder and wrapping his arm around Pedro's torso to support him.

Pedro winced, gripping his side as a litany of curses escaped his lips. Caleb rushed over to Pedro's other side.

Then all at once, Jordan fiercely embraced Pedro. Caleb stepped back. Pedro held Jordan against him and started mumbling something to him. Caleb turned to give them their privacy.

The cops and ambulance attendants finished up, and to Caleb's surprise, they left. It was all so odd and without any fanfare. There they were left standing on the side of the street. Off went the only authorities who made it official: something unusual and negative happened here.

He asked Ian, "The cops just leave them and drive away?"

"They did ask who would be in charge of their care, and I told them they would be at my house, Jordan's sister's. I promised we'd monitor them before I gave them all the necessary information."

"Oh." Caleb was miffed when he glanced towards his brother, whose head was still resting on Pedro's shoulder. "Where do you think the cops went then?"

"I hope they left to search for the sons of bitches that did this."

"Someone has to pay for it."

"I don't see how they can't." Ian's tone was quiet and neutral, but his eyes sparked with something Caleb had never seen before, a gamut of emotions. Anger. Sadness. Shock. Ian felt the same as Caleb.

Jordan lifted his head and motioned to Caleb. Quickly as possible, he placed himself under Pedro and helped him hobble towards Caleb's truck. Pedro didn't object to being taken to Ian and Kailynn's at least.

Jordan ducked in the back along with Ian and Caleb drove. The silence that descended was impenetrable. Tragedy. Shock. Hatred. Pedro stiffened, grunting or shuddering whenever the truck hit a pothole or a bump, which happened often on the unpaved road. They exited the long driveway of the ranch and headed down towards the river where the family had several houses built.

Kailynn appeared immediately when Caleb came in, saying he had to help Pedro out. She gripped Jordan in a tight hug as she convulsed with sobs. "I can't believe this. I can't believe this," she sobbed into Jordan's chest. He nodded as he patted her shoulder before Ian stepped forward and quickly took her against him.

Jordan smiled faintly as he approached Pedro's other side and they helped him limp towards the front door. "Oh, my God," Kailynn said softly behind them. "Look what they did to him. Why isn't he being seen at the hospital?"

"He flatly refused," Ian said quietly.

Kailynn called to them, "Put him in our bed. It's the biggest, and the most comfortable."

They helped Pedro sit down on the edge of the bed. He winced and groaned, but tried to remain stoic.

"You'll need to call my sister."

Josefina. Caleb jumped, he was so startled. *Shit!* News of this could destroy her. And it would. He dreaded her finding out so soon.

"I'll call her," Kailynn said from the doorway. Caleb wanted to make the call, and his heart thumped hard while he resisted the urge to insist that he call her. But he was too busy still helping Pedro get comfortable in the bed.

Ian and Kailynn left the doorway and Jordan sat down beside Pedro, face down, and his head kept shaking. He was still in shock. Caleb set a hand on his shoulder. "Maybe it wouldn't be a bad idea if you went to the hospital? Get checked out by someone? I think you're in shock."

Jordan's face lifted, and he jerked out from under Caleb's hand. "Fuck that. I'm not in shock, Caleb. I'm in a rage. A fucking rage. Look what they did to him. For what? Why?" Jordan screamed out the last bit. A figure appeared in the doorway and Caleb straightened up and stiffened. His gut churned after hearing the pent-up rage and injury in his brother's angry tone.

His dad was standing there.

Jordan's head jerked up and Chuck and he shared a long, neutral-faced, dead-locked stare. Caleb put his hand on his brother's shoulder before turning and going over to his father. He pushed him out as he gently shut the door behind him.

"If you say *anything,* anything at all, I will take you outside and flatten you with my fists and leave you lying there crippled and unable to get up," Caleb said, gritting his teeth in a daunting tone. "Test me. One derogatory word and I won't be responsible for my actions."

"What the fuck happened?"

"Three bastards jumped them."

"Where?"

"About two blocks from their house, down on Lenore Street."

Chuck didn't say anything, and his stony expression didn't melt into sympathy, shock, or concern. For once at least, he didn't say anything. Caleb rolled his eyes, wondering how he could have been so stupid all those years. He now saw an uncaring, unfeeling man even about his own child.

No wonder he'd been a lazy, mean, drunken loser for so long.

Frustrated, he stomped out towards Ian and Kailynn, who was just hanging the phone up. "Josie will be here soon. I don't have their dad's number."

Caleb spoke with confidence and replied, "She'll have it. I'm sure she'll take care of everything."

Slowly dropping his weary body onto the sofa, Caleb stared down at his feet as the last hour of his life sunk in. Defeat. Rage. Hurt. Shock. Everything congealed, and he teared up and had to push both of his fists into his eyes. He never cried in front of anyone before. The intense pressure and pain of the situation they experienced was humiliating and… necessary.

"It's Kailynn. Come to the ranch. Our brothers… they were jumped. Attacked by three guys. Get here as fast as you can."

Josefina's entire body froze before she instantly started to sweat. *Not this.* With her hands shaking, she fumbled with the keys, trying to get her small, old, unreliable sedan to move forward. She was shaking with fear at what she'd find when she got there. She came to a screeching halt when she got to Ian and Kailynn's driveway.

Caleb looked up and turned as Josefina rushed in the door. He was pale, and his stubby growth of facial hair appeared darker against his pallor. He'd been pacing the living room.

"What happened?"

"They're both going to be okay." Josefina appreciated that Caleb didn't add, *and calm down.* His mouth tightened and Kailynn came in from the hallway. Her face was pale and grave just as Josefina expected hers to be. She pushed past all of them and started down the hallway to the open door. "Pedro?" her voice whispered with panic and concern.

Pedro heard her and flinched as he struggled to sit up. He winced as he gripped his side. Josefina cried out and rushed forward.

"I'm fine. I'm fine, Josie. Don't worry, calm down."

"What happened?"

"We went to the tavern for a drink. Stayed awhile, and when we started to walk home, we were both a little drunk, and three pricks jumped us. Being cowards, they fled like cockroaches when a neighbor's porch light came on and their front door opened. The couple ran out to offer help because they'd already dialed 911. So it wasn't a total shit show. Someone cared. They helped us and brought us into their home to wait for the cops and that's when Jordan called his brother."

She glanced around. There. Jordan was standing at the back in the corner, his gaze riveted on Pedro. His eyes appeared unfocused. He didn't look well.

"We should have been more careful."

"How? We were being careful by not driving after drinking. So that's horseshit. You have to stop blaming yourself." Pedro's voice was hard as a rock.

She glanced at both of them, sensing huge undertones

and growing even more curious. "Why aren't you at the hospital? We need to go there now."

"We're not going to the hospital. The paramedics already checked me out. I have a couple of bruised ribs. Believe me, I know, I've had them before. Stop acting like it's so appalling. They're only bruises. I'm fine. I don't want the extra attention, okay? I just want my family. You guys. Let me handle this how I want."

She gripped her brother's hand, her tears falling as she nodded slowly and said, "Okay, okay, Pedro."

His cracked lips barely moved but he squeezed her hand. She squeezed his back and whispered, "I love you, Pedro."

"I love you, sis."

She shook her head. "This shouldn't have happened just because you love someone."

"It doesn't usually," Pedro said, his tone flippant. She lifted her head. He still had a twinkle in his eyes despite the sad look on his face.

"Don't be flippant. This… this isn't funny."

"No. It isn't. But that's why it's so necessary."

She sniffed and nodded, trying to hold back her tears. He leaned back and sighed. "Damn. They insisted on going after my chest."

Kailynn came in carrying a first aid kit, ice packs, and bandages and nodded at Josefina. Josefina nodded back at her before they both got to work on her brother and Jordan.

Quietly. Not a word was spoken.

Caleb and Ian stayed in the living room, but oddly enough, Chuck Hayes came into the bedroom and stayed there too. In the corner, sitting in a chair, he just remained there. She kept glancing his way without a clue as to what he was doing there or why.

Was he revealing something about himself? She didn't know. Hardening her heart, she kept her gaze off him. The hatred that flowed through her was seething. Her own father, she knew, would take the news pretty hard.

She and Pedro talked it over and decided he'd call their dad first thing tomorrow morning. He easily tired and she worried over how much the news could upset him. Calling him at one in the morning would not have solved anything and would only scare him.

Pedro lay down again. Jordan approached him and sat on the side of the bed. She sensed they needed a private moment together. Probably just to touch base and connect over what happened to them. She smiled at Jordan with love and understanding before she kissed her brother's cheek as he nodded at her and smiled. "I'll be right here in the living room. Take as long as you need."

"Take him with you," Jordan muttered while waving in a careless gesture towards his dad. She blinked in surprise.

"Okay," Josefina replied as she turned and approached Chuck. "They would like a few moments alone. Come on."

She put her hand out to pull the old man up and realized she'd never seen him up close before. He had hair like a mad scientist, almost to the point of being cartoonish with bushy white stalks and bald on top while being much too long on the bottom. Overweight and having a ruddy, purplish complexion were testimony to his love of alcohol.

One leg appeared visibly smaller compared with the other in the boxer shorts and white t-shirt he wore. He took her hand and she grunted at his heftiness but purely out of pity and decency, she allowed him to hold her arm and helped him hobble into the large living room where Ian, Kailynn, and Caleb sat.

They all glanced up and Josefina's attention fell on Caleb, whose eyes looked moist and glassy. Wow. Had he teared up?

They exchanged a long look before he got up and took Chuck from her as gently as he could to assist his father to the recliner. Chuck grunted without saying a single word and Josefina watched Caleb. Chuck couldn't even say thank you or offer a look at him, yet Caleb didn't seem to find that strange. Odder still was his gentle manner and touch with the old, fragile, crusty asshole. Her heart thumped.

Caleb wasn't *anything* like the demeanor he doggedly portrayed. He wasn't callous, heartless, stupid, lazy, or mean. He was, however, neglected and unseen. Uncared for. There was no softness shown to him, no moral support, and something inside him still yearned for it, wanted it, and craved it.

She shook her head. She might have missed all that about Caleb before, but there was no denying it now.

"Who did it?" she whispered, breaking the sad, distraught, but mostly tense silence. It was odd so many people were in the room, but no one spoke at all.

"Drew Nichols. Hank Percell. Tanner Norsday." Ian answered in a neutral tone. His gaze was already fastened on Caleb. Why?

Caleb jolted upright. "You knew who they were? Why didn't you tell me? Why wouldn't he tell me?"

"Jordan told me when we got back here. He didn't want you to do anything stupid."

"Drew Nichols?" Kailynn's voice cracked. She shut her eyes in horror. "I dated him. He came to our house... and hung out with Jordan. He... he really did this?"

Ian's hand rested on Kailynn's shoulder. "Yeah, he was one of them."

Josefina wanted to jump up and hurt them... someone... anyone.

How could a friend of the Hayes deliberately hurt her brother?

Caleb's frantic pacing increased, and his fists tightened. Josefina forgot her own anger temporarily and wondered

175

how hard it must have been to have once claimed these assholes as his friends.

Caleb paced faster now, stomping with rage.

Their friends.

Their friends could have done this? Caleb shook his head and muttered as he kept pacing.

Then he stopped abruptly. "They hung out at our trailer all the time, on our land, drinking our beer, and eating our food. They spent a good twenty years hanging out with us, especially Jordan, always riding around the hills, hunting and fishing, or swimming in the river. Ever since we were all in middle school. They weren't like any new acquaintances. They were our oldest friends, they were—"

Kailynn grabbed his hand. "The police will get them. It'll... it'll never be okay, but we... I mean, they will get justice and eventually be punished and forced to pay the consequences for their heinous crime."

"Justice? Our friends? Your ex-boyfriend for God's sake? They went after our brother right here in our own town. How can that be okay?"

Josefina's heart was pounding in her chest following their conversation. She agreed with Caleb; how could that ever be okay? Their brothers were ambushed, almost beaten.

They had been Jordan's so-called friends.

Caleb caught her gaze and stared into her eyes for a long moment. Nothing twitched or moved on his face until he barely shook his head. Swallowing, he shuddered and practically fell onto a chair. "I can't believe any of this."

"What do we do now?" she asked, her tone sounding hollow.

"We wait. Wait for the police to let us know as soon as they've caught them. They promised to contact me." Ian said, his tone growing authoritative.

Caleb glared at him in response and Josefina instantly

sensed clashing undertones between them. She recalled Caleb's sneer a few times when he spoke about his brother-in-law. An obvious power struggle existed between them, one which, she was sure, Ian must have won. He had the money, the land, the house, and the cush job. He was, therefore, the boss and the main authority. Josefina knew Caleb didn't like it.

"Why the fuck would they contact you?"

"I know the sheriff. He and I went to school together. I called him, and he said he'd let me know as soon as they had anything to report."

"Yeah? And you're a Rydell too, huh? That just about makes you damn near royalty around here," Caleb muttered before he started pacing all over again.

"If it works in our favor, Caleb, can't you stop please? Not today. Did you forget I'm a Rydell? I love you and I love my husband. Let me do that, okay?" Kailynn all but begged. Her throat sounded raw, and her eyes were red again and blurry with tears. She looked exactly how Josefina felt: on the tipping point of losing it altogether.

He ignored Kailynn's hand when she held it out towards him, and chose a chair before he flopped down. Silence. From not only both of them but the entire room.

Josefina picked her thumb cuticle. How could this be happening? After she came home that evening, she made herself some spaghetti and heated up some garlic bread. She ate dinner while glancing through all the paperwork she needed to catch up on. She downloaded a new ebook and started reading it before getting into bed and curling up to go asleep. The evening began as a normal, ordinary night. Like always. But now, it was like nothing before it.

The surrealism surrounding it kept it trapped inside a dreamlike vision.

When Ian's cellphone rang, all heads popped up. The

silence and tension that filled the room instantly dissipated and Ian rose to his feet and stepped away as he held the phone to his ear. Josefina could hear him speaking quietly.

She sat there, drawing her back upright and twisting her fingers together, her blood boiling inside her body whenever she imagined how they'd get them. Justice could be attained at least. She assumed they could get that. And soon too.

Jail sentences for all three rats. Hopefully, long prison terms without bail, and no plea bargaining.

Ian turned to walk back into the room. Looking solemn, he was a serious man Josefina rarely had any interaction with. Lynnie usually did the talking for both of them, especially with her. She understood in that tense, long moment how frustrated Caleb might have been with Ian's stoic demeanor.

He sat down, focusing his gaze entirely on Kailynn. He didn't waste words or time but said in a normal, everyday tone that was only slightly tinged with anger, "They... they found them. The three of them were drinking at the Tighten bar."

Kailynn exclaimed in a loud cry. "They got them? They really got them?"

"They found them, yeah." Ian confirmed and something in his expression softened. That small giveaway, that inconspicuous tell, conveyed he was sorry for her and Ian never revealed things like that. Something must have gone wrong.

Her face crumpled and she bowed her head, shaking it and repeating, "They... didn't get them?"

"They found them, yeah. And questioned them pretty extensively. Their alibis all matched up and their stories never changed. They claimed to have been at the Tighten bar since nine o'clock this evening until the cops found them. And worse still? The bartender, a waitress, and two regular customers backed up their story."

Silence. Death-like silence descended upon the room.

"F—four people backed them up? Supported their alibis? Were willing to bear false witness? Four people were willing to commit a crime to protect those three? Why? Why would anyone do that?" she wailed.

"Yes. I'm so sorry, Josie. At this time, they have nothing to justify anyone's arrest."

"Why?" she screamed again defiantly before she stood up. Her hands were fisted. "Why?"

"Because they're fucking locals," Caleb answered after her scream. His tone, however, was the polar opposite of hers. Cold. Quiet. Calm. Like a cool breeze blowing over her heated, flushed skin. How could he sound so calm at hearing that? So accepting?

"But it's wrong. All wrong. Locals? Who cares if they're locals? They attacked two innocent men who live here, which also makes them locals. It's—it's premeditated assault at the minimum and we all know it's also a hate crime. How can this be?"

Josefina was nearly hysterical. She kicked the couch with her foot, causing her to instantly cry out in pain and sending her crumpling onto the couch. Arms encircled her. Kailynn's arms. Kailynn immediately sat down next to her, and they both cried.

Her screeches of rage drew Jordan out. "What's going on?" he asked as he rushed out and stood in the entryway. She lifted her head, streaks of tears messing up her face. He stared first at her and then at Ian.

"How?"

"They bribed the bartender, the waitress and two others to vouch that they'd been there all night and never left."

Jordan wilted, but surprisingly, didn't cry or freak out or even seem the least bit surprised. She stared at him, her own cries lessening as she pierced Jordan with her glare. "How come you're not surprised? Aren't you outraged?"

"Of course I am. But I expected it might go this way. I'd probably be more shocked if things went our way."

"But... but how can that be?"

"Reality? Josie, come on. You should know why perhaps better than most people."

She started to cry again, and Jordan turned and walked back down the hallway. Her shoulders slumped, and her entire demeanor reflected defeat.

She and Kailynn cried together for a few minutes while Caleb just sat there, staring forward. Silent. No tears. No visible anger. He seemed indifferent to the unfolding news.

She rose to her feet. "I'm going to see my brother."

"Me too," Kailynn said, rising with her. Apparently, this event bonded them closer than sisters of the flesh. They gripped each other's hands as they started down the hallway.

Pedro saw her and patted the bed beside him. "Come here, Josie. It's okay."

"It's not okay."

He squeezed her hand. "Look at it this way. We beat hard on them. We might have fully taken them if I hadn't fallen down."

"Fallen down?" She all but screeched. "They caused all of it!"

"Yeah. But I'm not their fucking victim. Let's be clear on that. It wasn't fair what they did, but it was a fair fucking fight because Jordan and I gave it hard back to them."

Pedro nodded to his husband. Jordan smiled back and nodded as he walked forward and took Pedro's hand. "We sure fucking did."

Kailynn and Jordan sat together at the end of the bed. Ian came in and a sense of sadness and hopeless defeat instantly filled the room. They sat there for a long while. Shit. How could this be happening?

She was surprised when Chuck hobbled over. *Was it a caring gesture? Or was he mocking them? Was he glad it happened?* She stiffened and recalled Caleb's depiction of him.

Wait! Shit! Why wasn't Caleb in there?

Whipping around, Josefina pushed through all the bodies to rush out.

No Caleb.

The living room was empty. She rushed back to the bedroom and glared at Chuck before asking "Where is Caleb?" and addressing the entire room.

Jordan stiffened and stood up immediately. He ran out to the living room and then ran back, shaking his head. Kailynn glanced around. "He's gone?" she asked, tilting her head and shutting her eyes. "Shit. Do you think he went to find them?"

"You're goddamned right your brother did!" Chuck's voice suddenly announced in a fury behind all of them.

Startled, they turned as one to face him. "His damned brother was jumped and attacked, three to two, you're damn right Caleb went after them to right that wrong. Damn right that's my son doing right by my other son!"

Jordan's expression went wide-eyed before he slowly started nodding and shut his eyes. "Shit. Yeah, he did. We gotta go find him. He'll get himself arrested. Or worse." Jordan started to move but then stopped dead. Glancing at Pedro, his indecision was obvious. He didn't want to leave his husband.

Pedro's head was hanging as he said, "I'm fine. Go. Go and get your brother."

Jordan tossed a fleeting glance at his dad.

Then, to Josefina's approval and joy, Jordan touched Pedro's shoulders and leaned over, kissing him right on the mouth in a long, hard, yet caring, brush of lips.

Pedro's head rose, and he flashed a look of surprise before it turned to unmasked relief and comfort. "I'll be back as soon as I can. I swear, we'll find the cowards."

Jordan straightened up and glanced at Josefina, giving her a small, reassuring smile before his gaze went cool when it landed on his dad, still hulking in the back of the room. Jordan squared up his shoulders. "You have a problem here?"

His dad scowled back at him, crossing his arms over his chest. Jordan played chicken with their long, drawn-out eye lock. "Yeah, of course I do. That shit shouldn't have been done to you two. You don't allow any family member to take a beating and let the goons who did it get away with it."

The surprise answer moved like a wave through the room. "What? You agree with Caleb? About having a good reason to go after them?"

"Fuck, yeah. No one messes with a Hayes. Not without facing the consequences of it."

"Even a gay one?" Jordan's tone was demanding as he clenched his fist.

Josefina's eyes widened in disbelief and she glanced at Pedro. He, too, stared up at Jordan and his mouth dropped open. Jordan taking stance agains this dad was huge for him. Tragic he even had to, but huge that he was.

Chuck glanced from Kailynn to Jordan. "You're still my son, ain'cha?" Chuck said in a grumpy rumble.

"I don't know. Am I?"

"Yeah," Chuck said, but his tone was no kinder as he lifted a hand towards Pedro. "And if he is your… your choice for a spouse, then you gotta do what you gotta do. You can't let anyone do shit like that. If I were younger and healthier… and well, I'd do what Caleb's already doin'."

The whites of Jordan's eyes flashed. "You would do that for me?"

"Yeah. Family's family. Nobody fucks with my family.

That's my general motto in life." Chuck swallowed and looked away. "I just mighta forgot it for a little while. I won't forget again."

Jordan swallowed, ending his glaring eye lock with his dad. There were no hugs, nothing like Josefina would have expected a more normal, affectionate family to have exchanged. She had a startling revelation why Jordan and Caleb were the way they were.

Ironically, she and Pedro were the ones that softened them from the harsh, tough shell that characterized Chuck Hayes all this time. The Ruiz family taught the Hayes brothers how to ease up, and show affection, becoming half as abrasive and harsh as their father. They were light years ahead of Chuck and she clearly saw that now. Even if their interpersonal skills were light years behind the average person, now Josefina had a deeper understanding of *why*.

"But things aren't like the old days anymore. If your brother manages to get a hold of who did this, he'll just land in jail. So you should probably try to stop him."

Okay, hearing that comment from Chuck surprised Josefina. Chuck leaned back to sit in a chair in his subtle attempt to halt their stare-off. Surprisingly, Jordan was winning; of that, she was sure. For once in his life, Jordan defeated his father.

"Yeah," Jordan said as he nodded with a weary glance before he shot out of there.

Kailynn gently pushed Ian and said, "Please go with him and stop them, Ian. If Jordan finds Caleb first, Caleb might very well convince Jordan to help him. Please. Keep my brothers out of prison."

Her stomach twisted again. First her brother's injuries and now, Caleb and Jordan going after them. Panic clouded her brain.

No. No. No.

All of this was happening too fast. She didn't like any of it. The violence directed at her brother and Jordan; and now Caleb, going off primed for a fight. What? Three men to one? Even he couldn't prevail in a match like that. And now Jordan wanted revenge too. Josefina was pacing and fretting. Waiting. That's all she could do now.

Wait.

CHAPTER 12

*C*ALEB WAITED IN THE now empty living room and stared out at the dark night. He couldn't get Josefina's tortured cry and shock at the world out of his mind. He wasn't shocked. Not at all. Not because the perps were former friends of theirs, nor the other "friends" that lied for them.

The Hayes family wasn't like the Rydell family. They didn't have the blind loyalty of all the residents and thus, weren't protected. But ever since Jordan came out, there was some blowback from a few of the so-called *friends* he once hung out with.

However, the issue that ate at Caleb and made him feel even worse was: at first, he was right there with those friends. He used to hang with Hank and Tanner and fucking Drew.

Fucking fake alibis.

He paced some more, clenching his fists.

He knew how it went down. Rude goading and jokes at Jordan's expense as they dared each other to do more. Fueled

LEANNE DAVIS

by alcohol and mob-think. Peer pressure combined to propel them towards attacking his brother.

And afterwards, they went back to the bar to drink and everyone pretended they never left.

But they did.

They left, and they fucked with his little brother. And his brother-in-law. They hurt his brother. That thought was on an endless loop, going around and around in his brain.

They also hurt Josefina. Her wails and crying echoed in his mind. He grabbed his temples.

But now he wasn't being driven out of his head by rage. Or emotion. Or the unfairness of it.

No. Fuck no.

He was clear-headed and completely coherent of where and who he was.

He also knew exactly whom he was going after and what he intended to do to them.

He glanced down the hallway and his heart felt heavy in his chest. He'd probably lose Josefina. She would never condone his response. She should never either. He knew it was wrong. The demon returned, the one whom he tried so long and hard to exorcise from himself. His rude, crude self, the one with irrepressible urges and dangerous abilities. The one Josefina first saw when she had no interest in ever dating or being with him, much less, becoming his friend.

But these three had deliberately gone after Jordan. And now? No one seemed willing to do anything about it. They were about to go unpunished for their crime.

No one cared except Caleb. He would not let that happen. He was dead set on going after them.

His steps were quiet, and his heart heavy, but his head was crystal clear when he stepped out the front door, opened his truck door and got in and left. He knew exactly where the likes of Drew, Hank, and Tanner would be heading about now.

The same place he used to go.

JOSEFINA ENTERED the main living room and paced and fretted with Kailynn. Damn. This was scary. Now both Jordan and Ian were gone. The room was taut with nerves and still they waited. There were very few words spoken.

Two hours passed before her phone vibrated with a new text message. It was now past three in the morning. Where once her rush of adrenaline was keeping her high, now she was wilting. Kailynn had called Ian a half dozen times and they still hadn't found Caleb.

Josefina glanced at a new text on her phone. *I'm outside. Down at the beach. Don't tell anyone I'm here. Please. Can you come out? Alone? I need to talk to you.*

She jerked her head upright. He was here? What kind of condition was he in? Why did he want to see her alone? She sighed with relief to at least know he was still alive. "I need some air. I'm going to take a quick walk." If Kailynn thought it odd or strange that Josefina went walking in middle of the night, she didn't voice it. Shrugging and nodding her reply, she was obviously so rapt in her thoughts that Josefina's excuse to go out barely registered with her.

Josefina ran towards the beach, stopping dead in her tracks when she spotted Caleb's tall figure. His wide shoulders were illuminated by the moonlight. The moon beams trailed over the river, making it flow all white and shimmery like a ghost or a mirage. Caleb looked almost mythical. He was so handsome, and so tragic. His shoulders were hunched forward, and his hands were in his pockets.

It was not the stance of a man returning from fierce battle or a warrior intent on avenging a wrong. No. Caleb looked defeated. He didn't find the three guys. Perhaps that was good. At least he wasn't in trouble with the law or heading to jail, which, she reminded herself, would have only made everything worse. Two wrongs don't make a right and all.

Right?

Yes, her addled mind insisted. Even if it broke her heart that no one would avenge her brother.

"Caleb?" she said, closer now to him. He turned slowly. "Are you okay? Ian and Jordan are scouring the valley for you. Everyone is so worried. Y—you didn't find anyone, right? It's okay. You shouldn't go after them all alone. Not like that. I mean, maybe we can still get those other assholes to tell the truth and change their stories."

He lifted his hands up as she spoke, exposing his knuckles to the moonlight. Bloodied and with his left hand swelling, Josefina could only gape in disbelief. *Shit! He'd done it. He must have done something. What was this?* Her mouth opened to ask, and she lifted her face to his. "You… you found them?"

He gave her a tremulous, scared look. "I found them. I know where they live. I know where they hang out. I know how they think. I'm sorry, Josie. I also know this was wrong. I'm right back to where I started. I was pacing here, thinking about it… and recalling that two of those assholes were my best friends at one time. They hung out at our place and partied with us all the time and—and then they dared to do this? To Jordan? Jordan who never hurt them and was also their friend? They attacked him."

Her mouth was opening and she whispered in a soft tone through the shock. "What did you do?"

"I beat them up." He hung his head down.

"All three of them? How? Did you use a—a weapon or something?"

"No. They were all drunk. One was already passed out. I found them. It wasn't hard. They could barely stand up. Collectively, it was easier than fighting one sober man. But it was far fairer than three against two."

They stared at each other in the moonlight for a long, poignant moment and he shook his head. His eyes were solemn, scared. "I'm sorry... I'm so sorry... I know you hate me for doing this. I knew it before I left. I didn't do it in a rage though. I thought the whole thing out first. I meant to do this, Josefina. *I meant to do this.*"

"To avenge our brothers... my brother?" she whispered. The lump in her throat made it hard to swallow and she was on the verge of tears, ready to burst into wretched sobbing. Her mouth twitched however at her characterization. "Though, my brother won't appreciate the white-night treatment. He's quite sure if he hadn't fallen down he and Jordan would have beat *them* up. He's quite sure he is no victim."

"No. They are pretty messed already too. Impressive. " He nodded and hug his head. "As for what I did... I—"

He couldn't finish his sentence because she suddenly flung herself into his arms, directly against his chest. Taking his face between her hands, she pulled him down and touched his lips with hers. She ground her mouth against his and opened it before she pushed on the back of his head. She wanted to press against him even harder and fuller as she kissed him to convey her sincere gratitude and she did so with all her heart.

To her surprise, the heat they generated was nuclear. Her knees trembled, and her heart pounded furiously. Taken aback with surprise, Caleb lifted his mouth from hers and with a gentle push, he took her in his arms and moved her away from him. "You're not mad at me?"

"No. No. I—I only wish I had the physical strength to do it myself."

"It was wrong though, Josie. And definitely not the best way to handle it."

Her eyes widened and what worried him most clicked into place. "You're concerned that because this is not following the letter of the law, it makes you wrong?" She leaned forward, taking his hand in hers and kissing the swollen, bloodied knuckles. "No. You helped make it right. Sometimes doing the right thing isn't always obvious. You never stopped growing but only excelled and accelerated the change as far I'm concerned. Thank you," her voice broke with emotion as she said the last two words.

She watched him gulp and his gaze clung to hers. The former confusion and panic shifted to relief. He cared so much about what she thought of him. She seemed to have quickly become the bar and standard by which he measured his own actions, behavior, thoughts, morals, and emotions. It was startling he elevated her to such a strange pedestal. It struck her right then, how highly he regarded her opinions and attitudes. "I thought you'd be mad at me for sure. It was all I could think about as I drove back here. You'd hate me... and..." His voice stopped as if he'd been choked off.

"And what?" she prodded softly. She surprised herself when she asked, because until now, she drew a clear boundary and insisted she did not want to be told.

"And I couldn't stand to know you hated me."

She lifted up onto her tiptoes and brushed her lips with his again. Raising her hands and clasping them around his neck, she lifted her chest to press against his. "I don't hate you at all. I am so grateful for you now." She started kissing him again and they both heated up. Once again, he pushed back from her, lifting his face off hers and moving out of reach.

In a straggled voice, he said, "I don't... I don't want you to approach me purely out of gratitude. I want you to be here strictly because *you want me*. You have to feel something for me, and not because of what I did tonight."

She responded with a kiss on his collarbone above his shirt, gently brushing her lips across his salty-tasting skin. He groaned at her sensual contact and her entire body was on fire at the close proximity of his.

"It's not."

"But everyone—"

"Can wait."

"But..."

She licked his skin and he grew hard against her. "I want you. Right now. You once were known as the king of doing whatever felt good right there and then. I need that. Right now, Caleb."

He tilted his head back, and she saw him take in a deep breath with his eyes shut. When he seemed to relent and clasped her hand with his, her heart virtually drummed with joy. Excitement was beating a happy rhythm between her legs.

The air was cooling down, but it still felt warm around them. Pleasant. Perfect. She grabbed his shoulders to steady herself and kissed him, closing her eyes and breathing in a deep and satisfying manner. He kissed her back. "Are you sure?" he asked before he kissed her again.

"I'm very sure," she breathed between kisses. Her hot tongue entered his mouth and Caleb moaned, sweeping his arms around her and tightening his embrace.

"What if this is only a form of gratitude? I don't want you to regret it, if we do."

"It's not for gratitude. Or for the wrong reasons, so please don't stop."

He eventually caved to her demands. Who knew she'd

have to beg Caleb to suddenly desire her, and do what his body so obviously wanted? Who knew he'd fret over it so? Worrying over her reasons and trying to talk her out of them? She smiled against his lips and his sweet concern and felt a little surprised at the level of his restraint and respectfulness.

He quit trying to analyze or stop them. His hands surrounded her waist and he held her, anchoring her there and embracing her even closer. Their mouths were open as their tongues engaged and she combed the silky strands of his hair with her soft fingertips. Stepping back, she tugged her shirt off, then her bra and shorts, after kicking off her sandals.

He blinked at her in surprise and shock. She stepped towards him and started to tackle his pants. He emerged from his temporary astonishment and started pulling his shirt over his head. Her hands slipped beneath the cloth and she touched the bare skin on his chest as the cloth exposed it. He groaned when her hands slid up high, nearly to his nipples while he still struggled to negotiate a way of kissing her while also tugging the shirt over his head. His chest was covered in soft hair and her gentle fingertips made the muscles beneath them flex and sway as he pushed upwards. She undid his belt buckle and worked it off before she unsnapped his pants.

They fell onto the sand at their feet with a soft plop. He had to pull away temporarily to remove his boots and pants and she patiently rubbed her arms as she waited for the moment to pass. He also pulled out a wallet and a condom. She glanced at it before nodding her approval. She only hoped he had a condom, now that her body was getting wetter in preparation and excitement. He faced her, and his body was long and strong. She gazed with admiration at the ropey thighs and his fully erect penis, jutting towards her from a bed of dark hair.

Stepping closer, she shuddered when his hands encircled her waist. He pulled her closer, burying his face in her hair and hugging her close to him in a long and poignant moment. Her naked breasts smashed against his hairy chest and abraded her hardening nipples. She grew wild with need, lust, and sheer excitement. It was becoming difficult for her to pause and enjoy the softness of his tender touch and embrace. It thrilled her to realize how eagerly he held her and with such obvious passion and feelings.

She leaned back, and his gaze sought out hers. "You're very beautiful."

Her smile was real and genuine because she knew he meant it. Not a long string of kind words, but a very heartfelt message. He believed she was gorgeous. She reached up and cupped his chin with her hand. "Thank you."

"Are you sure you want to do this here? Right on the beach? If... when... I always wanted it to be... different. Special. Like you."

Her breath caught. She wasn't so special. Not one other person ever thought so. Maybe Pedro did but no one else. Caleb treated her as if she were the world's guru on all things moral. She never expected him to feel so strongly about her. Did she feel that way toward him?

No. Not really, although she was insanely attracted to him. She enjoyed their hours together and the way he always managed to leave her grinning. Her heart swelled with relaxation and joy. She loved seeing him and talking to him, so unlike their initial meeting. But she also cared deeply about him. She did want him sexually, and had for a while.

Now, she wanted it more than ever and would have gotten down on her knees to beg him not to deny her needs any longer. She was pulsating in anticipation, clouding her vision and her mind.

"I want to do this. Here. Right here and only with you." That was as honest as she could be. It was raw. Real. Maybe not love. Or commitment. Or forever. There was no promise or debt involved. Just the two of them now. Here. Alone.

That would have to be enough and she prayed it was. "Please…"

He nodded before his hands drifted from her waist and cupped her breasts. They were large and full as he pushed them up, supporting their weight. His thumb drifted over one and he bent forward and latched onto it with his mouth. She closed her eyes in sensual bliss and held his head closer to her, her hand repeatedly pulling the strands of his hair.

She scooted her bottom forward, aiming more towards his head before she cried out in bliss. He groaned too when his mouth devoured her, and his hands moved her breasts around like they were Play-doh he intended to mold and shape. He worked them over so vigorously, her limbs started to tremble, and a rush of feelings bolted through her.

She grabbed his wrist and pushed his hand downwards. In desperate need. *Now!* She cried out, "Please touch me."

He immediately slid two of his fingers into her wet, steamy core. There was no slow stroking or curious probing. He intended to conquer her. Her legs parted wider as he nipped and bit her nipple. His tongue rolled over it while his thick fingers plunged deep inside her, going in and out.

Using her own weight while standing there, she started riding his fingers in a way that might have been considered shameless and wanton. She was so close to orgasm, selfishly, crazily, greedily determined to get there.

And then? Oh, right then… she tightened around his hand and grasped it to hold him steady and still inside her. Throbbing over his unrelenting fingers, she tilted her head back, crying out when the hot, long, intense orgasm flowed through her like light. It seemed to beam right out of her fingertips, toes, and ears.

His mouth left her naked breast and he touched her hair line while drawing her closer to his chest. His other hand stayed inside her soaking, throbbing, wet core. She kept clenching and milking the pressure his fingers created inside her. A potent mixture of warmth and heat seemed to flow through her entire body, lubricating and coating her muscles and tissues in what felt like liquid gold.

She lifted her mouth to his and he started kissing her, making her desperate for more. More contact. More of him. His lips. His tongue. His hands. She moaned, and her eyelids fluttered open. She was all buzzing and excited. She wanted more. So much more.

He'd already exceeded her expectations. She was over-whelmed by how much she wanted him as she slid her hands down to his hot, hard length that was straining against her. She let his heat fill her hands and slid her fingertips along the length of him. He kissed her furiously in response.

She eventually parted her mouth from his and started kissing his chin, his neck, his collarbone, sternum and hard stomach. She let her breasts drift down his body, and the friction of it made him groan when one breast slowly brushed across his erect penis.

She felt the heat between them as she kept kissing his chest. His startled response did not faze his pleasure. She let her hands drift around to his bare, tight buns, which she brushed over before dropping her head and kneeling before him.

She sensed his hands growing restless and increasingly harder when they combed through her hair and down along her shoulders.

She smiled to herself as she kissed his length and slowly

LEANNE DAVIS

took him inside her hot mouth. She tasted him, and he jerked forward, seeking the nuclear core of her throat. She held even tighter to his butt and he strained to keep from ramming into her mouth as hard as he could. She released him and slid upwards, her mouth beside his ear. "Now. Oh, do it now, I can't wait any longer."

He nodded as he scooped her up in his arms. She cried out in surprise when he gently turned and sat down on the soft, cool sand. He lay down flat, setting her on top of him and letting her feel his entire length beneath her. Moisture pooled from between her legs and fell onto his leg as she adjusted.

He put the condom on and she leaned over and braced her hands on his chest for support. She lifted her bottom over him and then slid down his hard shaft just as she lifted her head up. His hands grabbed her face so gently and tenderly, she paused for a moment, and he set his lips on hers, filling her mouth with his tongue and mimicking their union below the waist.

She stilled when he completely plunged his hard knob deep inside her. Hot. Hard. Pulsating. She paused, instantly drawn to the long, tender, passionate, loving kiss more than the final act she so desperately ached for. Suddenly, he let her go, and she blinked, dazed for a long moment while their gazes met.

She was startled by the depth she saw in his eyes. All of his attention was riveted on her. She wiggled her bottom and he groaned as she lifted herself completely up and down. The long, slow movement educed more moans of passion and satisfaction from both parties.

She squeezed him as tightly as her lower half could, drawing out more explosive feelings in her nerve endings. She lifted herself up and down again. And again. Slowly. Long and slow and tortuous.

It was the most exquisite pleasure and pain she'd ever experienced. She pushed against his chest and held her own breasts. Cupping the nipples with her fingertips, she tossed her head back and started bouncing up and down more vigorously on him.

He yelled her name out as he watched her arousing herself and listened to her soft groans. When they switched positions, it felt different, yet much better inside her and she cried out as his mouth harshly shoved her hands away.

He took a big, hard, ripe nipple inside his feverish mouth and tugged on it with his teeth. The viciousness of it, and her need for more, as well as the crazy way he grabbed her waist and shoved himself deep inside her should have been hard enough to knock the breath out of her.

But instead, it sent her reeling over the edge of another orgasm that rocked her from her core and jolted every one of her nerve endings.

Nipping and swirling her bitten, abused nipple in loving kisses, he was trying to soothe the burn with his mouth when he suddenly stopped moving and his entire body strained towards her before thrusting inside her with body-shattering force.

She sighed, leaning forward to rest her forehead on his. She was breathing crazy hard. Their mouths reconnected. He blinked open his eyes and she saw the obvious passion, which she felt too.

He lifted his left hand from her waist and gently brushed over her nipple in soft, loving strokes. "I'm sorry. You... you were so hot, touching yourself, and I lost control... I'm sorry. So sorry." He brushed his lips to her forehead and she closed her eyes at the soft touch on her abraded skin. Smiling, she raised her lips to meet his for a moment in a quick, tongue-filled kiss.

"It was hot and your savage need of me was even hotter. I love it. Even the biting and all."

He still caressed her although it was sore and raw, and every second instantly reminded her of each stroke, kiss, and heat-filled moment of the crazy high from sex she just enjoyed.

"This was like nothing I've ever experienced, Josefina."

She smiled and hugged him closer to her, still sitting on his lap. He slipped away from her and she scooched forwards, all the while straddling him. He lowered his head to rest in the crook of her neck and she was surprised at the vulnerable way he clung so tightly to her, his hands gripping her back while bending his head down. She kissed the top of his head. Wow. Who knew that Caleb could be so affectionate and tender in his need to have her? Not like anything she could have predicted.

Maybe she was wrong. They sat silently for five minutes, their feverish bodies cooling, their breaths slowing, and their heart rates regulating a steady rhythm again.

Caleb took in a deep breath as he lifted his head to stare into her eyes. "I wish we had been somewhere better. Someplace more special. And under better circumstances. But this was the best. So much better than anything I've ever done before."

She brushed her lips through his hair. "I doubt anything like this could have been planned to increase the sensuousness and spontaneity of it. The combined passion. It was absolutely perfect."

"Perfect? I'm sure I've never done anything perfectly before."

She kissed him again. "This was. And the way you took care of our brothers."

He lifted his face and gazed into her eyes. "And you. The way I care about you."

Her heart beat harder. *Shit. Crap.* What... what could she say to answer that? She couldn't think of a single word so she kissed him again. Her answer was a long, passionate kiss that soon had both of them stroking each other's hair, faces and shoulders in soft, sensuous caresses. This time, it was much slower and lasted much longer and maybe it was even better.

CHAPTER 13

*S*HE NOW HAD TO face what she started and wanted so badly. Josefina fell silent as the night sounds entered her consciousness. The river's consistent babbling was not far from where they lay on the cooling sand. Together. Wrapped up like two sausages in a casing. Only the crickets and the river provided the music of the night.

"We need to go back. People were so worried about you. They didn't know what you were doing. In fact, there's a whole bunch of stuff we have to deal with."

He squeezed her next to him. "Including this. But I'm sensing, maybe not now. You want to ignore it and pretend we didn't just…?"

She took his hand in hers and kissed his knuckles. "No. I don't want to do that. I'm just glad you no longer like the types of people who you just beat up."

Caleb's entire body winced. "I would never have done such a thing to anyone. Ever. I mean it. I might have talked out of my ass, especially when I got drunk, but I was never violent towards anyone. But… but is that why you just had sex with me? Because you were so grateful?"

"You must realize by now that there is nothing that could induce me to sleep with anyone unless *I* wanted to. I certainly wouldn't do it just to thank you."

She felt his chest shaking under her like he was laughing. "I guess, well, that rings pretty true about you."

"Yeah, duh. Of course it does."

She got off him and rustled around, looking for her clothes. Caleb did the same. She eventually got up and so did he. He stared at her for a long moment with only the moonlight to illuminate them. "I wanted to do this with you from the very first time I saw you."

She tilted her head and resisted rolling her eyes. "Yes, I recall that. At the time, your eyes never rose above my chest."

"Sex was all I wanted from you then. I was pretty close to being drunk and the wedding made me so uncomfortable that I wanted to leave. Then there you were. You looked so pretty across the aisle and all I could think about were your plump breasts."

"Um, again, I know. Not exactly the best way to charm me, Caleb, in case you haven't figured that out yet."

"But now I realize I almost ruined it with the best person I could ever know. That superficial stuff is shit. I also learned a bunch of other things I was previously wrong or lazy about realizing. It's been very unpleasant to actually see myself, and reflect on my former actions, beliefs, and behaviors. It wasn't heroic, Josefina. It was me facing me. My demons as well as my past."

"But not your future."

He stepped closer to her and his hand slid to her waist as he pulled her in tightly. She felt him take in a deep breath. "I hope that will not be my future. I hope… I hope, Josefina, that you are part of my future." He pressed his face in the crook of her neck and shoulder and breathed out so softly, she almost didn't hear him. "I also doubt that will ever be."

She could not answer him. Her tongue felt thick inside her mouth. Something stopped her from responding. She wasn't sure what. She definitely liked Caleb. She had always been attracted to his physical appearance and especially now, after all the things he told her. They were better than any aphrodisiac to Josefina. But love?

She believed that's what Caleb didn't understand, but it was what he was describing and feeling, although she couldn't say for sure. No. Not yet. Maybe not ever. She just didn't know.

Holding him closer to her, she gripped his shoulders, seeking his comfort and presence just then. When they separated, he took her hand without a word, and started for his sister's house.

When they returned, they found everyone sitting in the living room. Ian. Kailynn. Jordan. Chuck. It was the middle of the damn night and all of them were waiting. Josefina was ashamed she kept them waiting when everyone stared at them with shocked faces.

"How's Pedro?" Caleb asked to break the overbearing silence.

"Sleeping. Got him some pain meds," Jordan answered before he jumped to his feet. He was all but chomping at the bit. "Did you find them?" He addressed Caleb. A long look was exchanged between them.

Caleb nodded. "I found them. Right where I knew they'd be."

Jordan stared and then asked in a hoarse voice, "And? What did you do?"

Caleb held up his knuckles, and in the overhead light, Josefina saw how bloodied and bruised they were. "I gave them what the law failed to do."

"Meaning?"

"An eye for an eye." Jordan nodded, seeming to understand what Caleb refused to say. Josefina didn't get it. Neither did Ian or Kailynn, judging by their puzzled looks.

"What does that mean?" Kailynn asked.

"It means he beat them up. He gave them the same treatment as they gave to me and Pedro," Jordan replied immediately. Josefina saw they were indeed brothers, albeit with a different set of values and ways than she was familiar with.

"They were baiting us. Drew. Hank. Tanner. They knew what they were doing when they went after you. They also knew what I'd do. Or maybe they thought I was still just like them." Caleb shrugged, flopping down on the sofa, hunching his shoulders.

Jordan came over and touched his shoulder. "You're not like them and you didn't take their side on this. That's all that matters now."

Chuck sat there too, listening. Caleb nodded towards him, and his shoulders looked rigid and taut. "How did you manage to stay in Ian's house?"

"Because those ugly asswipes should never have attacked a Hayes. Regardless of their reason, you took care of it. I woulda too, back in the day. When I was younger, no one ever messed with a Hayes. Just as it should be. Now, they still won't dare to."

Caleb's gaze went from unsure to puzzled. "What did you do? Finally realize your son means more than your stupid, shitty opinions on who he loves?"

"I sure as shit did. And of course, I'd expect you to go finish what Jordan and Pedro started. No use letting that lousy, trash punk, Drew Nichols get away with it. Growing their damn drugs out there in the hills."

"It's not illegal anymore. They are all licensed now," Caleb said with a tight smile.

"Still, trash is trash."

"And somehow, you think we aren't?" Caleb's tone was quiet, weary, and tired.

"Nah. We ain't. We don't let anyone mess with the Hayes family. So, no."

Caleb shook his head and Josefina sensed his confusion and need for comfort but restrained herself, seeing all the family members gathered there.

Caleb glanced at Ian and Josefina saw a flash of guilt and worry in Caleb's facial expression. "You can tell me to leave now and I will. But I don't regret anything I've done," he said.

Ian shook his head. "I would do the same if it were Jack, Shane, or Joey."

They exchanged a long look and Caleb gave Ian a jerky nod. She saw something change in Caleb's entire disposition and facial expression. Disbelief. He never earned Ian's respect before, and she was sure it was something he always wanted although he pretended otherwise. He nodded, his face stony but also a little shy.

He took her hand in his and squeezed it.

"I'm going to go check on Pedro." She exited the room and found her brother asleep. Seeing him settled and quiet she felt the overwhelming emotions finally slam into her. Exhaustion and grief over took her. She pressed a hand to her mouth to suppress her sobs.

Choking on her tears, she stumbled down the hall into Caleb's room. Of course, she should not have gone there. Everyone would know they were together; and yet, there she stayed, curled up on his bed.

His room was a mess and his sheets were strewn haphazardly on the bed. The room could have used a serious cleaning, but she didn't care. She curled up and just cried and cried and cried.

Caleb came in and he stood there for a moment. She

stopped long enough to open her eyes and found him staring at her. He suddenly stepped forward and scooped her up into his arms, pressing her against his chest. She wrapped her arms around his neck and cried harder. He didn't try to shush her. He knew. He saw. He felt it too. He made three people bleed to relieve some of his pain and hurt and frustration, where all Josefina could do about it was cry. And talk to him. It wasn't enough. It didn't make it right.

She wished she could have been Caleb for once and done the wrong thing.

Exhausted, she stopped crying, but still remained in his arms. He gently kissed her cheek. "We thought you were with Pedro still."

She glanced up and shook her head. "I'm staying here now. I'm too tired to face them. I just want to be here. With you. Like Pedro just wants to be with Jordan." He nodded, tucking her hair behind her ear and kissing her lips softly before disappearing.

He held her against him tightly. She spoke after she was calmer, "I always thought I had a firm grip on reality. I feel ruined by this."

He kissed her forehead. "That's okay, I feel that way too, Josefina. I feel exactly the same way."

"How do we go forward now?"

"Together? All of us, I mean, you and me, our brothers and the rest of our families? We all move ahead together."

It was simple and naive, sounding oddly sweet and beautiful coming from Caleb. It solved nothing, but his words melted her entire heart and insides like nothing else could have.

Together. It was better than being alone.

They all maybe learned something.

Maybe others could too. Right then, Josefina doubted everything she ever knew or thought she knew about the world. Everything except for Caleb. He managed to teach her more than anyone else when he changed. He made her believe for the very first time, that people could change. She hugged him tighter and kissed his mouth. "I'm glad you're here with me."

It was the only thing that made the night tolerable.

CHAPTER 14

*T*HE NEXT MORNING, THE sun shone, even though it felt as if the world had gone pitch-dark to Caleb. He no longer knew what to make of it. It felt so changed, completely and utterly different.

From an initial, naive sense of right and wrong, to his understanding that lots of things did happen even though they weren't fair or instigated, maybe there was more than one side to everything.

The only factor that made it tolerable was the woman sleeping beside him. Turns out she was a bed hog and not a snuggler. She avoided his touch during her sleep, tossing and turning and murmuring occasionally. Her active slumber would take a few nights for him to get used to. He found himself backing off and grinning at her whenever she spoke any incoherent words.

After lying awake for hours, Caleb got up early. He had to get up anyway to go to work. Naturally, there would be extra chores with Pedro being out. And Jordan being so upset. Caleb was ready to pick up their slack. He could work hard if he put some more sweat into it. He was a strong guy, coordinated and enterprising, when he felt motivated. It didn't happen too often in all his years of existence. But that was before now.

Flinging the covers back, Caleb started to quietly move about his room, slipping clean clothes on and sitting down to pull his boots on when Josefina's eyes blinked open. It took her a moment to figure out where she was, and he felt his heart stop.

Nerves agitated his stomach. What if she didn't like waking up with him? After what they did yesterday? It was something solely perpetuated by high emotions. Calmer now, what if she blamed him? Worse still, what if she hated him?

Dropping the boots, he slowly rose to his feet and her gaze followed him, without revealing much expression. Trying to ignore his suddenly clumsy sense of self, he sat on the edge of the bed and kept his gaze down. "You regret it, don't you? I knew I shouldn't... we shouldn't have. It was out of sheer relief about your brother, and not because you wanted to do that with me."

"Since when is Caleb Hayes wondering whether or not a woman wants him?" Josefina's voice came out gravelly and sleepy sounding.

He glanced her way. "Since the one woman I want doesn't want me."

She stretched her arms out and came up behind him, putting her arms around his shoulders, pressing her chest into his back and grazing his bare neck in a soft and tender kiss. "I want you, Caleb. I'm glad this happened. I'm not glad about anything else that happened yesterday except this. You've got to quit doubting me—us—this."

He paused and covered her hand with his. "It's just never been..."

"What, Caleb?" she asked, and her breath was right next

to his ear, sending shivers down his spine. He turned his head just enough to catch her lips in a warm kiss.

She fell back, tugging on his torso to follow her down until he was leaning over her as he kissed her. She stopped long enough to whisper, "What? It's never been what?"

"Important. No one girl or woman has ever meant anything important to me."

She kissed him and then smiled. "It's never really been important to me either. But this seems like it is."

"It is." He stopped and rested his forehead on hers as they stared into each other's eyes. She was a first for him. Her naked chest was visible now above the blanket line. He cared sincerely about her. She aroused him, of course, but her dark, intelligent eyes never failed to capture his interest, as well as his heart. He was scared, and unsure of how she'd feel this morning, so his relief was palpable.

"Where are you off to so early?" she asked as she leaned up and kissed his mouth again. A soft smooch was the only thing to break their long eye lock.

"Work. Both our brothers are out, and they need more days off. Busy time of year right now for us, and I can take up the slack for them, at least for a few days anyway."

"You are not the Caleb Hayes I heard rumors about."

"I hope not," he said softly, but with solemnity in his tone. "I hung out with the creeps that caused all of this. I was like any one of them. I *was* them. I hope to God I'm no longer like them."

He pried himself away from her and turned back around to put his boots on. When she spoke, her tone was final. "You are not anything like them. Again, you have to realize what I see, *you have changed*. But Caleb?"

He glanced back while lacing his right boot up. "Yeah?"

"Could there be any police units coming for you? Do you

think they might be looking for you? I mean, what about the family members of the guys…?"

"I highly doubt it. It's kind of an agreed-upon, unwritten code around here. They won't discuss it or press charges just as they never expected us to tell the cops."

"What did you do to them?"

He paused, wincing. "Do you want to see?"

"See? How?"

"I'll take you to them."

"Can they… I mean… they can still walk… can't they?" Fear and apprehension rippled through her and it was evident in her tone.

"Sure, they can still walk. But I doubt they went to work. They're most likely still in a drunken stupor or nursing terrible hangovers. They were so drunk, half of my blows to them didn't even resonate. They were like unfeeling rag dolls."

He glanced back, and she grimaced. "If I had to witness any of it, I would probably feel different. I don't… I mean, violence is not usually my first choice when dealing with nasty people."

"It was a fair fight. No worse than I've had in the past. I fought with one of them a long time ago. They'll heal up and be fine. Besides, what they did was far worse."

"I know. I really do, and I agree."

He finished lacing his boots. "I'm going to get started now. I was thinking, could we go out on a date? I'd like to do this seriously, and for real. This wasn't anything I intended to happen between us, if there is an us, but I want it to be special. Different. Not out on a beach. Or in front of everyone we know and love."

"Well, it wasn't in front of anyone, technically, and in its own way, it *was* very special. But yes, of course we can."

He leaned over and kissed her before opening the

bedroom door and shutting it quietly behind him. He tiptoed down the hallway and listened at Pedro's door, hearing the murmur of voices.

Where once it could have freaked him out to hear any intimate or quiet talk between his brother and this man, now, he took comfort in knowing they had each other. He hoped they were feeling relatively okay this morning. When he entered the living room, his sister was already up and eating a bowl of cereal. She looked as tired as he felt.

"Caleb?" she said quietly when he kissed her cheek. "Why are you up so early?"

"Getting an early start. Jordan and Pedro will need a few days off to recuperate, and Pedro will need even longer; and besides all of that, there's a lot of work to do right now."

"I'm sure Ian doesn't expect you to carry—"

"I expect to. I expect to earn my living. And make sure my brother has a job to come back to."

"He's our brother too. We aren't going to stiff him out of his job."

"It's something constructive for me to do," he murmured softly. He was unsure how better to describe the discomforting oddness about the entire world he now felt. The earth seemed to be tilted askew on its axis this morning. "And who knew or could have predicted that the idea of going to work would become a source of comfort to me? It's something I need to do. You shouldn't discourage it." He found that comment funny enough to grin over.

Kailynn's eyes filled with tears. "I do encourage it. I understand. I feel the same way."

He fell silent, at a loss for anything else to say. Sipping his cup of coffee from the pot Kailynn had already made, he grimaced as he stared into it and leaned back onto the counter.

It was time for him to do something different. Time to

211

grow up and be his own man. Not the blundering, trouble-causing, ignorant boy he had been.

"So… Josefina, huh?" Kailynn said after a long silence. He glanced up and found her smiling, as if she liked the news.

"Um, maybe. It's too new. We've been friends and gone on dates but I just don't know."

"I've never seen you like this with anyone. It's refreshingly nice."

"Like what? I told you, it's too new."

"No, it isn't. You've been dating all summer. For several months. That's a lifetime for you, Caleb. She's great. I can't tell you how happy it makes me. I'm just as happy as I am seeing Jordan and Pedro finally together." She grinned but it turned into a sad, world-weary smile.

He considered his sister with a new perspective. "The last thing you wanted was to be back here, living and working permanently."

"You're right, not my first choice. But after the fire, and Dad losing the trailer and you guys, even, not to mention when Jack's son lost his shit, along with Jack, Ian had to step in and take control of the ranch. So now, I am approaching the plate."

When the fire swept through and burned all their homes and land, it changed everyone's world forever. It brought his sister home in a way he now understood nothing else could have. It was only now, however, that he realized why and also finally understood her.

"So, you guys are dealing with it from both Ian's family and yours?"

A smile slipped over her face. "I think that's just grown-up life, Caleb."

"Yeah. I guess it is. You let Dad stay here even knowing how he felt about Jordan?"

"I did. Because he's my father. What else could we do?"

"And me? You tolerated me. For years. You made sure I had a job and could freaking fend for myself. When in truth, you and Ian were carrying me the whole time."

She shrugged. "Yeah, maybe. But now? No. You don't need me for that."

"I'm sorry I was such a fuck-up for so long."

"I'm glad you're no longer that way too."

"Yeah." He set his cup down and nodded. "On that lovely note, where is Ian?"

"Up at the barn, in Jack's... former office."

"All right. I'll go check in with him and get started. AJ will need the extra labor. Gotta harvest the apples soon and the alfalfa has to be baled and ready for fall." He slipped out the front door and left the house.

JOSEFINA SHOWERED and when she appeared downstairs, Kailynn was all alone. She ducked her head down, blushing.

"Morning, Josefina. Coffee?" was all Caleb's sister said to her. Josefina smiled through her blush and gratefully accepted the cup Kailynn handed her. They exchanged a smile, which felt awkward at first to Josefina, but her small smile spread into a huge grin.

"You clearly figured out—"

"Yes. And I think it's wonderful."

"At least someone does. My brother? Not so much."

"Your brother only wants what's best for you." Kailynn shook her head. "How ironic that Caleb was always the one who couldn't handle change. He would have kept us all living together in Dad's dinky trailer until we were senior citizens. It literally took a fire to end that dream. He's oddly sweet that way. He speaks and acts like he's tough as nails, but his heart is a big marshmallow. He never wants any member of his family to leave or move elsewhere."

"I've learned that about him. He's loving and sweet and he tries harder than anyone I've ever known to please me. It's pretty difficult to resist." She shrugged.

Both of their heads whipped around when a door opened, and a voice sneered, "Oh great. Caleb made his move."

She gave her brother a cheeky smile. "No, brother. I did. And like you never asking my opinion on Jordan, same goes here." But then her smile faded. "How are you?"

"Fine. It sucked. But I'm going to be fine. Stiff and sore, but so will the bastards who did this."

She got up and hugged her grumbling brother. "It never should have happened."

He snorted. "Well, of course not. But they are shitty people. The gutter of citizens of River's End. They aren't everyone."

She nodded. "No. They aren't. But still it's been so shocking."

Pedro sighed. "We need to tell Dad." He announced. He grimaced and sighed as he pulled out his cellphone.

Josefina stayed back as Pedro turned and spoke softly to their dad in Spanish. There were lots of nods. When he hung up, his shoulders were drooping. Then he hobbled over to the couch and slumped forward. Josefina went towards him, but he didn't lift his head. "He started to cry."

She lowered herself into a chair opposite him. She understood what it meant. Dad never cried. Not once, that she could remember. He was always quiet, much like Pedro, and kind of remote. He was mostly nice to all of them, but never very vocal or much of a factor in the molding of their lives. Pedro cleared his throat and got to his feet. "He wants to come over when I get home."

She nodded. "I'll go and get him."

"Thanks," Pedro said in a hollow tone before he started down the hall. She watched him. Kailynn did too and they exchanged glances.

There were few words to say this morning. It was much harder to accept in the daylight.

She rubbed her gritty eyes and sighed when she remembered she had to tell her clients she wasn't available for interpretation services today. She had to call in before she left to get her dad. She needed to…

What? What could she possibly do to make any of this okay? Nothing would ever seem okay again.

CHAPTER 15

*P*EDRO AND JORDAN RETURNED to their house later that day and Josefina skipped work along with Kailynn. They helped their brothers home and put Pedro to bed. Jordan stayed nearby. Josefina picked up her dad and gave him and Pedro plenty of privacy. She could not ignore the haunting knowledge that reminded her of how a house feels after a funeral. Quiet. Exhausted. Emotionally drained. And yet there were no words left to say out loud to each other. Neither she nor Kailynn made a move to leave and Jordan and Pedro preferred that they stay.

She took her dad home before dinner. He was quiet, solemn, and stony-faced. In Spanish, he said to her, "Pedro handled this very well."

She squeezed her dad's hand, glancing at him for a moment before focusing on the road and agreeing, "He did."

"He... he makes me so proud."

She blinked. Her dad rarely expressed any emotions toward his kids. She had always felt alone and independent, totally on her own. "Did you tell him that?"

"Yes."

She glanced his way. Dad rarely did that either. "I'm sure it helped him."

"But will no one go to jail for this?"

"No, nobody will."

"Did Jordan's brother beat them all up?"

"Well. Yes. Way I heard it Pedro and Jordan got a pretty good start on that."

"Yes. But the brother? He finished it?"

She grew bug-eyed and had to concentrate on facing forward lest she give that away to her dad. She didn't expect Pedro to rat on Caleb. "Um... yes."

Her dad faced forward and not a word was spoken for a few miles. Then he said, "Good."

She smiled to herself and walked her dad inside his house. Only her stepsister, Constance, still lived at home. Her father sat down, looking older than she remembered as he rocked back and asked, "You're dating him? This Caleb?"

She paused. *Damn Pedro!* She nodded. "It's pretty new..."

"Bring him to dinner sometime."

She blinked and nodded eagerly. "Yes. I will. Sure. To one of our Friday night dinners."

He nodded before flipping the TV on and that was that. She left him watching his show and shut the door behind her. Huh. Dad could still surprise her. Fridays were traditionally an open invite for her stepsisters, Pedro, Jordan, and Josefina to visit their dad. They often met at Dad's place or a restaurant. And now? He purposely asked her to bring her new date? Huh.

Still slightly subdued, Josefina returned to check on her brother.

Caleb came walking in at five o'clock with several bags of food for dinner. She smiled at the thoughtful gesture.

He smiled back at her, but only after his brother turned away. "Hey," he said softly. He was so at odds with the old, blustering Caleb she used to see carousing around town. Or the same man who could beat up three men and yet her heart blipped, and she felt all weird and warm when a rush of emotions flowed through her.

"Hey," she replied in the same tone before they shared a long, lingering smile. He stepped forward and placed an arm around her waist as he leaned down to kiss her mouth with a quick swipe of his lips. It was both odd and thrilling. She fought the urge to glance around at their siblings, and reminded herself she was an adult and allowed to do that.

Even with Caleb.

Releasing her, he passed around her to set up the take-out on the table, smiling at her when she followed him to help. "Not exactly the romantic dinner I'd like to have with you."

She shook her head. "You don't get it. I'm not about fancy, impressive dinners or gifts. I'm only about you. And me. What's real? Both of us. Nothing could be much more real than what we saw last night."

"And what I did."

"And what *we* did," she added low enough so that no else could hear. He lifted his head and a hand to grab hers, which he squeezed tightly. Then, he felt flushed, like he was blushing. "What *we* did," he repeated softly.

She held his hand tighter. "I wanted to. It wasn't a thank you. It was real."

His entire expression changed. Going from strained and unsure, his face seemed to be made of elastic.

"Okay?" she pressed.

"Okay," he answered with a smile.

"Guess what?"

"What?"

"My dad wants to meet you."

Caleb winced. "Okay. Are you sure? What if he learns about what I did last night?

"He already knows all about it. Know what he said?"

"I can only imagine."

"He said, 'good'."

Surprise filled Caleb's face. "Really?"

"Really." She took his hand and squeezed it hard. He squeezed hers back as their gazes hung on each other in a long, goofy eye lock.

Pedro hobbled out from the bedroom and scowled when he caught them holding hands with their heads bent together. Everyone paused at seeing Pedro observing them. She and Caleb let go of each other and Pedro rolled his eyes as he flopped into a chair and reached for the take-out bag. "Quit groping my sister and pass me some ketchup with the fries."

"I was holding her hand."

"Groping, holding hands, it's all the same to me. It hurts my eyes."

"It's not the same to me," Caleb muttered but he let her go and passed Pedro the ketchup.

Josefina was pressing her lips tightly together to restrain her laugh. After the stress of the last twenty-four hours, unbelievably, she started to laugh, even nearly spitting out her food. She had to hold her stomach at one point, it hurt so badly.

"What are you laughing at?"

"Holding hands," she gasped out between more fits of laughter. Could Caleb still find her attractive after this? Panting for breath, she said, "He... he's upset because we hold hands, when he's... he's all black and blue and hurt and knows his attackers will get away with it. Meanwhile, Caleb beat the shit out of three guys... and... and... hand-holding is upsetting my brother!"

Caleb reached over and gripped her hand again, starting to chuckle with her, and seeing what managed to strike her as being so funny. Slowly, one-by-one, everyone else joined in the laughter and the horrible tension of what they had endured was winding to an end in a collective laugh. They controlled it that way. In many ways, that was the moment when they didn't let it define or hurt them.

～

JOSEFINA STAYED in close contact with her brother and her brother-in-law. They all seemed to feed off each other's company. Everyone was raw and vulnerable, not just her. Caleb, Ian, and Kailynn went often to visit Jordan and Pedro.

Even Chuck Hayes came out to visit them a few times. Flanked by Ian with Kailynn behind him, shrugging her shoulders, her eyes bugged out as she whispered to Josefina, "He insisted on coming. I don't get it." Chuck didn't say much to anyone. He never apologized to Jordan despite how often he now sat in their house. He was just there. It was odd. But also proof that people could change.

However, no one had changed like Caleb Hayes. He successfully carried the workload for his brother and Pedro, eagerly assisting them while they eased back into the farm work. He came and went, planning things around Josefina's work schedule along with his own.

Things were lovely and like nothing Josefina ever expected to have in life. Especially considering how the summer started compared with how it was ending. Pretty epic. New. Strange. Wonderful.

～

SHE GLANCED up when Caleb stood before her and said, "I just thought of something."

He was grinning like a child with a secret. Like the good, exciting, can't-wait-to-tell kind of secret. "What?"

"You mentioned on your bucket list you wanted to see salt water."

"Uh-huh."

"And you never went on any summer family vacations. Right? Never a single one?"

"Not a one. So…"

"So neither have I. What if we took one together? There's a park I heard this guy in town mention, so I asked him, and he told me all about it. Well… I reserved a campsite." Caleb beamed. "For you and me to spend four nights camping there and it's right on the Sound. Salt water. He said it was super nice. He's a fisherman too, and he was out there salmon fishing, but it is salt water and not as far to drive as getting to the open ocean from here."

She stared at him and her mouth dropped open. "You want to go camping? You and me?"

"Yeah." His gaze wavered and started to lessen in its intensity and happiness. "You mean, you don't want to?"

"I don't know. I've never camped before or even considered it." How could she have thought about vacationing with Caleb Hayes? It just seemed so unlike any reality she ever pictured for herself, including, of course, sleeping with him. He was the last man she would have imagined doing such a thing with.

But here she was. "I'll have to check my work… and can you get the time off?"

"Ian already gave me the time off."

How could she not go? Besides, she always longed to see salt water and had never ventured to the western side of the state. In fact, she'd never been anywhere. Ever. Not even fifty miles from there.

"Okay. Then let me check work and if they say yes, we

can plan on it. But what about all the camping stuff? Costs?" Neither of them had money left over at the end of each month. Their weekly outings ate up most of their discretionary funding, which they truly should not have wasted although they often did.

But God help her if Caleb wasn't one of the most fun people she'd ever hung out with. Being with him was all that alleviated her boredom from her own predictable life. She liked the time she spent with him enough to devote her precious money to it.

"The Rydells have all the camping stuff we could want. Kailynn says we can borrow it. So, all we have to pay for are two tanks of gas, our food and the campsite fee. We can scrounge that up together, if we split all the expenses," he said as his expression tightened and his eyes glinted. "I'm sorry I have to say that. I should have been able to pay for all of it."

She scoffed at his concern. "Don't, Caleb. Don't go all he-man, making me the little woman you provide for. We make comparable salaries. You don't owe me anything. So, don't regret that. Yes, I think we can afford a camping trip."

"Do you want to go?"

Her heart skipped a beat. She did want to go. No one had ever asked her to go on vacation before. Who cared that she had never been on a vacation? Who listened to her lifelong desire to see salt water? Caleb. He consistently noticed and remembered and cared what she said and what was important to her.

"I do. I would like to go. Very much. Thank you, Caleb, for thinking of that."

His expression morphed from apprehensive to blushing with unmasked pleasure. Her heart beat harder in response. No. She refused to let his glee and boyish enthusiasm to please her lure her into forgetting this was just temporary.

There was nothing about their relationship she expected to last in the long term. She intended to go far beyond the circumstances of her birth and plain life now. She could not forget that dream. Caleb would be the kind who settles for whatever he gets, and she refused to do that for anything or anybody. Even a killer smile with super sweet intentions behind it.

She arranged to get the time off and put her house in order before she packed to leave. They decided to take off right after work and he showed up promptly at five o'clock to get her. The back of his truck was loaded with the camping gear strapped in. She was pleased that he could take care of the gear so seamlessly.

When she first met him, she would have doubted he could handle the task of organizing and packing multiple items. They shopped together and she found that his expertise proved invaluable. Having camped multiple times with his brother and friends, Caleb knew how to tent camp and cook in the outdoors.

"Easy. We won't have a kitchen, remember that," he said when he noticed her pile of produce before she put most of it back. Her gastric health would have to wait until after she returned, she discovered.

She brought her duffel bag out to his truck and he came around the hood and met her, grinning from ear-to-ear. He leaned down and his lips grazed her mouth while his arms wrapped around her waist. "Ready?"

"I have no idea what to expect."

"Me neither." He chuckled. "I brought lotsa stuff… hopefully, it's the right stuff."

She glanced at the pile he referred to. "Bikes? Where did you get those?"

"Rented 'em. You said you wanted to go bicycling, remember?"

"I did. But you remembered that? And rented two bikes?"

"I think people often do that at places like this."

"And we're just a couple of people going to a camping park? Weird, huh? But seriously, thank you, Caleb. I can't wait to try them out." And it was true.

"It's not like a trip to Hawaii or Las Vegas. There's no reason to be that grateful. At most, all we can hope for is that it'll be better than working."

She stared at him from across the distance of the truck bed. He leaned his elbows on the rim and gazed at the assortment of gear tied down before them.

"Caleb?" He raised his eyes to hers upon hearing her serious tone. "You're very wrong. This is an exotic trip to me. I have nothing to compare it to, remember? I've never taken a vacation except for a few days off work or school when I just stayed at home. This is as big as Hawaii or Vegas to me. And you thought of it, and planned it out, and executed the whole experience for me. You can't possibly expect me to take that lightly."

Shrugging, he blushed as he hemmed and hawed, acting as if it were no big deal, but she detected a glimmer of pleasure in his eyes. She knew that what she said pleased him. All that he'd done for her made her feel the same sense of affection. He actually rented bikes for them to ride. Who thinks about fun activities like that?

"Where did you even find bikes to rent around here?" River's End and Brewster weren't exactly tourist traps. They settled into the cab of the truck, cranking the AC to ease the heat outside as he pulled out. "Chelan. Lots of tourists go there and they have all kinds of rentals like this."

"Oh." He thought about doing it and prepared for it. She was puzzled and awed by his ingenuity and all the effort he invested in doing small things for her as well as bigger things. Why was she so quick to assume it was abnormal for him to do those things? From the first time he asked her out, hadn't he shown extra concern for her? Yes, of course he had. So why did she cling to her erroneous, previous assumptions when he continuously proved they were incorrect and she was underestimating him?

She wondered for a long time about it and it made her rethink everything she thought she knew. They headed over Highway 20. Another place she'd never been before. He marveled at her frank admission. "You've got to be kidding me. It's like… I mean, everyone in Brewster has been up here at some time or another."

"Everyone except me." She gazed at the startling peaks and craggy heights that clawed at the sky. The rocky tops were like spears above the vast depth of forest that went on forever.

"Shane and I, back in the day, used to bike over these all the time. We'd go for day rides and sometimes, week-long rides."

"You had a motorcycle?"

"Oh, I wish. Desperately. But we could never afford one. We'd… well, you know, we'd just borrow a bike. Shane was always fixing them and that was in the days before he got so formal about it. He used to lie about the date he would be finished with the repair and then we would take off for a few days."

"Riding someone else's bike? That's horrible. Disturbing. And you never got caught?"

"Oh, yeah, we were. Once I thought this guy would kill us. Seriously. Big, old biker. The *real kind*. Not the fake, wannabes just seeking fun, and harmless like Shane. This guy? Well, I had to hightail it outta here for a while."

Josefina shook her head, trying to suppress her laughter but to no avail. Glad too, that stunts like that were no longer part of Caleb's life.

The ride was beautiful over the mountains under a deep blue sky that cast long shadows and provided cooling temperatures. Traffic was light and the twists and turns seemed unending. She felt like a pendulum inside the truck, swinging back and forth. Lowlands, another river, and unbroken acres of trees.

Every species seemed on display, and all were hugging the road. Leafy, green sycamores as well as conifers, Douglas firs, cedars, alders, and maples filled the spaces between the houses. "I imagined it would be far more crowded."

"This area's out in middle of nowhere. It won't be long before all you'll see are endless tracts of houses and commercial buildings along with more traffic."

Sure enough, passing road after road of strip mall neighborhoods, they encountered bigger malls and low buildings as far as the eye could see. The flood of traffic was unlike anything she'd ever experienced at home. Her head kept whipping around as they entered the freeway. They were on it for only a few minutes before exiting onto another highway, and crossing over a huge bridge.

"Puget Sound," Caleb announced as she stared out her passenger window in awe and admiration. Salt water. Marshy edges surrounded a small marina and farther off, all that could be seen was the water, which filled the horizon.

The road turned suddenly away from the water and she lost her view. They breezed through the small, idyllic town of Anacortes. It was quiet with small shops and businesses lining the street. Water and a huge marina glinted in the sinking sunlight as glimpses of the land flashed from across the way. "It's incredibly beautiful."

He took her hand in his and squeezed but she noticed he didn't agree with her. They drove a few more miles, going through the outlying neighborhoods before reaching the water's edge and driving past all the multimillion-dollar homes that offered multimillion-dollar views.

Passing the ferry terminal, she saw a hulking, white and green trimmed boat idling and being loaded with cars. She'd never seen one before and kept staring at it until it vanished from view.

They pulled into the park eventually. A park filled with trees. That was the first thing she noticed. An unbroken chain of huge fir and cedar trees bordering the winding road that led to all the campsites, which were located up a short hill. The light instantly dulled, obscured by the canopy of conifer tree limbs that shielded them. The temperature also dropped a good ten degrees in the few minutes it took to drive from downtown Anacortes to the park. "Holy shit. How could the temperature drop so fast?"

Caleb swung into the campsite he reserved, and Josefina remembered this was all for her. Their campsite was longer and slightly more private than others with nothing but the woods surrounding the pull-in. A simple, wooden picnic table and metal-rimmed fire ring were the extent of their accommodations. "Miles of cold, icy water flowing just through those trees, and it probably works like natural air conditioning."

She swung her door open and shivered when the cool air blew over her. Wearing only a pair of shorts and a tank top, since it was in the nineties when they left home, she immediately got goosebumps all over her skin. *Crap.*

She wondered if she packed enough clothes. She did bring warmer clothes than she wore at home, but this? It had to be sixty degrees and dropping rapidly. She rubbed her chilly arms as she approached the tailgate.

Caleb noticed her discomfort and he smiled. He jumped up onto the bumper and rooted around. He unzipped a bag and turned to hand her a jacket. "Here, put this on. Before you start turning blue."

Gratefully, she pulled the jacket on and jumped up and down to stop the shivers. Caleb let the tailgate down as he started grabbing all the stuff. He made quick work of it, placing all of the cooking items on the picnic table, and putting the tent and inside gear in a stack beside it on the sleeping spot.

He heaved the packed ice chests and made it look easy while she struggled to lift one side in her effort to help. He waved her off and did all the heavy lifting himself. She was clueless as to how to set up the cook stove or the tent. But Caleb had the whole routine down.

She unpacked the different poles and clothes while he laid out a tarp before quickly lining up the poles. Within a few minutes, the whole tent popped up. "Shelter." With a huge grin, Caleb unzipped the door and started to step inside. She followed him. It was roomy, a ten-man tent. She still felt cold, however.

"Here, let's put some air into the mattress." Using a hand pump, Josefina began to add air to what turned out to be a double air mattress. She tossed their sleeping bags and pillows on top of it before she brought in their duffel bags filled with their clothes, shoes, and personal items. She organized everything inside the tent while Caleb worked on the outside. Placing chairs around the fire pit, he also stacked the few loads of firewood he brought along.

At home there had been a burn ban in effect for three months. Not here, however. She stuck her long pants on and huddled under his coat. Her coat wasn't half as warm as his was. The fire was flaming and she went over to warm herself up next to it. Pushing her hands towards the flames, she rubbed them together and turned when Caleb chuckled.

He came up behind her and wrapped his arms around her

before resting his head on top of hers. She snuggled into the embrace, still startled by all of the affectionate gestures he initiated, like this one.

They amounted to many and they happened often with Caleb Hayes. Not something Josefina could have ever predicted from him. He was crazy affectionate. She would have expected it to be lewd or rated R and not so sweet.

He was sweet and warm in his affection. They held hands often when they weren't hugging, holding, or embracing. His hands rested just below where his jacket ended, and he held onto her hip bones, but not in a salacious manner.

She tilted her head to look at him. "Did you camp a lot as a kid?"

"No. Never with Dad. When Jordan and I were teens, we'd go off a lot and do it. For us though, at least at first, it was a pair of sleeping bags on the ground and a fire, so this is sheer luxury. We always went hunting in the fall but those camping trips weren't anything like this."

"How were they?" He let her hand go to stoke the fire, and she sat in one of the lawn chairs, hovering closer to the heat source.

"Lots and lots of beer. Some hiking. Some hunting. A few cans of pork and beans over a fire, and voila, camping."

"Just Jordan and you?"

"Always." He smiled to himself, staring at the fire, one boot resting on the grill. She stared at his face, which was so contemplative and beautiful in the waning light and glow of the flickering fire. He was an extraordinarily handsome man.

And the longer she knew him, the more his personality emerged, and the more well-rounded he became. "But back then, Shane Rydell was always with us, along with Drew, Tanner, Hank, Barry Kenwit, and a few others."

"Trouble with a capital T, all of them. As we found out too

late now. What about Barry? Isn't he doing time in jail right now?"

Caleb frowned. "Yeah, he beat up his girlfriend. I had no idea he was as mean as that. I'd have beat him up if I'd known then." He shook his head, shrugging. "I guess you never *really* know anyone."

"No. Not always," she agreed softly but she wasn't talking about Barry, she was staring at him, and thinking of him, in an extremely positive light.

"You and Jordan were always very close?"

"Brothers. Best friends. I felt kinda lost when Pedro turned up and he became both to Jordan and... even more."

She froze. The light suddenly dawning. "You were jealous. You hated him so much because you were jealous."

He ducked his head but said softly, "Yeah, I was pretty green with envy. I mean, I wasn't sure how to accept my knowledge of Jordan, but in the end, it meant losing him as my perpetual... well, sidekick, but don't forget that I was also his sidekick. Know what I mean?"

"I do. And yet, look how far you embraced Pedro. You seem to be over your jealousy."

"Only because of you. You did that, Josie."

"No, actually, I didn't. I didn't even like you at first. You convinced me to like you because you changed. That's the only reason I could start liking you, so no. It was all because of you."

They went to bed soon and zipped their sleeping bags together, so they could cuddle up close and do much more. Oh, so much more. Josefina clamped a hand over her mouth to keep quiet in the public space since they had no real walls around them.

Morning found Caleb already out and about, heating the water for hot chocolate before she even stretched her limbs. She ran to the public bathroom, disliking that aspect of camping, but thoroughly enjoying the rest. He cooked her bacon and eggs on the outside propane cooking stove and they huddled under their coats. The morning was clear and sunny, but the sky was far away and only visible through the breaks in the tree canopy.

"I can't believe this is already the end of August." She stared into the fire, letting it warm her legs. She was so glad she had Caleb right there to help her or she'd have been a disaster attempting all of this.

"Not like home, huh? Well, should we go see it? That salt water that you've always wanted to experience?"

She nodded eagerly, and they got on the pedal bikes. She quickly found her balance and waited while Caleb struggled first with the pedal and then to get going. He muttered and swore under his breath and she laughed out loud at him. Calling the innocent pedal bike any number of bad words like *fucker, shithead,* and *asshole,* Caleb finally got going. Scowling at her, he cautiously made his way down the road, braking every few minutes.

She pressed her tongue inside her cheek to restrain her cackles of laughter. "Didn't you ever ride a bike as a kid?" she asked, trying to hold hers as slowly as he meandered. His knuckles were turning white as he gripped the handlebars, always at the ready to use the hand brakes.

"I rode dirt bikes. Not pedal bikes. You saw where I lived. Where the hell would I have ridden these damn things?"

She couldn't help the sneaky laughter that kept escaping her, but he looked so funny. He was a big, hulking man in heavy boots and jeans, barely managing to keep the bike pointed straight and upright as it wobbled all around. His speed was excruciatingly slow.

She zipped ahead and flew down the hill that led to the road. She caught a glimpse of the water through the thick strip of tree trunks and bushes. He got off and walked his bike down the hill as she spun circles at the bottom, and her heart swelled with mirth but also awe when she saw how adorable he was.

And he did all of this for her. Just to please her. He located, rented, and brought the bikes for her even though he struggled to stay upright. It was all for her. He only wanted to heighten her enjoyment.

When he reached the flat road, he smiled wearily and nodded. "Okay. I think I can do it now." The bike path was mostly comprised of small hills, going up and down but only for short distances. Josefina could have walked faster than Caleb rode, but she shut up and enjoyed his kind intention and everything he provided for her.

When they got to the boat launch and kids' park, they saw a clear, grassy field with a long, clean beach filled with people. She smiled in undisguised pleasure. The air warmed up as soon as they emerged from the darkness of the trees. The sun felt hot and the air was fresh and moist and clean.

Puget Sound was huge, going far beyond the opposite shoreline. Tall mountains were covered in trees but nothing like the mountains of home. These were lower and rounded, yet much more than minor hills. She looked up at the clear, blue sky and full of bliss, she breathed in the cool, fresh air. It was so different from the dry, stifling heat and pine-scented air of home. The stale scent of dead grasses that were singed last year wafted upwards to taint the air in Brewster. This smell was salty and soft and different.

They stowed their bikes and sat on top of a picnic table, watching all the boats of various sizes, from huge cargo ships, to the personal yachts, and smaller fishing and ski boats. Kayakers paddled by leisurely. People milled around on the beach and kids climbed on the playground equipment. Soon, the picnickers began using the covered areas to cook.

Boats dotted the horizon, and some were huge, so the

ferry eventually had to cut a path through them all and she saw little tugboats pulling enormous, fully-loaded barges chugging by. "Let's go down and feel the water."

He followed her with an indulgent smile on his face as she reached down and touched the water. It felt like regular water. But very cold. Oh, it was so cold. "It's just about freezing."

"Yeah, Puget Sound doesn't warm up like the river." His smile was sweet and apologetic. She could tell he liked the interest and pleasure she showed in it. "It's a smidgeon deeper."

She laughed, and the salty air tickled her nostrils. She could taste it on her lips. She wasn't sure what she thought of it yet, but it made her skin feel sticky. The water, itself, was impossibly clear and clean. Big swaths of kelp undulated beneath the surface. Spots of sand and small, smooth pebbles reflected under the sun's rays until the water's depth turned it black.

They walked along the shoreline. A black, rocky outcropping rubbed smooth by tidal forces made it an easy walk. Up and down the craggy shoreline they followed the water's edge. There were plenty of shells and pebbles to find and Josefina was like a kid collecting Easter eggs. She'd never touched a real shell found on a saltwater beach before. The rocky, hard coast soon became a sandy cove and she took her shoes off and sunk her toes into the soft, moist sand. Waves drifted in and out. They sat down and watched them. The tide was coming in. When they walked back to collect their bikes, they were both relieved to find them still there.

They brought a picnic dinner to the beach and sat for hours in the cool but pleasant—a high of seventy degrees—afternoon. She never enjoyed the sun like that before. It was finally tolerable. The breeze was cool and as the evening wore on into the night, it felt frigid to her. She shivered and snuggled up to Caleb, relieved that his body heat was warm enough for her to sleep.

The second day, they took a long ferry ride to Orcas Island. They toured the town and beach before coming back. The ferry ride was wonderful and terrifying to Josefina, who had never been on a boat before.

Going out to the middle of a body of salt water and knowing it was perhaps hundreds of feet deep, was way out of her comfort zone. The water below her was dark and black and deep and very cold.

She shivered whenever she imagined it engulfing her and pushed harder into Caleb's arms as they stood against one of the front rails. He put his arms around her, resting them on the railing and surrounding her. "Afraid?" he asked before he felt her tremble and shudder.

"A little." She grinned up at him. "Never been on a tin can floating on nothing but water." She turned to enjoy the views and the salty spray on her lips. Despite Caleb's warm embrace, she felt ready to die at any moment. On the way back, the ferry stopped moving and she gripped Caleb's hand in alarm. Straining while glancing around, her heart thumped in panic. What the hell was happening?

Someone announced a pod of orca whales was spotted ahead. She stared to see them despite the glaring sunlight and exclaimed, along with many others, while lifting her hand to point, and yelped when she saw a huge, tall, black, very distinct fin poking through the surface of the water.

Then another one broke the water, but it was a much smaller fin. She grinned and squealed as she stood up on her tippy toes, trying to get the best picture she could. Nothing could exceed the sight and reality of watching them in their natural habitat and glory.

They soon swam out of sight and the ferry started its engines to move forward again. It was something so spectacular to Josefina, she was sure it would survive in her heart for the rest of her life. She'd seen whales in nature, real life orcas.

Back at the campsite, Caleb was enjoying the evening when, right before dinner, a little kid kept coming into their campsite and talking to him. She was grinning when the little boy wanted nothing to do with her and talked only with Caleb. The family across the way noticed he was gone as they'd been trying to set their tent up. The father crossed over and grabbed the little boy's hand and they started to talk.

"I work at Microsoft. Getting out just to enjoy a little hiking and bird watching. What about you?" the father asked them. "This little guy, however, always tries to go exploring the moment we turn our backs."

Caleb stretched his legs out. "He was pretty intrigued by my cowboy boots."

The guy looked down. "Oh, yeah, he would be. Loves horses right now. You like to ride?"

"Not much. I work at a ranch in eastern Washington."

"Really?" the guy's interest was obviously piqued. Caleb glanced at Josefina and she suppressed a giggle. She could tell Caleb was confused as to why the guy was so interested in him. His job, from his point of view, was nothing special or extraordinary, and low paying as well. Not like working for freaking Microsoft or living in Bellevue. Even she knew what that meant: money. Real money, the kind they couldn't even imagine.

"Really."

"What's that like?"

"Lots of lifting and operating machinery and animal care."

"Wow." Then off he went with a litany questions for Caleb, who shifted, growing increasingly uncomfortable at all the attention. She stifled another laugh. He didn't get the guy's interest in him. Nor did he particularly like it. She knew it made him feel less than the obviously suburban middle-class man with his designer shoes, clothes, and a vehicle that exceeded the cost of their rent for several years.

The guy's wife eventually joined them, and it took a while longer before they wandered back to their own tent. Josefina had to muffle her giggles and smirks but finally let loose and expressed her amusement. The sun was setting, and her stomach rumbled, getting ready for Caleb's next camp cooking endeavor. He glanced at her and squinted with a frown at her incessant laughter. She couldn't help it, so she walked over and nudged his legs apart. She just sat in his lap and kissed his mouth as he scowled his annoyance. As usual, that did the trick and she coaxed a small smile out of him.

"I'm not a circus show, you know."

"Well, apparently they thought so. They never met anyone who purposely wears a cowboy hat all the time," she said, lifting her eyebrows up. He swept the hat off and flipped it to the ground.

"Yeah, I gathered that, and may I thank you, Ms. Ruiz?"

She tugged on his hair and in a more serious tone asked, "Hey, really, why are you so annoyed?"

His mouth twitched. "I don't know. Guess I'm not so used to feeling 'different' and… and all I could think of was…"

She kissed the side of his frown. "Was what? How pretentious they sounded?"

He rubbed her butt through the jeans she wore. "No. Not at all. I just thought that's the kind of guy you should have. Someone who could give you all of that. And much more. I don't even know what life in fucking Bellevue would be like. Cultural opportunity, whatever that shit is, isn't readily available where we live. I don't even know how much I don't know, but judging by this little interaction, it's got to be a whole damn world full of new stuff. I don't belong here, on this side of the mountains, and I don't even completely understand why. But I do know that is why you deserve so much better."

She frowned. "What are you talking about? I'm from the same place you are. I'm like you are. I'm no better than you. I'm not like them either. So why would you say that?"

He hugged her and replied, "I just know how special you are and when I'm reminded that I'm not enough for you, it's irritating."

She slid to her feet and put her hand out. "Let's eat dinner and forget the God-awful Smiths from Bellevue, okay?"

He nodded. And they did, but Josefina had a sneaking suspicion that something about the Smiths from Bellevue made a big impression on Caleb.

MEALS WERE EATEN outside and mostly prepared by Caleb. He was by far the expert. It was easy food to prepare, mostly just chili or beans and burgers and hot dogs. She tried to throw a few apples in here and there and even cut up a watermelon in her longing to eat something that was not prepackaged. He rolled his eyes but dutifully ate some of it. She gathered mementos of the sea life remnants she saw when she walked along the salty beach.

They rode their bikes up the hilly cove road, reaching the pinnacle at the top where they beheld an unobstructed view of the San Juan Islands and the Olympic Mountains as well as the backside of Anacortes. It was breathtaking to see where the water hit the horizon before disappearing and joining the open ocean.

She watched huge cargo ships slipping away as if they were falling off the edge of the earth. It intrigued her how the boats seemed to disappear when in reality, they sailed or motored off to other places of commerce. It seemed so exotic to her. The sheer vastness of the water intrigued her, but also freaked her out too.

They spent one day in town exploring the marina and shops but the thing that stuck out most to Josefina's happened at the main grocery store when they ran in for some milk and cheese. She noticed Caleb grabbing a half case of beer but didn't comment, and was surprised when he set it down on the conveyor belt to pay for it. She hoped it didn't turn into a problem. She'd have no idea how to handle that.

ON THE LAST DAY, Caleb decided to test himself with a case of beer. He didn't consult Josefina, but chose to indulge in the alcohol for the first time since the day he promised to quit. It had gone fairly smoothly and therefore, he wondered if he were truly an alcoholic. He'd always been prone to drink a lot and often. He had already realized some of the benefits of not drinking. But being addicted to alcohol? He wasn't so sure he was.

Besides, drinking this time felt different. He wasn't escaping anything. He wasn't bored. He wasn't trying to cause any trouble. He wasn't miserable or surly, drinking to feel better. No. He was just the opposite, totally relaxed. It was a beautiful day and the sun was high and bright. The air smelled clean and pleasant and he felt at peace. Happy. So, he drank a few beers to enjoy it.

By evening, he had a nice buzz going, and it warmed up his brain. Josefina took off on her bike to ride along the water line. She loved it so much. He enjoyed their trip, sure, but mostly because of her. She made him much more aware by saying how much she liked the views, weather, and ambience of the area.

Sunset covered the land in sinking, golden sunlight and a

white, dusky sky. He walked the rocky coastline she adored. Then he saw where she was, a petite, tiny figure, sitting on the edge of the water, watching the waves pound in. Sometimes the Sound was calm and serene, like a lake, and at others, it could be robust and choppy like the open ocean. The golden sky turned the islands across the way into no more than black lines of silhouettes and Josefina herself became shadowy.

He sat down next to her, his breath catching when he saw how lovely she looked while staring at the water. She was a haunting beauty with long, dark hair and a clear, perfect face. She had a coat and blanket tucked over her shoulders, finding the place far colder than he did, which only illustrated how unfamiliar with it she was.

A soft breeze accompanied him when he plopped down next to her. She was startled at his presence. He cringed, realizing he was a bull in a china shop next to her. She was a soft, subtle, quiet individual who didn't raise any attention to herself in most places where he was. She didn't act obnoxious or loud or boisterous. And here he was, usually right on the verge of doing that. His uncouth manner had to irritate her no end. He tried to rein it in. Especially, right then after he'd indulged in way too many beers.

"What're you doing?"

"Enjoying the sunset," she said softly, pushing back a hair that sprang over her face.

"Wanna share some of that blanket? Kinda nippy down here." The wind at the camp was impeded by the density of trees that acted like a wall against the cold wind and sunlight. She gave him half of the blanket and he tucked himself in closer to her, wrapping his arm around her shoulders. She didn't stiffen or pull away like she might have done once before. Back then, she struggled getting used to him. He understood that and tried to lessen her unease in any way he could. The signals he received might have needed some adjustment or change, and he wasn't always sure what to do. He spent a lot of time on his toes, uncomfortably clear he was doing something wrong, but failing to identify what it was.

She sighed as she leaned her head on his shoulder. His heart expanded with warmth and the thought of how much he loved to have her so close. Like no one else he'd ever been around. He adored her. Worshipped her. He couldn't even find the words to describe his feelings for her. She was so much more woman than he was man. Truly the finest, highest quality person he'd ever known. So smart, so funny, so hardworking, so everything he could ever want.

Well, he sure as shit wasn't everything *she* could ever want.

He, however, accepted her head on his shoulder and pulled her closer to the side of his body. "It's pretty, huh?" he said, staring out over the water she seemed to love so much. He didn't find the salt or anything else particularly exciting. Perhaps the shells were pretty. He understood why people collected them, but he'd prefer a river with fresh water any day over the Sound.

But if she liked it, he'd be right there with bells and whistles on.

She tilted her head up his way, and sniffed, wrinkling her nose. "Enjoy a few beers while I was gone, honey?"

His heart swelled at the casual endearment coming from her. And the reserve that said she cared. He knew she hated his previous life and reputation, much of which was done under the influence of beer. Lots of beer. He had flirted with being a drunk and now he counted himself lucky that his twenties hadn't created that as a consequence.

Judging from his little experiment here, he felt sure it hadn't. He enjoyed the way he felt right then, but he didn't feel panicked about it. And if Josefina asked him to never do that again, he would have consented. He could choose not to drink. He could live with that choice.

"I did. Is that… does that bother you?"

"You have to be yourself too, not just what you think I want."

If there were more to her message, his fuzzy thoughts failed to hear it. He leaned in and nuzzled her neck, unable to stop himself as he watched her gazing at the sky and landscape. She looked like a poem or something more profound. He just didn't have the words or the creative means to portray what he saw in her. Settling for the ordinary and obvious, he groped her.

She leaned into his mouth and sighed as she tilted her chin up to let him touch her. His hand left her waist and cupped her breast, hidden by the blanket and she sighed softly when his mouth worked its way to hers. He shifted so he could deepen the kiss and she had to wrap her hands around his shoulders to hold herself up.

Darkness descended over where they sat. There was not a soul nearby for as far as he could see with a quick scan around. She started laughing and pushed him back. "Not here, Caleb."

"Okay." he said, still kissing her. She didn't stop him when he insisted on kissing her again until she groaned. Combing her hands through his hair, her mouth opened to speak again.

He grabbed her hand and said, "If not here, then let's go someplace where we can." He dragged her up from the sand and she laughingly followed his quick, clipped pace. Through the brush beside the road and then up the hill to their camp they fled until he all but threw them into the tent. They fell onto the sleeping bags together as she giggled and laughed at his eagerness and passion. Thank goodness for the air mattress which broke their fall.

They both enjoyed the deep, long kisses and groping. He pulled off her clothes and she did his. They groaned and moaned softly, enjoying each other's bodies. Their clutching and touching grew more earnest. He held her naked body and enveloped her in his arms as his head spun in a wonderful alcoholic buzz which freed him and enhanced his experience with her. But there was something else, something more. What was it? His heart was as full and ready to burst with joy as the rest of his more engaged body parts. He stopped for a moment, cradling her face in his hands, while staring down into her eyes, and stopped her frantic movements in response to him.

Startled, she glanced up at him. Her eyes were liquid chocolate that shone so luminous in the shadowy tent. He closed his eyes for a long moment as his feelings grew more intense, deep, heated, and the passion overtook him. He never experienced a moment like it. Alcohol-induced? Perhaps, but he'd spent years while being drunk and never once felt this way.

There were so many emotions inside him for her, every inch of her: her body, her face, and her hair as well as all of the details that comprised her. He liked her smile and quick wit and the way she stuck her tongue in her cheek when she didn't want to say something to him. Or rolled her eyes when he teased her. And the way his heart lifted at just seeing her wave hello to him. It was her. Every part of her, from the inside to the outside, and he'd never experienced anything like it before, not for any other person. His heart swelled with so much affection toward her, he feared he might tip over, since it was too much to quantify. What was it?

Love.

What else could it be? What else could arouse those feelings? But the flat words were too weak and inferior to describe *this*. All that he felt for Josefina. She was in his arms and he had her pinned down as he leaned forward. His warm lips touched hers in a soft, long, forever kiss that was tender and gentle and deep and passionate. His clumsy groping and hasty pace just a few moments ago were abandoned.

When they broke apart, he rested his forehead on hers. Her hand felt soft and cool when it came up to touch the side of his face. His heart accelerated at her touch. Never had he experienced any gentleness from anyone. No one considered him worthy or was even interested in it, but as it turned out, he craved it, needed it, and maybe he even deserved it. His mother never offered it, and Chuck Hayes couldn't even hug him, while Lynnie and he didn't have that kind of relationship. His sister was nice to him, sure, but she couldn't provide this kind of tenderness for him.

"You okay?" her soft voice whispered in his ear. He nodded, lifting his face until it hovered above hers.

"I was such an ass; for years I was. I did things, really bad and careless things. I said things to people that were mean and hurtful just because I could. And figured it would earn me a laugh from other creeps. Because I was bored. But really because I was just mean."

She obviously was shocked at hearing his confession. Her gaze wavered. "Caleb?"

"You're the first person to ever ask me if I'm okay. I mean, like *really* okay. You know? No one ever asked me before. Maybe… maybe if someone had even once asked me that, I wouldn't have grown up to be so mean, lazy, useless, ignorant and—"

"Caleb, stop. You're not that way, not at all. I wouldn't be here if you were."

"Now, maybe, but only in the last few months. You wouldn't have been here before then."

"Oh…"

"I'm not a great person. Not even close to it. Not like you."

"Stop." She pushed her fingers on his lips. "You're not useless. You're not a victim of your former reputation and if you were, can't you admit you aren't now?"

"I'm not, but only because of you."

She let out a small, soft laugh. "Oh, Caleb, no one can change another person that much. Stop it. Stop giving me credit for your achievement. I see it. I see you. Why can't you?"

He leaned down, burying his head between her naked breasts and breathed in the scent of her skin deeply, letting it fill his nostrils. Holding her waist in his hands, he flipped his head up and started kissing her forehead before dropping down to her mouth. "I can't."

She put her hands on his chin and tried to pull him up towards her. "You can't now, but I think you can try."

"You give me hope that I can be better. That my life can be better, more than I ever knew. You make me feel like I've touched the sun and I never knew I wanted to so badly before."

Her breath caught, and he was shocked to see tears falling from her eyes. Startled, he lifted a thumb and brushed them away. "Why are you crying?"

"Because of what you said… it was so beautiful. No one's ever felt that way about me before. I've never been special to anyone, anywhere. And, Caleb, you're special too. You aren't special because of me."

He shrugged and said, "I love you, Josefina." He whispered it softly and his mouth touched her cheek, then her eyelid and landed softly on her mouth. Shifting his body, her legs opened to him, as well as her mouth and arms. He plunged inside her as far as nature and the laws of attraction would allow. He finally understood that sex was about love. There was nothing comparable between making love and getting laid. He wanted it to last, to be long and deep, slow and profound. His body tried to show her what his heart felt.

Her cries were muffled only by his mouth as she clung to him passionately. He held her, and they curled up together, alone against the world but also together in a way he never knew was possible. Worn out by the buzz, he was flooded and overwhelmed by all the feelings he never tapped into before. He held her closer, his arms wrapping around her and tugging her back even more. His mouth touched the top of her head in a soft kiss. Sleep flirted with both of them.

"Josie?" he said moments later, feeling groggy, tired and hung over.

"Hmm?"

"If six months from now, you're still with me, you have to… well, you can't be. You can't end up with me. I can't be in your story. And I won't be, but I won't let you go because I'm selfish and always have been, so please don't wind up with me."

His arms tightened around her before he fell into an exhausted sleep. He was unclear how she responded or if she even did and he hoped she wouldn't remember it the next day. But in his drunkenness and stupor, he needed to make sure she understood the real truth.

CHAPTER 16

*C*ALEB HAD A KILLER headache the next morning when they got up and started taking down the tent. Josefina had to press her lips together to hide her mirth. He hadn't touched the beer he bought until yesterday afternoon and then he plowed through a lot of it. It shocked her to smell it so strongly on his breath when he came and found her. But it also drew a surprising eloquence out of him instead of sloppiness and drunken ramblings. It made him say things she couldn't quite find a way to process yet. Every word he said was tender and deep and absolutely a compliment to her.

He thought the opposite about himself. She had no idea his self-loathing ran so deep. He hinted at it before, but she never understood the full extent of it or the lack of support in his life.

Was it any wonder Caleb Hayes acted the way he did for so many years? And what greater compliment to her than that he was so desperately trying to change because of her? She was starting to see the strength of his character that had been buried for so long start to shine through.

Before he dropped off into a drugged stupor, he uttered a plea that gave her pause. He most likely didn't remember anything he said. He certainly couldn't remember everything, or could he? Did he mean any of it? She could not say for sure.

They had the truck and camping gear loaded up and tightly strapped down. Caleb leaned on the tailgate. "So, are we ready to head home?"

"Of course. But I do hate to leave. I love it here. I hope to come back again."

His mouth twitched. Wearing a hoodie, he pretended to rub his arms as if he were cold. "I had a feeling you were going to say that. Why would you wanna come back to this ice box?"

She grinned at his sarcasm and appreciated it as much as anything else. He was so easy to get along with, and he had no trouble making her smile. The casual banter they engaged in made the most ordinary things more fun. Up until then, her entire life was nothing but ordinary. However, with him, it became much less so.

THE RIDE back to River's End was almost traffic-free and Caleb felt as if he could breathe again after returning to an area where the sheer volume of the land far outweighed the population. People were not Caleb's primary interest. Land and space were. But Josefina liked it.

Probably because she liked people more than he did. When he pulled up to her place, he got out and lifted her luggage out, bringing it around to her front door and waiting until she unlocked the door and set it inside.

He tapped his foot, feeling uncharacteristically awkward. All of this, and everything, really, that involved Josefina, moved him way out of his comfort zone, yet he cherished all the time he spent with her. He was the aggressor, always trying to spend more time with her and embracing all the changes that brought.

But now they were, once again, different. A couple. They were having sex now. And they shared an intimidate vacation together when he'd never experienced an intimate relationship with anyone.

Caleb would have laid down his life for any number of his friends and certainly for Jordan, and now Pedro and Lynnie and Ian.

But letting anyone know anything personal or intimate about him? He had always held tight to his innermost thoughts and feelings and never let anyone see his vulnerabilities. Everything changed with Josefina. He felt raw inside. And weird. Like he would blush at knowing she saw him so clearly. He repressed the urge to run from her.

But the urge to turn around and run away from her because she *did know* those personal things about him, and because she knew how to draw them out of him, never left him. He didn't know how to act now with someone who might be for real, with warts and weaknesses and all.

Before it never mattered. His perpetual insistence on spewing arrogance and bullshit blocked anyone from ever grasping what he might be feeling or thinking about anything. But the worst part was he doubted that anything he thought was worth knowing.

Yet, this smart, articulate, witty, clever, interesting, funny, beautiful woman, inside and outside, seemed to find spending time with him rewarding.

He now grasped all the things he wasn't, and he knew deep down she should not be with him. She should be with someone better. Not him. He didn't have anything to offer except for being kinda pretty on the outside.

Not exactly the foundation for a life partner.

And yet, after they were inseparable for a few days, he hated to leave her. He only wanted to be with her. And stare at her. Or talk to her. Or listen to her. He was in awe of this connection they shared. He rejected Shane when he suddenly changed and became like this for his wife, Allison. Or Jordan after he began spending all his time with Pedro. Or Ian, freaking leaving his entire life to live with Lynnie in the damn city. He realized, just maybe, if Josefina asked him, he could possibly consider doing the same thing. He just hoped she never asked him.

But now he didn't want to leave her, which was completely asinine. Having lived alone for his entire life, with his family for company, he never felt needy for anything or anyone.

He felt needy for her now.

She was busily setting her stuff down, glancing at her messages before she turned his way. "Um... well, I guess I should go and get that gear all unpacked. We've both gotta work tomorrow, so..."

She stepped towards him and put her hands at his waist, pulling him closer to her. "I had an amazing vacation with you, Caleb."

He sighed and wrapped her up in his arms, his hands kneading her spine. "Yeah? I did with you too."

There were so many more words he wanted to say than those innocuous ones. A deep, panicky need urged him to say so much more. But she kissed him and let him go. Casually. Easily. Sure, why not? No big deal.

He had to force himself to withdraw from her. He liked her. Too much. There was no way she could develop the same kind of clinging hunger he had for her. He doubted she'd ever feel the same intense passion he did. And that was no way to live, always wanting her to want him.

A sense of hollowness followed him back to his sister's house that was deep and pronounced. *No. Damn it.* He smacked the wheel when he realized the truth of the situation now. He loved her. He was in love with her in so many ways that he didn't even know existed until he met her. He felt an irrepressible, gnawing need to constantly be with her, and he thought about her, always longing for the next time to be with her.

It was difficult for him to suddenly be *that guy*. The guy he always made fun of, and never thought he would be like: a responsible, working, non-drinking, serious guy.

SIX MONTHS CAN BE a long time or feel like the blink of an eye. For the first time in his life, Caleb found it interminable. For once, he worried about the passage of time because it mattered. It mattered to him every day now, because he had a chance to see Josie. He longed to see her smile and hear her complaints about someone she just met or something she saw on the news. She was well read and always up on current events and Caleb learned more in the time he spent with her than he ever learned in school.

He didn't always agree with her, however, and surprised when he found himself arguing with her. They discussed politics and stuff he'd never given thirty seconds of thought to before, yet when she got going, which was often, something would tweak his interest and he had to ask questions. After pointing out the differences in how he saw it or calling her attention to the outright flaws in her logic, they had some heated debates.

But being able to articulate his thoughts long enough to *have* heated debates was exciting and new. He didn't even know he had opinions; and agree or disagree, she never ceased to inspire him to think. He had to articulate the facts and back up his arguments because she could easily outrank him with her own ideas. Now he was gaining on her. Rarely could he win, but he did get her to acknowledge some of his crucial points at times.

No one ever told him or could have convinced him how hot debating could be. Watching someone else disagree with him provoked such hot, sensuous images and worked like no foreplay he'd experienced ever before. It was a new dynamic for him. He was as attracted to the person as he was to her looks.

He also never failed to realize with each passing day and continued exposure in knowing Josefina better than anyone else, she was destined for far more than he could ever offer. She deserved someone who would amount to more than he would.

He remembered his drunken stupor and telling Josefina that if she managed to stay with him for six months, she had to let him go. She had to leave him.

But he saw no indication she would dump him. It puzzled him to the point that he often found himself evaluating her in silence. He was usually confused over why she was there with him, and talking or laughing, lounging on the couch or falling asleep beside him in bed.

Why would she continue this thing with him? She was everything he could ever want or ask for. But unfortunately, he wasn't what she deserved.

He now understood why Pedro was right; he wasn't good enough for Josefina. He was not at all the best guy she could end up with. Sure, she was dating him exclusively and seemed to like and care about him, but did she love him? He wanted her love as much as he wanted her, but he dreaded hearing the words come out of her mouth.

He could never leave her if she said those words. But

leaving her was the only possible outcome. The problem was: he wasn't the same guy he was when they first met, and to do what he needed to do, he had to be that guy again.

CALEB WASN'T LIKE anything she ever expected but somehow, it all worked out and in ways she couldn't have predicted when he first introduced himself to her. Their vacation together solidified something between them. Surprisingly, they were very much alike. Most of the time, Caleb avoided alcoholic beverages and the difference in him was drastic.

They spent most of their weekends together along with several nights a week.

He made an arrangement with his sister; he asked for six months to get the old family land into something livable again. Plus, he even began to pay them rent. Pedro begrudgingly admitted Caleb had been doing all of his work and was even asking for extra.

Soon after he brought in an old trailer he bought from the Rydells, Caleb set it up on the family plot.

"It's not much, I know, but remember, it's only temporary and it's all mine," he told her as if to keep her from expecting too much.

Josefina drove up to the Gunderson Hills and stopped where the gravel ended. The trailer was set up on its stabilizers. The area around it was neat, clean, leveled and cleared. He opened the door at her knock and when he saw her, he smiled sheepishly.

"Hey." His expression seemed as nervous as a teenaged boy asking a girl to the prom. "So... another trailer..."

She smiled right back. "Yes, but at least it's not at your sister's house."

He nodded. "No, it's not."

She walked in. It was older, but he must have just finished cleaning it, if the smell of vinegar were any indication. "You have your own residence now, Caleb. You have every right to take pride in that. And look at what you did to this place. It's nice up here."

And it was. He cleared out all the garbage and rubble from the old buildings and scrapped the metal car and tractor pieces into piles. Everything was either burned or hauled to the dump, and at considerable expense. He re-routed the irrigation lines and planted grass, hauling in boulders and rocks to surround it. His reason, he explained, was that if a fire ever came through there again, he'd have established a wide enough, significant green belt and rock barrier around it for a fire break.

She walked up to him and grabbed his face in her hands. "This is wonderful. You thought of everything."

He tilted his head.

"I'm so proud of you."

He'd covered her hands with his own. "I live to hear that now."

Naturally, she believed him. And more than that, she *was* proud of him.

CHAPTER 17

*T*IME FLOATED BY IN a haze that Josefina could never have guessed she'd enjoy. Tinted in a rosy glow, she fell victim to all she hated the most: cheesy first dates and budding attitudes. They held hands and cuddled, spending all their spare time together, and Josefina even saved her errands, so they could go running all over town and do them together. She often cringed at her own clinginess since she'd always been independent until now. He came to her place most weeknights and she usually went to his trailer on the weekends. Fridays were the one day of the week they rarely got together because she often had dinner with her dad and whichever sisters were available. Sometimes, Caleb joined them; sometimes, he didn't.

When Josefina had to work late on Friday, she skipped the family dinner and grabbed some take-out before driving to Caleb's. It wouldn't be that shocking to him. Anytime she worked late, she usually grabbed food and came to him.

She spent a lot of time out there recently after never traveling up the roadway to River's End. She still preferred the crowded valley in Brewster. The dusty, barren, isolated fields and hills against the tree-topped mountains of Gunderson Hills were way out there for her taste, but River's End was growing on her.

It was dark before she pulled into Caleb's driveway. She'd been called in by a local CPS case worker to help with two kids who were being taken away from their abusive dad and stepmother. Neither kid could say more than "hello" in English. She hated cases like that. It was impossible for her not to get emotionally involved after hearing what the kids said and seeing the emotions, fear, and confusion in their expressions.

Already down from her depressing day, she was relieved to be free when her headlights swept over Caleb's trailer. She jumped out of the car with her now cold take-out. But as her stomach rumbled, she thought at least it was some kind of dinner.

She walked in without knocking. Caleb recently added a modest multipurpose outbuilding, which he was often found tinkering in. He told her to come and go as she pleased without knocking or asking. Whatever was his, she was welcome to use as her own.

Walking in, she didn't feel odd because it was dark. She set her bags down and clicked the small light on over her head, instantly brightening the entire living area. There was a basic kitchenette in the back, where the couch and a two-seat table were. The interior was dark mauve and burgundy, and Caleb mentioned once that it used to belong to Erin Rydell. Now, Erin owned the entire ranch. They sold the old trailer to him for a grand or so and it provided Caleb with the necessary shelter, privacy, and independence he preferred.

She stopped dead when she realized the divider that separated the bedroom from the living area was shut. It was a white, accordion door made only of fabric, so noises and lights were not muted, although there were some sight limitations. She thought it odd he'd close it since he never had before. She stepped up to it and jerked the accordion door open.

Two forms moved. They fucking moved. She blinked, her hand still resting on the edge of the door. What? Her brain couldn't compute what she was seeing, but she was seeing it all the same.

Caleb. In. Bed. With another woman. It could not have been more of a cliché. There he was, lying with a strange woman in his arms, and they were both naked. The covers were all twisted around them. Legs and upper limbs were ensnared, and their torsos gleamed with sweat. She saw white breasts and legs and skinny hips and blond hair.

Standing there, she wondered if she were in shock. Perhaps. She could not decide what to do. Or where to go. She closed her eyes and swallowed.

No!

Caleb wouldn't—No.

He made such a convincing case of how much he cared about her. Repeating that she was too good for him. He wouldn't cheat. She was the woman he wanted most of all. But there he was with a naked, blond woman in bed beside him. Sleeping. Nude. It was only ten o'clock. Sure, maybe he didn't expect her to come over tonight and it was much later than she planned to, but no.

It didn't make sense.

But there he was.

She let out a gasp and jerked the stupid, cotton fabric door further open. It was enough to awaken him, and he lay still for a moment. She was that in tune to the man, and she knew he was aware it was Josefina standing there. He barely lifted his head up, his neck straining.

Their gazes met and locked. He didn't jump up to deny

anything or offer lame explanations. He didn't start apologizing either. Very slowly, he let his head fall back to the pillow and... and that was it.

His chest expanded as if he were releasing a long sigh, but he just lay there.

Blinking back the tears that sprang to her eyes and slid freely down her cheeks, Josefina always thought if she encountered a situation like this, she'd know what to say and do. She would never just accept it quietly or slink away. But now that it happened, nothing came to mind. Her shock and confusion were that great. God. The blinding hurt in her chest was so heavy and suffocating, he injured her in ways she couldn't have imagined.

She backed up a step. And then took another. And another, falling down when she stepped off the small three stairs that led up to the tiny bedroom. Sprawling flat on her butt, she cried out before scrambling to her feet.

No. No, she couldn't see Caleb ever again. She could not bear to see his lying, cheating face or his naked body coming towards her. Clambering to her feet, she all but sprinted out of there, racing to her car and taking off. When her headlights beamed over the trailer, she saw nothing stirring. He didn't even try to come out and catch her. Or apologize. Or explain himself. How could that be?

How could it hurt her so much?

But it did. Her hands started to shake, and her chest was heaving as pitiful sobs escaped her mouth and tears fell from her eyes. She didn't know how much she cared for him until then. She didn't realize how gradually and blindly she'd come to trust him and believe in him.

Perhaps the most shocking revelation in that moment, the worst moment of her life, and certainly the worst moment to have to realize it, she had to admit that she'd fallen in love with him.

Admitting that, an aching moan from a broken heart escaped her lips.

She knew all along, didn't she? The moment when, at Pedro's wedding, he walked up to her all drunk and smelling of booze and his eyes fell onto her breasts. She recalled how he sneered, and the lazy, insulting way he approached her.

She saw him very clearly in that moment. That unforgettable scene was testimony to his true character. How could she have forgotten it so quickly? How could she ignore what she *knew* to be true? How did she manage to forget that introduction? How did she fail to expect this very scenario happening only months later?

Of course, Caleb Hayes did that. She was the fool. Falling for his lies and pickup lines and believing what? That he changed? After being threatened with joblessness as well as homelessness, his motivation was not so noble, nor his claim that he desired to change whom and what he seemed to be.

That he lasted as long as he did might have been the only surprise.

That didn't affect the sense of drowning that afflicted her chest, nor did it muffle the heart-wrenching cries that escaped her mouth or the tears that fell from her eyes. Oh, God. Pulling into her own place, she walked in, dragging herself inside and sobbing ceaselessly. She fell onto her couch and cried even harder. So hard, she started to hack and cough.

She was tired of living the oldest story in the book. The humiliation she felt at realizing their relationship was so stereotypical was harder than recognizing how right she was about Caleb all along. From the very beginning.

Her shaking legs collapsed, and she had to move. She had to get out of here. She would do something big to make herself feel better. But first... *Crap!* There was a knock at the door before her brother's voice said, "Josie? Open up."

Annoyed, she flung the door open. "How did you know?"

"Caleb called Jordan and said you were upset."

He called to get backup for her—why? To comfort her about his cheating? Huh. Weird. Strange.

He took one look at her and grabbed her in a hug. "What happened?"

"Caleb—"

"Caleb what? What did he do to you? Shit. Are you pregnant? Did he run?"

"No. I'm not pregnant. No... he... he cheated." She cringed. As if that should be a surprise about Caleb Hayes. She was the fool. Thinking she was so damn important, he'd change his ways and stay faithful to her.

"Ah, damn, Josie. How do you know that?"

"Caught him in bed with a blond. A fucking blond."

Pedro rubbed her back and she started to cry against his shoulder. "Go ahead and say it, I know I'm a fool. Not a shock anymore. It's Caleb. It's more surprising that it didn't happen sooner. I just thought, no, *I believed*, he was really changing." She turned her head into his shoulder. "Go ahead and tell me what a fool I am. He never changed. You were right."

He rubbed a hand over her shoulder. "No. I was fooled by him too. I believed he wanted to improve. I thought, no, I believed him too. And you know I wasn't as vulnerable or easily hoodwinked by him as you were. I had nothing to gain by trusting him. I've always been slightly wary of him because of Jordan's history with him. It wasn't okay with me when he started dating you. But I started to trust him, so yeah, I fell for it, too."

Another knock sounded on her door. She rubbed her eyes as she turned away. Jordan came in. "What did he do?" Jordan's voice sounded cold and robotic.

"I thought you weren't coming."

"I realized it was Caleb and he'd done something, so I had to," Jordan answered Pedro. "What did he do to you?"

"He cheated." She took in a shuddering breath and faced Jordan. "Had a girl in bed with him when I stopped by his trailer tonight."

Jordan nodded, and his gaze held hers. He replied, "I believed the self-improvement act, too. I'm so sorry, Josie."

He turned and disappeared into the night and she stared after him. Pedro looked as concerned about Jordan as he did about her.

"Siblings shouldn't date other siblings. It's too confusing."

She gripped Pedro's arm. "I never set out to do that."

He scoffed. "Believe me, I know."

"What is he going to do?"

"I think the ultimatum he stated at the wedding is about to go into effect."

She sniffled, staring at the partially opened door. She wished his contempt for Caleb and defense of her honor mattered. But everything inside her hurt and nothing mattered to her.

"What the fuck is wrong with you?"

Caleb was out in his newly finished, prefabricated pole building. He used it as a shop and garage and workspace, and he glanced up at hearing the voice. The workbench fluorescent light flickered, and he dropped his boot on the cement floor. "Lots is wrong with me."

"Why? Why did you do it?"

He sighed. It was time to face the music. "You know why, Jordan. Because that's who I am. I don't mean to be such a fuck-up. I'm always sorry, but there's no changing it, is there? Not when it's who I really am. I'm just a fuck-up."

"You haven't been for a long time."

"Only because I haven't been drinking."

"You drank occasionally." Flat-toned, Jordan stepped closer. Caleb refused to turn or look at him. He kept staring at the fitting in his hands and working. He was currently installing a sprinkler system around the living area.

"I did. I'm not fully sober. I just drink a lot less than I used to."

"So, you got drunk and fucked some blond?"

Caleb's leg jiggled, and his knee bobbed up and down. Perhaps it was his nerves, or regrets, or because he'd hurt Josefina so much. He closed his eyes and tried to ignore the image of Josefina staring at him. She got so quiet. That bothered him more than if she just vocalized how she felt. It was so unlike her to be quiet or docile, and that scared him. When she tripped and scurried away from the confrontation, he was surprised. He'd never known her to be like that.

He did that to her.

"You know I didn't mean to."

"Who is she?"

"A woman at the bar I met tonight."

"You didn't even know her?"

"No."

"Did you know Josefina was coming tonight?"

"Doesn't matter."

"That's all you got to say?"

He flipped a glance at Jordan and got angry. "What do you want me to say? Make up some lame excuses? I can't. I know that. I'll apologize to her but you and I both know it won't do any good. She deserves an apology, okay? But not tonight. I'll go see her in a few days."

Jordan was silent and then he said, "That's it? After all you did just to be with her and tried to change and all that, that's it? This is it?"

"Guess so. Do you see her ever forgiving me?"

"No."

"Neither do I. But I'll apologize anyway."

Hands in fists, Jordan said in a scathing tone, "You're such a bastard."

"Yup."

He didn't turn around. Jordan stood there, wanting more out of him but Caleb had nothing more to say to him.

Jordan left, and Caleb's shoulders fell forward as he lay his head down. He shut his eyes and a wave of bitter regret washed over him. It hurt more than he could handle.

He shut down his brain. He was drinking tonight, and his head was pounding. His stomach was ready to regurgitate acid. Frustrated, he shoved the project he was working on away.

Then he stared at the workbench and used his arm to swipe it across the entire table top, clearing all the tools and sandpaper, boxes of nails and screws and letting everything crash and fall into a jumbled mess. Gripping the edge of the table with his fists, he breathed heavily.

He hurt the only person he'd ever really loved. He did the one thing she could never forgive him for. He didn't dare hope she would either. He knew she should not. Flipping around, Caleb walked away.

What was left now? A trailer? More trailer trash living on the hill? A job he didn't cherish but since he had no other prospects or choices, he felt obligated to it? No other prospects or choices. Why did he think he could ever change that?

Fuck change. Things just didn't change for guys like him.

CHAPTER 18

CALEB KNOCKED TIMIDLY ON Josefina's front door. Two days wasn't enough, he knew that. She would still be raw and hurting and angry. Filled with rage. Ready to cut his junk off and he deserved it, no doubt. But still, he had to try. He had to offer up a lame, sad, and totally worthless apology.

He was surprised when she answered the door. He stared at her and his heart pounded in his chest. She looked tired and sad. Her eyes were puffy and red from crying. His throat felt dry. He caused all the physical pain and symptoms he saw in her now.

"What do you want?" she asked in a hollow tone.

"To talk to you," he answered softly. She shrugged as she stepped back. He was astonished when she so calmly allowed him inside. He walked over to the couch and sunk down into it. He was dressed in worn jeans and a dark hoodie. He kept his hands in the front pocket and stared downwards. "I'm really sorry, Josie."

He didn't know what else to say. He wasn't ready to give her a long, drawn-out, horrifying description of what he'd done. Apologize for what she found? She knew what she found. She was there for God's sake. There was very little he could do now to save the situation. He knew that clearly.

"You're sorry?" she snapped steamily.

He kept his gaze down. "I'm sorry. Maybe I always intended to do it. I don't know. It's what I used to be. I don't want to be that guy, but it's so easy for me to fall backwards. What was hard for me was being with you and no one else. Yes, I love you. I only love you. No one else means anything to me. But I, well, I drink sometimes and do things I wouldn't normally do. You've seen me in action before. I shouldn't even attempt to excuse my behavior, but I have to try."

"I'll never forgive you," she replied, and her tone was sure and strong and passionate.

"I know," he whispered. Silence descended. "I had to come here and try. You were the best thing that ever happened to me. I wish I could undo it, or be better. I wish I could promise you that I learned from my mistake, and this wasn't worth it, if that would be enough. But I know it isn't. It couldn't be enough. I know that only too well now."

"Was she worth it?"

"No. Not even for a second. Of course not. She wasn't you. You're everything I could ever want in a life partner." He glanced at her and then looked away. "I swear to you, I've learned a lesson here. It won't happen again. Nothing compares to how bad this feels. I never wanted to hurt you. In doing so, I hurt myself the most. I want only you, Josie."

Her soft voice, surprisingly low and sounding kind, had more of an effect than all the shouting, yelling, or lecturing she could have done. He was ready and willing to listen to anything she needed to tell him. But her words were very soft, and they cut him to the quick. His knees threatened to buckle. "Your love hurts, Caleb. It hurt Jordan. It hurt your sister. And it also hurt me."

He nodded while slipping his hands from his sweatshirt and twisting them together. He lifted his gaze to hers and nodded. "I think I have a lot of my mom inside me. Her love always hurt us too. It doesn't mean I can't love, I just don't know how to do it right without hurting people I don't want to hurt. I'm sorry."

"Me too."

"That's it? You don't want to say anymore? Or yell at me? I deserve it. I'll listen to anything. Please just go ahead and say it."

"I'd just like you to leave now. I want to be alone. I'd like to get over you as soon as I can. You did enough damage already. I don't need to rehash it. I think you know what you did."

He rose up to his feet and stared down at her. Her face was turned away from him, so he had to look at her profile. He saw fresh tears on her cheeks, but when he reached out, she flinched. He let his hand drop. "I'm so sorry, Josefina."

"Please, just go."

He nodded. Tears filled his own eyes as he walked out, shutting the door quietly, firmly and forever behind him.

HE FELL to a new level of low. He was all but black-balled. It wasn't easy working with a former girlfriend's brother who always disliked you. Adding his own brother and sister's bitterness made for pretty miserable days for Caleb. Kailynn looked at him when he showed up for work on Monday and shook her head. She had a stricken look on her face. "Caleb, why? Why would you do something so idiotic?"

"I was just stupid. And drinking. I'm sorry." He spread his

hands out. "I don't know. I tend to screw up a lot. Ian plan on firing me?"

"No." She shook her head. "But I don't see how this can work between you and Pedro and I can't blame Pedro."

"I'll head out and finish the orchards. Send AJ over to deal with me. That way, Pedro doesn't have to see me."

And she did. AJ didn't say a word, but the cold, icy shoulder let him know, that yeah, he screwed up again. The anger was obviously percolating in all the rebuffs he received. But he ignored them and tried to contain his tendency toward surliness. That was so easy for him to retreat into whenever he felt threatened or weak and stupid, as he did now.

Towards evening, while hauling gear to one of the barns, Caleb was suddenly face-to-face with Pedro. Pedro stared hard at Caleb before he launched into a long litany of Spanish swear words. The rapidity of his words imbued them with a force and fury Pedro could never have achieved in English.

Caleb shook his head and started to pass Pedro when Pedro grabbed his arm. Caleb jerked away but Pedro grabbed him again. He took Caleb's arm and started to swing back his other arm. Caleb grabbed Pedro's fist before he could strike and body-slammed Pedro into the barn. They stared at each other, huffing and puffing, their chests rising and falling with adrenaline and anger. Caleb leaned into Pedro but lifted his weight off when he was sure Pedro wouldn't hit him.

"She's better off without me in the long term. You know that. You always did," said Caleb before taking a long breath and shoving Pedro one last time for good measure before he let him go. No lapse in volatility between them.

"Then why would you start this to begin with?"

"Because I'm as big of an asshole as you always said I was."

"But she didn't believe it. Why did you have to show her you were?"

"Well, she knows it now, huh? She'll believe whatever you say from now on. So, the damage is done and now we can all move on to happier pastures."

Pedro's breathing was still jagged and rough. "You're a cold son of a bitch, aren't you?"

"Yeah. I am. And you have to know your sister is so much better off without me. Knowing the truth now, you can reassure her that she dodged a mean bullet."

His heart had turned to ice. It was so uncaring, he should have just curled up and succumbed to hypothermia. Caleb would never have anyone significant in his life again. He could start drinking again now and see all the kinds of friends he attracted. Maybe some of his previous so-called friends would return, like the guys who beat his brother up. Or the ones who preferred to beat up innocent girls like Barry.

What new friends awaited him? Who might next be the woman in his life? His brother would surely side with Pedro, and even if their anger eventually cooled off, they'd never want him close to them again. The same went for Kailynn. Anyone would prefer to take Jordan's side against his because Caleb was the primary source of trouble. There was no changing his history or his future. Being a decent guy for a handful of months couldn't obliterate the three decades before that. Only now did he fully understand his primary error. At least, he finally got it.

He ignored the angry silence he received from Pedro, Jordan, Kailynn, and even Ian. He just hoped they kept their disappointment in him to themselves. There wasn't one thing they could tell him that he didn't already know by now. He knew he had to become a monster to Josefina. By ending it with a terrible finality, he knew she could survive without remembering any of the good parts. Caleb was the problem. As usual. Exactly what she should have expected.

He bowed his head.

It could drive anyone to drink.

But maybe not Caleb. And for now, not today.

JOSEFINA HAD a hard time with all the crying. She teared up, and plenty of tears had rolled down her cheeks, but she didn't sob any longer. An odd sense of calmness descended and a numbness that overtook her and reminded her of getting Novocain at the dentist's office.

She was aware of everything that was being said and done around her, but she couldn't *feel* it. She couldn't associate the events around her with her own life. She couldn't react to anything due to a perpetual numbness. It made it easier for her to work and function, which she did without missing a beat. She didn't go on a crying jag at the wrong time or sit down to eat a gallon of ice cream to alleviate her sadness. The suspended reality allowed her to float above it all.

Like a chant, she refused to let Caleb affect her. Ever again. She clung to that. She needed it and lived by it.

"You want to come over tonight?" Pedro asked her, speaking in rapid Spanish. He sounded highly strung.

"No. You don't need to babysit me."

"I just wanted you to know you're always welcome here. He isn't."

"You convinced your husband to ban his brother from your house? I doubt that. Now, perhaps, but not for the long term."

"Just watch me."

She let out a sad sigh. "You saw him today."

"Yeah, the fucking prick," he muttered.

"Did you leave him alone? Like I told you to do?"

"Yeah. I left him alone."

"Pedro…"

"Well, he couldn't understand what I said anyway."

Her lips tilted up and she imagined her small brother swearing in Spanish at the big, beefy Caleb Hayes. "How did he react?"

"Pushed me into the barn and strong-armed me. You dodged a lethal bullet. I think about it daily."

"Did he really? Did he hurt you?"

"No, he didn't. He just wanted me to leave him alone."

"And you're going to, aren't you? Please?"

"Maybe."

"Pedro, I need you to promise me. I can't handle anything more. I'm trying to put one foot in front of the other and pretend like Caleb never entered my life. But the thing is: he did. And I fell hard for him. I truly believed he was changing. Right down to the core. I saw something unique in him, but it wasn't real and never existed, at least not like I believed. It's pretty humiliating and it still hurts. So please, just stay away from him and let it die a natural death."

"I believed him too. He seemed so sincere. Jordan agreed. In fact, I think Jordan might be taking it as hard as you are."

"He thought Caleb wouldn't cheat on me?"

"He keeps repeating he never thought Caleb would do anything like that to you. He believed Caleb. Let's not do this anymore. Let's not rehash something that can't be changed and does nothing but hurt you. I'll leave the subject of Caleb alone if you will."

"I'm trying, brother."

"Again, do you want company?"

"Not tonight." She hung up and walked to her front window, glancing out. Nothing would make her feel better.

How had she done the exact thing she'd promised herself she would not do?

~

CALEB ENTERED the barn and turned to the left to go into the office where all the ranch business was generally conducted. Ian sat behind the desk and punched a keyboard, staring at the screen before him. Caleb felt itchy whenever he pictured himself doing that. He couldn't last five minutes. He stood there, quiet and waiting, and Ian had to know that Caleb stepped in, but he held a neutral face like nothing Caleb ever saw before. Finally, Ian tapped and clicked the corner screen before it disappeared. He stared at Caleb.

"You wanted to see me?"

"Yeah." Ian leaned back in his chair. "There're going to be some major changes made around here."

Caleb cringed, and his shoulders drooped. How many more changes could there be? How many more would he need to adapt to? "What now?"

"You work well with Ben, right?" Ben Rydell was the virtual heir to the entire farm, no doubt, but the guy was solid, and Caleb didn't have any attitude toward him. Ben had disappeared for a long time, and when he popped back up with some kind of drama to explain, Caleb didn't care enough to listen.

"Meaning: does Ben consider me a piece of shit who betrayed all that is decent in the world? No, he doesn't." Caleb sneered. "Besides, who is Ben to fucking judge me? Oh, I get it, the owners and the workers abide by different rules, right? I mean, Ben fucks a woman behind his wife's back on the very same night she's dying, so—"

Ian scowled. "Sit down," he tersely replied. "We're going to be expanding. We're planning to build a pretty big, covered arena that would also house a restaurant, more stables, and some conference rooms we can rent out. It'll complement the rest of the resort and we could eventually invite the local horse clubs to hold their shows and contests and exhibitions. You name it. We're looking at a huge expansion here, Caleb."

Caleb sat up straighter. This wasn't what he expected to hear from Ian. He wasn't sure if he liked it yet. What about all the alfalfa they grew? The family farm and family horses gave it a homey vibe. Now, they just wanted to keep expanding. First the resort, then rebuilding the resort, which was close to being done, and now they planned to add more buildings to it all?

Caleb often worked at the resort as the groundskeeper, doing maintenance or whatever AJ assigned him. Usually, he reported directly to AJ and rarely to Ian. It was the only thing that managed to keep them both professional and tolerant of each other.

"Kailynn's going to be in charge of it."

He sat up straighter. "The whole thing?"

"The whole thing. She's the leader. I'll continue like I have been since the fire."

"What about Jack? Isn't he coming back?"

"Yeah, he is, in a way. He's starting a horse rescue. That'll be a separate project, and he's going back to training horses again. He wants nothing more to do with the resort or the guests. He's downsizing and we're going bigger."

"What does that mean for me?"

Ian leaned back. "That's what we're discussing here. You can't work with two of my top guys. It's only you, AJ, Ben, Jordan and Pedro and now…"

"What do you want me to do?"

"I was thinking of assigning AJ and Ben to work on the new arena construction and also its maintenance. Joey's got the resort to deal with, but he also needs help now and then."

"And?"

"And I think Pedro's ready to take AJ's place as foreman on the farm and the one in charge of all the horse care. He's worked for us the longest. Since he was only eighteen. He's sharp and quick and loyal. He also—"

"Hates me."

Ian nodded and stared for a long moment at Caleb. Caleb looked away, ignoring him. Ian sighed. "I can't get a handle on you Caleb. I want to. You were working so hard and trying to be different ever since Jordan's wedding. But why did you screw up?"

His surprise at Ian's probing had him staring at his brother-in-law. Ian never asked personal questions and only in the context of how it affected Kailynn. Nothing was random with Ian. "What does that have to do with my job?"

Ian shuffled forward. "Lots, actually. Because your nemesis is my choice for foreman. What the hell am I supposed to do about that?"

"We can both be professional."

"You can. Which is funny, considering you never used to be. But I don't think Pedro can."

"Are you firing me?"

Ian shook his head. "I need more able-bodied hands, not fewer, for at least the next year with all the new construction projects we're planning. The rebuilding after the fire still isn't done. No. I need you, Caleb."

"What do you want me to do?"

He shook his head. "Can you blame Pedro? Look how you reacted to me and your sister sleeping together. You tried to beat me up. And I didn't do anything negative to your sister. You not only slept with Pedro's sister, but then you cheated on her."

He didn't answer. Why was Ian interested in all of this? Was it all work-related?

"Did you really do it?"

"Yeah. I really did."

"I thought you loved Josefina."

"I do."

"You just refuse to be faithful?"

"I guess so."

Ian shook his head. "I let your sister go a long time ago. I was worried that she needed something more than I could give her. We didn't even try to work it out. Are you doing that now?"

Caleb shook his head. "You let my sister go to college so she could fulfill her dreams. You'd have been a total prick if you hadn't let her go. Me? I'm still just a prick. I'll lay low around Pedro. He can boss me around all he wants, and I'll accept it. As long as he doesn't take a swing at me, we can get along fine. I can handle whatever he's gonna dish out. Go ahead with your restructuring and planned expansion. And please tell my sister congratulations on the new promotion."

"Okay, Caleb."

Caleb got to his feet and left.

Even his stupid damn job, the one constant in his life, the only thing that hadn't changed in a decade, even that just couldn't stay the same.

CHAPTER 19

*C*ALEB HEARD THE KNOCK and opened the trailer door. His mouth dropped open in utter surprise. *Josefina?* What the hell was she doing there?

"Can I talk to you?"

He nodded, feeling sheepish. How could he face her? He grabbed his coat and indicated that they go towards the fire pit. He couldn't take the small, cramped trailer. Not with her so close to him. She was bundled up against the cold temperature. He walked over to the fire pit and built a fire with the wood and twigs he'd already set in there. He slowly pushed his hands towards the flame, staring at them as they started to lick and sear the pieces of wood.

He rose up and turned towards her. She stared at him, her eyes hollow, big and injured. She looked so hurt. He flinched at the raw pain he saw in her eyes.

"Six months."

He was startled at her words. Genuinely confused, he asked, "What?"

She started to pace. "The day you fucked her was exactly six months to the day, to the night actually. Remember what

274

you said to me in Anacortes? That I had to make sure I wasn't seeing you. Do you remember that? I never mentioned it, thinking it was just a drunken ramble. And I supposed you had a deep sense of insecurity that you often covered with bluster and a brash ego, but it was just the opposite. You have a fragile ego and you rarely think you're good enough. For anyone. For Jordan. Kailynn. Or me. You always told me you weren't good enough for me."

He turned and sat down on the old, wooden picnic bench he found and placed next to the fire. Staring at the flames, he shrugged. "I'm not."

She stopped and flipped around so they looked at each other across the small fire. "You do remember that night. Don't you? You were drunk, but you do remember saying it."

"I remember."

She shut her eyes. "You did that exactly six months to the day. You did it on purpose. You deliberately tried to drive me away because you thought I'd be better off without you."

"You're stretching the truth now. Don't do that. Don't find ways to forgive something that isn't forgivable."

She shook her head. "I can't have been so wrong about us... or you. I can't be. Tell me you set this up just so I'd break up with you. Like you think you deserved. Like you think I deserve someone better."

He couldn't look at her anymore and stared downwards. "I did it, Josefina. I didn't make it seem like that. I didn't try to push you away for your own good. I did it."

"But I remember that night. It was exactly six months ago."

"It was."

"No denial?" She sucked in a breath. "You knew it was."

"Of course."

"You did it on purpose? The exact date?"

He lifted his head. "Yes."

275

She pressed her lips tightly and stared at him long and hard. Skirting around the fire pit, she walked up to him and grabbed his coat and pulled on it, tugging him to his feet. She held on tighter. Crying, she shook her head. "Tell me the truth, goddamn it. You didn't really do it, did you? You're just trying to push me away. Using your warped sense of right of wrong, and always trying to do the best for me. Like Ian did for Kailynn all those years ago, insisting that she leave him. I suppose you thought this was best for me?"

He had to flex his hands not to grab her and drag her against him.

"Tell me, Caleb. It wasn't the right thing for your sister and it isn't the right thing for me."

"My sister? You're trying to compare us to Ian and my sister? We aren't anything like them. For one, Ian fucking Rydell has an entire ranch and fortune to give to my sister. She runs the whole show now. Her life is elevated and thriving because she is with Ian fucking Rydell. Of course, he should be with her. This, I mean, us, we aren't like that. I'm not the best member of my family. She is."

"See? You think you're not good enough for me. Stop it. Stop this now. Tell me the truth. Stop lying."

He was weak, immoral, and selfish. He lifted his hands to her cheeks and rubbed his thumbs across the wet tracks of her tears. He leaned his forehead into hers and oddly enough, she quieted down. Her hands came up to his shoulders and she gripped him. They held each other for a long while, rocking back and forth and clinging to each other, their heads touching, the night sounds their only serenade.

She sniffled and her choked voice whispered, "I knew you couldn't hurt me like that. I knew it. I couldn't cry or react because I knew it wasn't real. Or true. You're better than that now. We're—"

"I did it," he interrupted her. He pushed his hands into her hair and held her against him. "I fucked another woman. That woman. That night. Only hours before you walked in."

"No. It was the six-month anniversary…" She held him while shaking her head.

"It was." He kissed her forehead with a gentleness that didn't match his words. "But I was loaded up on alcohol and found a stranger. A stranger I later had sex with. I did it, Josefina."

Her head shook. "You're lying to me. You want me to go, to leave… and what? Find a better man? You did this because of some warped sense of protection toward me."

"Yes. I want you to find a better man. Yes, I want to protect you. But no… no, I'm not lying."

"You have to be. Stop it. Please. Stop hurting me." She gripped his arms and shook her head over and over, her tears streaming. "Please stop."

"I'd like to. But I can't." He pushed her backwards. "I know we love each other. I was there. I don't deny it. I don't insult you or try to pretend what we had wasn't real. It was. But it was doomed to end no matter what. It would only end up hurting a whole hell of a lot more later on."

She pushed away from him, all but spitting on him. "How do you figure that? Who are you to decide what I should or should not want?"

His anger, the only thing that didn't hurt then, started to rise. "Look around you, Josefina. This is it. What I got. I ain't Ian. That trailer there? It's all I got. Probably take me five years to even upgrade it. Get over it. That stupid fantasy. Yeah, you're damn right I made sure you left me. What were you intending to do? Come live up here in the Gunderson Hills with me? In my old, used, small, cramped trailer? That what you want outta life? For real? I mean, really? I can't believe that. Not the woman I first met who was trying to change and enlighten me. The one who tried to make me grow up. Not the woman with plans and life savings. I knew she could not live in a trailer. Remember her? The woman who refused to end up like our families did? You weren't going to do that with me. You're letting your dreams of love cloud reality."

Her jaw dropped, and her body stilled. "You're admitting it?"

"Yes. It's not going to help you. But you want to know. Fine. What good does this do? It doesn't change the facts."

Her mouth opened. Closed. Opened. She shook her head, squinting her eyes shut. "You purposely tried to drive me away from you?"

"Yes. I knew you wouldn't leave me just because I suggested it. And I sure as damn hell wasn't going to let you go. It had to be something you couldn't forgive. I couldn't allow you to end up here. Forever. And how long do you think your love could manage to carry that, Josie? Remember that stubborn, little thing called reality? Eventually, it would have sunk in."

Her hair whipped around as she started to pace. She had to move. She was agitated. "What do you think? Poor people don't fall in love and get married? Maybe, oh, just fucking maybe, together, we could upgrade your stupid trailer in two years instead of five? Who asked you to provide anything at all for me? Who? Huh? You stupid, sexist pig!"

"Yeah! I am all of those things. I've told you before, there's a lot wrong with me. I might wanna fix them for you, but I ain't gonna change this leopard's spots."

"Who asked you to?"

"Not you. You stopped asking me. Seek something better for yourself. Don't you see? You were already starting to settle for less than you desired." This time, his frustration towards himself for what he did to her made him lash out.

"What is wrong with you? I get to decide who I'm with

and why. You don't have sex with someone else to push me away. No… you talk to me and consult with me. Act like an adult with me. I don't know what to do now. You didn't really do that."

"I really did."

Her pacing stopped again. She lifted her head to stare at him. "You had sex with her."

"Yes."

"Protected?"

Surprised and puzzled, he nodded. "Always."

"Except with me, you stupid fuck."

His entire body stiffened, and his mouth dropped open, but no sound came out. Then he gasped, "Josie? No. Are you saying…?"

"What if I am? What are you going to do? Go fuck the high school cheerleading squad?"

"No." His head spun. "NO! Are you okay?"

"Am I okay? No. Of course not. My boyfriend fucked someone else, and why? I think in some twisted-ass way it was for me, but then again, no, it can't be, not if you're having sex with someone else. I don't know what to do about this. If you were trying to somehow protect me from wasting my life with you, why would you choose to break my heart instead? Who does that? What kind of person does that?" She wiped her face. "But then again, I know you would do that if you thought it was best for me not to be with you. Because you're all fucked up, Caleb. I mean it. It's not normal to do that to someone you love."

"I know, I am fucked up. I know." He dropped down to sit before rocking back and forth, his feelings percolating inside him, and overwhelming him. "Ar—are you pregnant?"

"What would it matter if I were? We're poor, remember? I don't make much more than you do. We couldn't have a baby together, could we? You seem to think love is only a luxury of the rich or maybe the middle class? Those are the only ones who can afford it, right?"

He grabbed her hand. "Josie, are you pregnant? Of course, I'll be right with you. I'll... we'll figure out something. We'll figure it out. I promise you. I'll work my back to the bone. I'll find a way—"

She jerked her hand from his and answered, "And that, Caleb, is how you were supposed to love me. No matter what. Not by using arbitrary standards and material goods."

He stared at her, stunned. "So, you're not pregnant?"

She scoffed. "As if I'd let myself accidentally get knocked up. I have plans too, Caleb. And nothing will distract me. Not a baby, nor you. And if you'd have just believed in me, and in us, well, you would have known that."

"Why did you just say that?"

"Because we often lie to each other." She sneered.

He lifted his head. "Why are you doing this?"

"Because you think you're doing something *for me*. And I want it firmly established, you are not. If I wanted to live here in a trailer, that is my decision. If I wanted to stay in my place, that too, is my decision. You don't get to decide for both of us anymore."

Her breathing was labored and so was his. They stared at each other in the waning glow of firelight. Tears filled her eyes and she closed them as she said softly, "The saddest part is I think in the end, the person you most hurt is yourself. I think you broke your own heart, and what hurts me so much is that there was no reason to do that."

She stared at him for a long, drawn-out a moment, and then stepped around him and walked off into the night. Her car lights speared through the darkness before she disappeared.

Her words hit him like sniper fire. Sharp and painful in his chest, the uncomfortable sensation traveled throughout his entire body. He sagged and fell onto the bench, leaning forward and burying his face in his hands. Yes, she was correct, he had broken her heart, but hers would heal and she'd move on to someone better.

His heart, however, would be broken forever. He understood that. It was the best thing to happen to her, even if she was hurting because she had convinced herself that he would somehow bring her long-term happiness. He could not. He never brought it to anyone else, so how could he now?

She had walked away from him. Exactly as he planned. He despised and detested himself for making her leave, yet there was no other choice. This was the *only* outcome for them and he should have seen it coming a long time ago.

CHAPTER 20

*S*HE PACED BACK AND forth as her anxiety gnawed at her insides. She reviewed each and every little thing that Caleb had said and done since the very start of their relationship. From the day their brothers got married, to the day she caught him in bed with another woman. He never drank around her. But he did that night in Anacortes without giving her any explanation why.

Then she remembered the run-in they had with the Microsoft couple and Caleb acted sort of weird about it. And also on the night he set out to find a sex partner.

Caleb did it. Or so he claimed.

There was so much more to Caleb despite what he kept proclaiming.

He was nothing to himself.

And firmly rooted in that belief.

He admitted cheating and said it was only to push her away. He did it on purpose. He loved her and wanted something better for her. Most of all, he didn't want her to end up in an old trailer nestled in Gunderson Hills.

All of those thoughts and images swirled in her head.

Then she stopped dead. She just couldn't fucking believe him. Despite all the evidence to the contrary and his adamant claims that he had indeed cheated on her, she was not at all stupid or gullible. She rarely believed any guy's story, and this time, she knew she was right about Caleb. Why?

Simply because he had changed so much. She now realized what he did was just his twisted way of making things all right with her. He believed he was doing what was best for her. Instead of following his usual gut reaction of pleasure-seeking. He was so unschooled in being a good, decent person, he thought that was how to do it.

She walked to Ian and Kailynn's house and knocked on the door until Kailynn answered with a puzzled expression at finding her there.

"Who do you know who has blond hair? Perhaps a family friend? Or maybe an old school mate? Who does Caleb know who has blond hair, is about his age, and does not know me?"

"Uh… let me think… I don't know," Kailynn shut the door behind her after Josefina entered and started pacing. She refused to make eye contact. Or much sense.

Kailynn frowned until Josefina stopped dead. "What blonds do you know?'

"Do you… do you doubt that he cheated on you? Tell me what you're thinking. That he set it up?"

"Oh, yes. I know he did." Josefina waved it off dismissively, long past deciding that it was indeed the truth. Using that as her premise, she intended to figure out what she should do with it.

Kailynn's expression morphed into a smile. "Lauren Townsend."

"Who's that?"

"A girl who used to have sex with Shane Rydell a long time ago, when I liked him. She was their age, and she moved away a few years back. She comes to visit her mom every once in a while. She and Caleb were friends, but they never had sex because of Shane."

"Any chance you might have a picture of her?"

Kailynn turned suddenly and started searching in a closet down the hallway. Josefina followed her and watched her throw all kinds of stuff everywhere. She came out eventually with a yearbook and said, "This is Ian's yearbook. Lauren would have been a freshman when he was a senior. Ah, here it is."

Josefina took the book and stared at it. It wasn't clearly apparent. She shut her eyes and tried to picture the fresh-faced teenager being older and with longer hair, with evidence of a hard living visible on her face. "I think so. Yes, I believe that was her."

"What are you thinking now, Josie?"

"I'm thinking Caleb has shit for self-esteem and a total lack of self-confidence. He still has no idea how much he's changed. Six months to the day when he told me I should not be around or end up with him, and then he goes off and cheats? He has an inferiority complex about me and thinks I'm out of his league. So, he pushed me away before *I* could leave him. Or start to hate him. As I'm sure he expects I'll do eventually."

Kailynn's eyes bulged. "That's fucked up, but it also rings kind of true."

"That's because it is true."

"But how can you be sure?"

"Because I know him better than he knows himself."

"What will you do now? Just forgive him? What do you do with something like this?"

"I don't know yet. But I plan to do something. To start with, I'll arrange a little talk with Lauren Townsend." She shoved the yearbook back at Kailynn. "Thanks, by the way, too, that clears some things up at least." Then Josefina marched out of the room without another word.

"Good luck with whatever you decide to do," Kailynn said as she followed behind her.

One week later, Josefina showed up at the ranch. It was midday. She parked when she spotted Jack Rydell, who was working with a horse near where the old house once stood. She walked over to him and asked, "Do you know where Caleb is?"

"Back there, behind the furthest barn you can see. That mountain of manure from all the barns is getting too high. He's moving it today."

"Thank you."

He smiled, and she passed around him, spotting the dim light of the furthest barn.

She followed his instructions and found Caleb using a tractor. He pushed an impressive load of manure into the huge scoop located at the front of the machine before roaring off to a waiting dump truck. After releasing the load inside the truck, he swung the machine around to scoop up more.

She watched for a while but eventually stepped over the dusty lot that was devoid of grass. She waited until he took another turn on the tractor and that was when he spotted her. The tractor stopped, and he let it idle while staring at her from across the distance. He wore a hat and no sunglasses. She stared at him, unsmiling, and revealing no facial expression at all.

He lowered the tractor shovel and turned the sputtering, loud machine off. He sat there longer than necessary before rising up and lifting himself over the side until he reached the ground. Taking a deep breath, he slowly walked forward and stopped a few feet away from her.

"What are you doing here?" Caleb inquired.

She stared at him, twisting her mouth into a sneer. Her eyebrows rose high as she replied, "Lauren Townsend."

He blinked. Stepped back. "What?"

"Does that name ring a bell?"

"Yes. But how do you know it?"

"She's an old family friend. Who fucked Shane Rydell. Never you."

"That was back in the day. Shane's long since gotten married and is out of the picture."

"But you're not, huh? I know what you're doing, Caleb." She rested her hands on her hips, with a disgusted look on her face.

His eyes sparked with fire. "Yeah, I know what you're doing too."

"Me? What do you think I'm doing?"

"Trying to make me more honorable than I am... again. Is it lost on you that I'm literally shoveling shit right now?"

"No. It's not lost on me. Is it lost on you that I don't care?"

"You *should* care. You used to care. You changed."

She gritted her teeth and loudly exclaimed, "So did you, you idiot. Why won't you see that?"

"Because it's making you ask for less in your life." He shook his head. "I don't want to fight anymore. Let's just let it go."

"No, I came here for a reason."

"What? What is there left to say?"

"Here." She pushed a card into his hands.

Startled, he glanced down. "What is this?"

"The answer. Caleb, you have zero self-esteem. You have no faith in yourself or in me. What you did is one of the most fucked-up things I've ever heard of. You know that you planned it all out and pretended it was true."

"I didn't pretend—"

"Save it." She held a hand up. "I don't believe you."

"So, what is this?" he asked, looking down at the card she gave him.

"It's the name of a counselor."

Anger clouded his face. "A-a-a what?"

"You're fucked up, Caleb. I don't know exactly what's wrong, but you need to figure it out. This compulsion you have to push me away before I can leave you probably comes from your mom. And by insisting you are inherently unlovable, once again, you push me away. Whatever this is," she swept her hand around him as if encircling him, "it has nothing to do with me. You have to find the inner you that failed to get whatever the inner you needed and wanted most of all. You began to fulfill the inner you with me, but then you panicked and lost your focus because you filled your mind with self-doubt and then what? You decided if I caught you cheating, it would push me away before I could get to know the inner you? The version you've already decided I could never love. Why? Because Mama didn't?"

His eyebrows rose in astonishment and his mouth dropped open. "Wh—what are you talking about?"

"Basic psychology. That was one fucked-up stunt you pulled. You wanted me to hate you. Because you hate yourself. You suffer from having both your family and mine hate you. You were willing to go down a total scumbag. Yet, you knew you weren't that guy and you still aren't. Do you realize how deranged that sounds? Your commitment to your strange scheme is impressive, I'll give you that."

His mouth pinched up and he hugged his chest with his folded arms. "It wasn't any stunt. I did it."

She rolled her eyes. "Don't keep lying, Caleb, you'll just make it worse. I already talked to Shane, who told me to hide in the back of his shop if I wanted to see Lauren Townsend, your and Shane's old gal pal. I heard the entire story from her lips. She told Shane all about it without knowing I was listening. It merely confirmed what I'd already figured out. You lied. You freaking paid her to pretend that night was a sexual encounter but it wasn't. Paid her. I can't believe you wasted your money on something so stupid or that she accepted the money and helped you do it."

He winced. "How...?" He seemed to choke on his words, still somewhat in shock.

"I'm not stupid, Caleb and I got played at first, I'll admit. Even the Sad Sack apology you gave me almost confirmed your lie. Brilliant. You seemed so contrite and sorry, knowing I wouldn't believe you stopped caring about me and also knowing that if you cheated on me, I would never forgive you for it. But the thing is, you didn't do it. And for some really screwed-up reason, you keep trying to convince me to believe it."

"Then you have to understand how sure I am about us. We aren't a good idea. Not for the long term. And since I probably can't be monogamous, this stops it all before I can ruin it."

"First, it's a totally chauvinistic notion for you to think you can make any decisions for me. How dare you condescend and dictate whom I can or can't sleep with. I'm the only one who gets to decide that. But you just said what your plan was, you were deliberately pushing me away before it got too hard and too messy. You believed it wasn't going to be so much fun in a real relationship, after intimacy set in. You're running scared from digging into this and grasping it for all it's worth."

"That's because I can't do it."

"No, now you might not be able to. But you can't quit before it starts. I guess that's much easier though than staying with me, isn't it, Caleb? Easier than being in a real relationship with me. You're just scared. You have a lot of work to do. So there," she pointed at the business card. "You can start there."

"I can't though. What do you expect from me? You want me to talk to someone? Just sit down and start talking to some stranger? How can that possibly help me?"

She crossed her arms over her chest. "Well, do you have a better idea? Maybe some more fake cheating-sex? So far, your ideas suck. And I think the only reason you liked me was because you've never had true acceptance in your life. A soft place to fall. No mother to comfort you. Your sister felt abandoned too and she ran away to deal with her own problems. Jordan struggles just as much as you do in trying to maintain a semi-normal, intimate, and committed relationship. But you? You, Caleb, have to take the gold medal for acting out in all the wrong ways. You got a lot of shit to work out, Caleb. But I..." she paused for a moment, letting her gaze slide over him and softening her tone. "I would be willing to continue to love and support you while you figure it all out."

He stepped back, shaking his head. "I don't get it. What do you want? I mean, fine. So, you figured out who Lauren was. Whatever. Doesn't that elaborate ruse tell you all you need to know? I'm fucked-up. And bad for you. I use bad judgment. I have bad manners. I was mean to you before. Do you want to pursue someone like that?"

She stepped forward to get closer. His eyes darted around like two ping pong balls. "I don't. No, I don't want those things." She kept her gaze firmly riveted on him. She stretched out a hand to touch his, which he held tucked tightly against his body. He reacted swiftly by jerking back and stepping away even further from her, his eyes scanning around as if he were desperate to escape. She sighed inwardly and let her hand drop. "But I do want you."

"No. You don't. I would cheat. Because I pretended to

cheat. Does it matter? Either way, it isn't right. You deserve much better. Much more. You deserve—"

"You. I deserve *you*, Caleb," she interrupted with a gentle voice that swiftly ended his flustered, hurried words. His face turned red. His breathing was coming in gasps and she worried he was on the verge of an anxiety attack, but he shook his head defiantly. Again and again.

She shrugged and kept repeating, "I want you."

"You don't. You can't."

She sighed. "I do and I can."

He backed up so far, he bumped into the tractor. With a startled jerk, he rubbed his head, his gaze still fastened on her. He was half-hoping, and half-fearing her next sentence. "The thing is, Caleb, I love you, but this—whatever happened isn't part of my lifestyle. You have to figure some stuff out about yourself first and work it out so you *can* be with me."

"No one signs up for a relationship that's already broken."

"I've heard the story, you know."

"Which one?"

"How your sister left to go to college, until she had an epiphany and realized she could have Ian and still go college. She surprised him in the middle of the mountains and they had an epic reunion that re-established their commitment and love. You think I deserve that, don't you? And a house like theirs and a college degree and to live happily ever after enjoying their kind of lifestyle."

"You do. You do. You deserve all of that."

"I said that was *their* story. It's about their love, their relationship, their house, their college degrees, and their lifestyle. It isn't ours. I don't want it to be our story and I never asked you to make it so. So, quit *giving* me all the things you think I want and start *listening* to what I'm telling you I want. And it's us. Not them."

"What do I have to offer you? An old trailer. A plot of

incinerated land? I'm literally shoveling horseshit today. So, you're damned right that you deserve better." He ran his hands through his hair and kicked the machinery behind him.

She walked forward and set the business card on the tractor seat. "I know what you're doing today, including shoveling a mountain of horse poop. I know where you live. I know how you live. I know where I live. I don't want you to rescue me from all this. This, all of it, is my life too. I don't want you to save me from it. Hell, have you met me? Why would I ever need to be saved from anything? No, Caleb, all I want is a relationship. A real one. Equal partners. I don't expect it to happen fast with us. We have a lot of work to do. But one thing I do know is that I'm willing to figure out a way for us to be together. That is far more commitment than merely saying how I feel."

He shook his head and began pacing again. "Counseling is stupidly expensive. So yeah, poor people can't just be *fine*."

"It couldn't be more expensive than paying a woman to pretend to have sex with you," she spat out.

He winced, and his gaze veered to the left. His face was flushed with embarrassment.

Josefina drew in a long breath to calm her anger. "We'll split it then. Fifty-fifty. I think if there's even a chance we could make it, it's worth the investment. You have to decide if you do too. I can't force you."

"I don't go to… things like counseling. I don't even know anyone who does." She smiled, letting her eyes track him as he paced and moved his arms about in agitation when he spoke. Mostly, she saw the fear, which shone so brightly in his eyes.

"Neither do I. But I want a healthy functioning, intimate, trustworthy *relationship*. That is my only priority. If it's yours too, then come to counseling. Show up. Show up for me…

But mostly you have to show up for yourself. And first off, you need to learn how to talk *to* me, not for me, or about me, or through me. *Talk to me,* Caleb."

His gaze was riveted on the tractor seat. Her voice sounded sad and resigned when she said, "Next Wednesday at seven o'clock. Before either of us start work. Your choice. This is my version of coming after you on a mountain and telling you I love and want you. It's your turn."

She flipped around and walked away, giving it a fifty percent chance that he would take the card and crinkle it up in his hand before throwing it out.

She was willing to work through whatever he did. And also willing to support him and talk until they could figure out how not to do such things. But she refused to keep begging and pleading. He had to stand up and own his desire if he wanted to be with her. He also had to sustain it. To avoid ending up like their parents, any urge to cheat in order to push her away was not how she planned to spend the next twenty years.

So, she drew a line in the sand and there they were.

THE COUNSELOR'S card sat on the seat. He stared at it as if he were expecting it to burn a hole through the material. That's how inflammatory it seemed to him. Counseling? Him? What the fuck? Who did that? What could it do for him? How could a complete stranger manage to help him? What did he need help for anyway? Finding a way to let go of a woman who was way too good for him? She outclassed him and outsmarted him. She out... shit! The list of things she was better at than him was endless.

He didn't expect her to check out his story. But she dug down and discovered the truth. So maybe, yeah, he underestimated her, and that illustrated exactly why he shouldn't have been with her in the first place.

He stared at the card, and then looked back up at Josefina. Her figure was getting smaller as she approached the main barn, stopping to talk to... Shit. *Pedro.* She ran into her brother who would, no doubt, come after him in a hail of angry, Spanish slurs.

He stared again at the card.

He had too much work to do. Other things to get done. She shouldn't have come here, not to his work. But she'd already turned away from her brother and was headed back towards her old, dented, tired car.

Leaving.

As she should have. As he wanted to happen.

Gone.

Done.

He turned the tractor so he couldn't see her pulling away from the ranch.

The rest of the entire afternoon felt like a hot boil on his leg. It was just the presence of a small business card with a phone number and a name.

All she wanted from him was for him to show up.

He finished the day and tucked the tractor in the storage shed, locking up before he went to Kailynn's office inside the house. She was busy drawing up the plans for the big-assed arena they were starting to design.

He stared at her working in the office with a large set of plans before her and a computer behind her. How did she know what she was doing? She had no training in this. Yet, she had the leadership skills, the acumen and now, the confidence to accomplish it. Lynnie was a shy, unsure, quiet kid and teenager. Not so much as an adult.

Not like Caleb was. He just hid it by being the loudest, most jarring version he could be of himself. No one expected much from him or peeled off the layers to go any deeper. They hated or liked him. They rolled their eyes at his audacity or were charmed by his boldness.

No one had ever expected anything profound from him or challenged him to reach for it.

Only Josefina.

Kailynn glanced up, spotting him and rising to her feet before setting down a pen. They exchanged a long look. "Lauren Townsend? I'd have never investigated it. That Josefina did speaks a lot about how well she thinks she knows you. Why'd you do it anyway?"

"I think she's way out of my league."

"I see." Kailynn's head shook. "And what is Josefina's opinion on the matter? Did you ever ask her? She doesn't strike me as the type that likes people to assume anything about her."

Assume anything about her? No. Of course not. He wasn't assuming anything. He was protecting her by making sure she didn't end up with him. He was right about that. He was sure he was right.

"She figured it out. Now she thinks I pushed her away to keep her from dumping me later on."

"Uh-huh. And again, what does she want from your relationship?"

He stepped forward and threw the card down. He could have tried to explain it, but half of her words were jumbled in his head and he wasn't sure he could repeat them, not as Josefina said them.

Kailynn looked startled before she picked it up. She stared at it then looked up at him until a smile slid across her face. "Oh, my God. She doesn't mess around, does she?" Kailynn handed it towards him. "Go there. Do it."

"Me? Go to counseling? Talk to a shrink? What the hell would I say? I can't."

"You can, and you should. You faked having sex to hurt your girlfriend, Caleb. It's a pretty extreme way to manipulate her. She's willing to do this right along with you, I can't imagine why you have to think about it."

"I thought it was—"

"Best for her? Really? It's not. Destroying her faith in the one she loved. Making her think good men cheat. Maybe there is something about her that made you do it, but you could have permanently damaged her self-esteem, so no, it wasn't okay. That she'd ever forgive you again floors me, but this? She's right. She's an impressive woman you picked and instead of running from her or ruining whatever you've begun, have you ever considered just freaking embracing it? Or doing everything you can to keep her?"

"I never thought I was doing harm to her. I was—"

"Saving her?"

He winced and flopped on the couch behind him. "Yeah, I guess so."

"I'll bet she didn't see it that way."

"No. Not at all. She thinks my main problem is my low self-esteem."

"It is. I think you know why." She sighed and walked around her desk to flop beside him. "Don't lose her."

He gave her a weak smile. "That's it? You don't have any more to say?"

"No. You messed up because you *are* messed up. She's right, this is what you and she need. Do it, Caleb, so you don't lose her. In the end you just might learn something about yourself."

She took his hand and squeezed it. Then she got up and walked out of the room.

He left and ran up to the trailer, headed home.

He stared at it hard. The view was worth a million dollars. But there was nothing else up there, not for miles. A random hunting cabin amongst a few, off-the-grid mobile homes and some houses. One place had a cyclone fence surrounding it and a pack of snarling dogs behind it. It looked like some kind of drug compound. So as for neighbors, there were none. Some electric power and a well were all the amenities. It wasn't much to offer anyone.

This is what he'd have for the rest of his life.

Alone. Here. Staring down at the ranch where he worked. His siblings were married and pursuing their own lives, which only seemed to get busier. A dad who wasn't exactly going to relish becoming the twinkle-eyed grandfather to his grandkids any day soon.

Not that there would ever be grandkids. Caleb wondered if he ever wanted any.

Or didn't.

He didn't know.

But he didn't like being alone.

He felt it more ever since he quit drinking. And quit partying. And quit sleeping around.

But he never felt alone when he was with Josefina.

He thumbed the card.

Counseling. Talking. Exposing his inner self. Exploring his emotions. Self-reflection. He had no concept or idea of what to expect and no idea how to do any of those things. At all. Ever. No one he knew did such things either.

He sighed. It would require massive, exhaustive, changes from him. The mother of all changes. And the cost? He'd be paying to talk to a stranger about the most personal and painful issues of his past. All of which he had no idea how to begin. He was so tired of trying to change. How could he willingly sign up now and pay a professional for it? Why would he do that? What good could it possibly do?

When did Josefina ever steer him wrong? She seemed to always know more than him. What if she were right?

But then again, what if she were wrong? Her view of him was skewed. Her usual logic faded. What if she were not objective and seeing things that weren't there? What if this was the one time when Josefina Ruiz was all wrong? Wrong about him? And that reality struck more true than the idea of him ever being an equal partner with her.

Even though there was nothing more in life he wanted than that.

~

JOSEFINA TAPPED her phone with her opposite hand. She flipped it over and back, and turned it on. Two minutes since last she checked. She turned it off again and brushed her hair over her shoulder.

6:53.

If someone's future relationship hung on the balance of a 7 o'clock time frame, wouldn't they at least show up a few minutes early?

Maybe give it a five-minute grace period?

She jumped to her feet and walked over to the window and glanced out. Nothing. No one out front. She turned back, sat down, and shuffled her bag beside her. She crossed her legs and tapped her foot. Lights under the door indicated the counselor was already in there.

Alone. She was all alone. Going to say what? Talk about her heartbreak? Betrayal? The psychology behind the reason why she'd take back a guy who pretended to cheat by letting her find him with another woman, naked in bed, and—

Who was she kidding? Why was she there? Of course. Any guy who would go to those lengths to get away from her, wouldn't show up and do... what? Talk? The one thing that could have solved the entire situation long before it came to this? She scoffed. Yeah, right. Caleb was going to just show up and start a long, slow process of change with her, for her, and about her... but in the end, it would really be all about himself.

Wouldn't he show up a few moments early? Like right about now? If only to say *hey, hello* or something?

He let her walk away. The counseling card shocked him. Unpleasant. Unwanted. Unforeseen. But it was all she could think of. She longed to make the incident that led them there an isolated event. Otherwise, all she foresaw was more dysfunction. The one thing she wanted to avoid.

Then... his truck rumbled. She heard it. The loud, monstrous diesel was shifting gears before idling. She jumped up, dropping her bag and clutching her phone in her hand. Shit! There he was. Here.

Her heart lifted, bursting as she stared dumbfounded.

She didn't think he'd come.

He shut the monster down, opening the driver's door before his foot appeared and he was out. He paused for a moment, stuffing the keys into his jeans pocket. He pulled the cuff of his jacket up on his neck. The morning was cold, frigid even. Snow crusted the ground.

And Caleb was there.

Her former mojo had already evaporated. Now raw nerves filled her, and she bit her lip when she heard the door handle being grabbed before he jerked it open. Mad? Sure. He'd have to be annoyed to be there. After an ultimatum that essentially forced him to start talking.

Then he entered the cold, small waiting room and the goosebumps rose on her arms. Or else her nerves caused them to appear. Gasping for breath, she felt like someone knocked all the air from her chest. Her eyes bugged out.

He was there.

He doffed his hat off his head. He even shaved. His black hair was swept back, and his gorgeous blue eyes found hers.

He didn't smile. His shirt was white and clean, and tucked into a pair of clean blue jeans and new shoes. He wasn't at all dressed like he did for work.

He was dressed specifically for her.

His gaze scoured over her and she swallowed the lump of nerves bundling in her throat. "I didn't think you'd come." He didn't answer. She licked her lips. "I wanted you to come. I hoped you would come. I even prayed you would come."

"Is my being here enough? The gesture, I mean? We could leave now and go to breakfast? Or maybe a hotel? Anywhere?"

Her heart dipped. He was mocking her.

But suddenly, his face slipped into a smile and his eyes twinkled. "Judging by the angry scowl, I'm thinking not. Can't get mad at a guy for preferring sex over talking. So, yeah I'm here."

"For real? Not to joke around or blow this off?"

He stepped forward and his arm swept around her waist before he drew her closer. As she approached him, she had to tilt her head back more. He looked into her face with a gentle, tender smile and his eyes glimmered with passion for her. "You're never a joke to me. Even what I did wasn't a joke. It was my fucked-up way of telling you that I love you. I think you're right though and I need to find a better way of expressing myself. Correction, I *want* to find a better way. I'm here, Josefina. For real."

"For real," she repeated. Her eyes shut, and she swallowed. "I didn't think you were coming."

"You said seven o'clock."

She laughed before she threw her arms around him. "Yes, but I thought... oh, never mind. You're here."

"I'm here," he agreed, and his tone implied so much more than that he was just there at the counseling office with her. "I think... I think I have a mountain to return to you,

299

metaphorically speaking, of course. I have no idea how to begin, but I'm willing to learn." His smile was tender as he leaned down and grazed his lips over hers. She closed her eyes as her mouth engaged the soft, warm pressure of his.

She stared up at him and touched his cheek. "That's all anyone can do. That's what I'm going to learn too, it's not just you anymore. It's both of us."

The sound of someone's throat being cleared interrupted them and Caleb lifted his head. He softly whispered, "Uh, I think it's time to talk."

She smiled as they separated and turned, their hands still clasped while exchanging nervous looks as they glanced towards their new counselor and entered the room. In a strange way, they were more together now than they had ever been before.

"WHAT ARE WE DOING here?" Josefina asked as she fidgeted around in his passenger seat. Her tone was definitely annoyed. Caleb grinned and didn't answer. He jumped out of his old truck and, as expected, Josefina scrambled after him. The heat of the day started to recede, and the sunset made the otherwise average neighborhood they were in seem like so much more.

"Caleb? I thought we were getting some dinner? I'm starving. Famished. I skipped lunch because an older lady fell, and they had her in the hospital for X-rays. Guess what language she spoke?" Josefina was obviously not waiting for an answer before she continued without a breath, "She was German. Vacationing here. She was confused and scared. In lots of pain. I tried to explain I wasn't fluent in German, but I could help her enough to translate her needs back and forth. She didn't want to be left alone, so I sat with her the entire afternoon. Anyway, that's why I didn't eat."

He took her hand as she prattled on, coming around the front of his truck. Oblivious to the orange and peach hues on the horizon as well as the purple and blue clouds that further enhanced the unusual light and sunset, he tugged her his way until they were centered on the sidewalk.

"Caleb? Are you listening?"

"German. Scared. Hungry," he summarized, and she rolled her eyes, smiling.

"Yes, mostly hungry. Where are we?"

He turned her forwards and she stared at the ugly, little house she saw before them. It had a single garage, with the door all bent and cracked like a car had recently run into it. The lawn was dead. Dust and rock particles led all the way to the front door with a sad, gravel walkway. There was a shabby front door and a cracked window next to it. Single story, boxy, without a trace of curb appeal. It was the color of puke that maybe once was a shade of beige. It was ugly. Truly.

And cheap. It was also a single-family home. One that they could afford.

"We are home."

She frowned up at him, then stared forward. "We are home? What the hell are you talking about?"

"Well, we could be home. It just would have been more dramatic if I could have presented it to you. But that'd put me back in couples counseling again. Instead… oh, there's the realtor. We're meeting a realtor. Take a look inside to see how bad it is. See what they want—"

"Caleb. What the hell are you talking about?" She jerked her hand from his as she whipped around to glare at him.

He grinned and touched the side of her face. She quit scowling. "What?"

"I'm talking about selling the land and trailer, and investing in something more like this… with you. You said you had some money saved up. We could share the expenses. All of it. The down payment. The monthly payments. Upkeep. Fifty-fifty. Both of us. And we could live all our lives together. I mean, it doesn't have to be this particular one. It's just a starting point. A symbol. An idea."

"Selling the land? Your family's land? Buying a house… Have you gone mad?"

"Yeah, a long time ago, right after I met you." She bristled but a small smile tilted her lips upwards. He continued pulling her forward and kissing her mouth before explaining. "But as for the land, they all agreed I could have it. It's all I got that's worth a damn, in assets, I mean. But what good is it? Up there where you don't want to live anyway? When I could invest it towards buying a real home, with you?"

Her eyebrows arched and then lowered. "You want to buy a house?"

"Isn't that what you always wanted? Spent your twenties saving up for?"

"Yes, but you didn't and—Caleb, what are you doing?"

"I want to now. I never had a reason to before. I do now. Us. I want to build a life with you, Josie. I know it's ugly." He turned her head towards the house they stood in front of. "But we could fix it up. It won't look like that for long."

Gaping first at the house, then at him after what he said, she gripped his hand. "You want us to buy a home? And live together?"

"I do. But only if you want to."

Her hand tightened on his. "Fifty-fifty?"

"Together. Us. Like we do everything else."

Her eyes shut. For two years they'd been dating and learning how to interact with each other. They'd both gone to counseling, first together and later, Caleb went alone. He began working on things he never understood before and growing from them. But he soon figured it out and that was when he started to blossom.

"Did you talk to Genevieve about it?" She was their counselor.

"No. I didn't. I'm talking to you about it. I'm asking you. What do you think? Too soon? Too strange? Too ugly a house?"

She smiled and gazed at the house again. "It is ugly."

"But it's a nice, quiet street."

She glanced around. "It is. We're pretty good at working together. We could probably do wonders with it."

"We could. Do you want to look inside?"

"You living in Brewster? In a suburban neighborhood?"

"With you. Yes."

She started to smile, and he smiled back. It was impossible not to. His heart hammered. He was nervous but excited. He wanted this, but also didn't want to push. But he mostly wanted to have a home with Josefina always.

She stepped forward, walking towards the house. The realtor parked in back and was now opening the front door, smiling and waving at him in recognition. "Come on, let's go see about a house."

And they did. They looked at everything and argued and talked and laughed. They spent months of looking before they found the right one. A small, two-bedroom, single-story house that they'd have to take down to the studs to re-do and make livable, but they were up for it. Together.

They tore it down and destroyed it before they rebuilt it with their meager funds. Living in it as they worked and slowly accomplishing the remodel one step at a time, they crafted their tiny home. It changed as much as Josefina managed to motivate him. By the time they started it, he was pretty sure their relationship was solid enough to stand the test of time.

ABOUT THE AUTHOR

Leanne Davis has earned a business degree from Western Washington University. She worked for several years in the construction management field before turning full time to writing. She lives in the Seattle area with her husband and two children. When she isn't writing, she and her family enjoy camping trips to destinations all across Washington State, many of which become the settings for her novels.

Made in the USA
Las Vegas, NV
31 March 2024